GEORGIA GHOSTS

GEORGIA GHOSTS

by Nancy Roberts

John F. Blair, Publisher
Winston-Salem, North Carolina

Fifth Printing, 2002

*The paper in this book meets the guidelines
for permanence and durability of the Committee
on Production Guidelines for Book Longevity
of the Council on Library Resources.*

DESIGN BY LIZA LANGRALL
ALL PHOTOGRAPHS BY THE AUTHOR UNLESS OTHERWISE NOTED

The Library of Congress Cataloging-in-Publication Data
Roberts, Nancy, 1924–
      Georgia ghosts / by Nancy Roberts.
           p.   cm.
      ISBN 0-89587-172-6 (alk. paper)
      1. Ghosts—Georgia.   2. Haunted houses—Georgia.   3. Haunted
hotels—Georgia. I. Title.
BF1472.U6R6318   1997
133.1'09758—dc21   97-13697

TO MY HUSBAND, JIM BROWN,
WHO NOT ONLY HAS BEEN SUPPORTIVE
BUT ENTERPRISING ENOUGH TO FIND SEVERAL
GHOSTS FOR ME TO WRITE ABOUT!

CONTENTS

Colonial Coast and Golden Isles

SAVANNAH

ST. SIMONS ISLAND

ST. MARYS AND CUMBERLAND ISLAND

Magnolia Midlands

Atlanta Metro

Presidential Pathways

Historic Heartland

Classic South

Northeast Mountains

Northwest Mountains

INTRODUCTION

With a history and landscape as rich and varied as Georgia's, it's no surprise the state is teeming with ghosts. From the coastal sea islands to the northern mountains to Atlanta, the South's largest urban center, tales of the supernatural abound in the state.

While I was writing earlier collections of ghost stories around the country, I longed to write about the ghost lore of this uniquely Southern state. For one reason or another, the project kept getting put off, but now the opportunity has finally arrived. When I started the project, I knew there was a rich source of material in Georgia, but even I did not realize how rich that source was. Halfway through the process of collecting stories, I decided my problem would not be finding material, but determining when to stop writing. I not only wanted to cover the best of Savannah, but the rest of the enormous state of Georgia as well.

The final result, I believe, does represent the entire state. Considering publisher deadlines, to which all writers are subject, I have tried to make the book as comprehensive as possible. Savannah and the Atlanta Metro area have the most stories, but there are stories from all the other parts of Georgia also.

During the course of my research for this book, I was privileged to hear one fascinating story after another, many of them first-hand interviews with people who had encountered ghosts. Unless you have experienced the supernatural yourself, or know someone who has, it's difficult to describe the feeling you get when these experiences are described. Can you imagine what it is like to talk with a young lawyer from Washington, Georgia, who saw four Confederate horsemen in the morning mist? It's the type of thing you see on television and read about often, but you get an entirely different sensation when you encounter someone who has witnessed such an event with his/her own eyes.

Besides the many people who told me their stories, I owe debts of gratitude to a long list of librarians and newspaper people throughout the state. Without the wonderful help and support of these people, this book would not have been possible.

For convenience and ease of use, I have arranged the stories according to the region headings used in the *Georgia on My Mind* publication available from the Georgia Department of Industry, Trade and Tourism. This is the official travel guide for the state of Georgia and is available by mail and at Georgia welcome centers.

It is my hope that people will take my book with them as they explore this wonderful state and visit the many interesting places described in the book that are open to the public. I am sure you will find each place a worthwhile stop and your hosts along the way as gracious as I have.

–NANCY ROBERTS

COLONIAL COAST AND GOLDEN ISLES: SAVANNAH

JIM WILLIAMS'S FORMER HOME

Mercer House, 429 Bull Street, Savannah

Paul and Ginny Crandall were filled with anticipation the Friday afternoon they arrived in Savannah for the holidays. As lifelong New Yorkers, this would be their first venture into the ambience of a truly Southern city.

"There's so much of the past here," said Ginny as they drove down Abercorn Street. "Such magnificent old homes and buildings. This is going to be a new experience, Paul." And she was right.

After browsing through the shops in buildings on River Street that were once cotton warehouses, they dined at The Boar's Head. After dinner, Paul spread a city map on the table and was soon absorbed in the layout of Savannah. As they drove around the city later, he regaled Ginny with details of the city's history.

"This General Oglethorpe was an exceptional man. He not only founded the colony of Georgia, but he laid out a very orderly design for Savannah. His plan included a series of squares at regular intervals along the streets, and the settlers

Jim Williams's house

built homes around them. Each square was meant to serve as a market place, or a small stockade in time of danger."

"Danger?" questioned Ginny.

"This was Creek Indian territory. But Chief Tomochichi and Oglethorpe hit it off so well the colony was settled without a single massacre. Over the years the squares evolved into parks, and magnificent houses replaced those of the early settlers."

Ginny listened to Paul intently, for old homes always fascinated her. As they drove, they approached a tree-shaded park that appeared to be the most elegant one in the whole city. They noticed a metal sign and stopped to read it. "This square is called Monterey," said Ginny. She then turned to look at the Italianate mansion that seemed to preside over the exquisite square. The mansion was dark red brick with tall, arched windows, lacy ironwork balconies, and palms on either side of the front entrance.

"Look! They're having a party inside, Paul. Slow down a little." Each window on the first and second floors of the magnificent house was ablaze with candles, and every room brilliantly lit by chandeliers. She lowered the car window and stared.

"Oh Paul, wouldn't you just love to see what is going on? It must be crowded with people."

"Probably having a Christmas party."

"The music is lovely. I can hear it out here. Stop. I want to get out Paul." Something seemed to draw her to the house.

"Your ears are better than mine," he said. "I don't hear a thing."

"Wait. I won't be a minute." She got out of the car and stood at the side of the house looking through a window.

"Ginny, this is ridiculous," called Paul. "Come back to the car. We can take a tour and see all the homes tomorrow." But Ginny didn't move.

"Well, what did you see?" he said when she finally slid in beside him.

"Candlelight everywhere. Butlers in white jackets and women in gorgeous dresses. And the most fantastic looking young man—*very* handsome."

"Should I be jealous? I suppose I'm lucky you didn't try to crash it," said Paul teasingly.

In bed later Ginny said, "Does it seem strange to you that no cars were parked around the house, and that the front entrance was dark?"

"No. There's probably a place to park at the rear."

"But why would lights be on inside and not at the entrance?"

"Were they? I didn't notice. Honey, I'm almost asleep. Can't we talk about it tomorrow." Paul quickly slid off to sleep. Ginny, though still perplexed, soon followed.

The next morning they took a harbor cruise on the Savannah River and then lunched on crab cakes at the Bay Street Inn. "When do we see the graveyard with the beautiful statues and the ghost story?" said Ginny, her face as excited as a child who's been promised a treat.

"Do you mean Bonaventure? Later. Remember, we take the tour of homes in an hour," said Paul.

On the bus Paul remarked, "I once thought tours were for unimaginative people too dull witted to find their own way around a city, but we're seeing places we might never have known about."

"That's true, honey," Ginny said, "but don't forget some of the most interesting places we've seen were when we were exploring on our own."

The tour bus driver interrupted their conversation. "Now this house was built by General Hugh Mercer during the Civil War," he said. "Songwriter Johnny Mercer grew up in it, and Jacqueline Onassis once offered two million dollars for it. It overlooks Monterey Square, which is considered one of the most beautiful squares in the city."

"Monterey Square! That's where we were last night," Ginny exclaimed. "And he's talking about the same red brick house we saw."

She leaned forward in her seat. "Driver, we drove around this square last night and that house was ablaze with candlelight. There was a party going on."

"Lights and a party inside? Ma'am, you must have been seeing things."

"Not at all! Who lives there?"

"I don't know now. The Mercer House is the one that once belonged to Jim Williams. Haven't you read about him in the book *Midnight in the Garden of Good and Evil*?"

"No."

"Well, Mr. Williams used to throw the grandest parties in town, and there haven't been any parties on the same scale in Savannah before or since his Christmas galas. Unless dead men throw parties." The driver smiled at his macabre joke.

"What happened?" asked Paul.

"Williams was tried for the murder of a young man who lived in the house and worked for him. They tried him four times, and I heard he spent millions in legal fees before they finally acquitted him. After his acquittal in 1989, he threw one more lavish Christmas party. Let's see. When was that party? Five years ago last night. Less than a month later he was dead. Possibly from a heart attack."

"Five years ago last night!" exclaimed Ginny.

"That's right. He always held it the night before the Cotillion's Debutante Ball, and I remember because the Cotillion Ball is tonight."

"What goes on in the house now?" asked Paul.

"I've never heard of anything happening there since then," the driver replied.

"But I saw formally dressed guests through the window,"

said Ginny, "and chandeliers ablaze with lights."

"You've got the wrong house then, ma'am. That is a private home, and I don't even know who lives there now. There are many parties in Savannah during the Christmas season, and tourists easily get mixed up about which house is which on these squares."

"But the style, the tall windows, the palms on each side of the front door. It's the same!" Ginny exclaimed, sure of what she had seen the night before.

"I'm sure you think that, ma'am," the driver said, gunning the motor, "but if anyone ever gave a party in that house as elegant as the ones Mr. Williams used to give there, the whole town would know about it."

The driver pulled away from the curb and was off to the next house. Ginny was too upset to hear much narration for the next few minutes. "It had to be the same house," she said to her husband. He patted her hand.

The week after Christmas, on the day the Crandalls were to leave, they drove over to Monterey Square for the last time. It was a cold, gray day, and the house looked as gloomy as the weather. The light rain fell on a drooping arrangement of purple-and-white satin ribbons on the front door. There was something about the ribbons that appeared more funereal than festive.

Paul parked the car and watched a tour bus stop opposite the house. They could hear the guide's muffled story about Johnny Mercer having lived there, and how Jacqueline Onassis wanted to buy it.

And they could almost hear the hushed comments of the tourists to each other. "You remember the man in the book? Yes. That was his house, where it all happened," they would say staring out at the dark windows of the mansion.

Their final trip to the house held no answers, and soon it was time to leave for New York. On the plane Paul said, "Do you believe that energy or rage or strong emotion can remain somewhere in the atmosphere, perhaps enabling the spirit of the dead to cause an event in the world of the living?"

"I don't know," Ginny replied. "Remember our bus driver saying how we couldn't have seen a party at the Mercer House 'unless dead men throw parties'?"

"Yes. Why?"

"He may be right, but if Jim Williams ever did throw a party, when do you think it would be?"

"On the night before the Cotillion Ball, of course," said Paul.

THE GHOSTLY LORD
OF LAFAYETTE SQUARE

Hamilton Turner Mansion,
330 Abercorn Street, Savannah

"You seem to be admiring the Hamilton Turner Mansion," said a gray-haired little lady in a black coat. I was standing in the middle of the sidewalk in front of the house, mesmerized by its style. The woman paused a few feet away from me.

"It reminds me of a monstrous beast as it prepares to spring," she continued. "Passersby can't help looking at those windows; they look like sinister eyes staring out over the square. As it says in the book *Midnight in the Garden of Good and Evil,* locals speak of this mansion as the Charles Addams house."

I gave a little shiver and replied, "Yes, it has the haunted, decadent look of an Addams sketch. It looks so menacing I can't help wondering if it is haunted."

"Of course it is. I've seen a ghost as I walk past here at

Hamilton Turner Mansion

night," she said. Delighted to learn of an unfamiliar Savannah ghost, I turned and introduced myself as a writer of ghost stories. The lady said that she worked in one of the businesses on Abercorn Street.

"I didn't know there were any spirits in this house," I said, "but then, I've not yet talked with anyone about it or seen the interior."

"Oh, the ghost I've seen is *outside* the house."

"It is? Where?" I replied anxiously.

"Before I tell you about seeing the ghost would you permit me to share something about the Southern blockade runner who built this house?" she asked courteously. I indicated I would, delighted to learn the house's history.

"His name was James Pugh Hamilton, an adventurous man who often slipped right through the Yankee blockade into the port of Savannah during the Civil War. The profits from these daring escapades were enormous, and after the war, he used them to help rebuild this wrecked city. By the time the war had been over five years, James Hamilton was a Savannah business tycoon and city councilman. At a time when many places in the North were suffering bank failures and financial panic, and people were starving right here in Georgia, Hamilton was building this home, one of the grandest in the South. People call the style Second Empire Baroque, but as the years passed, Mr. Hamilton made many changes corresponding with contemporary styles."

"He sounds like a fascinating man," I said.

"Would you like to know what the inside of the house was like?" the woman asked.

"Very much."

"From the main hall, a broad stairway with a carved mahogany balustrade swept upstairs to the sleeping quarters. The immense master bedroom ran the length of the house, and speaking tubes connected all the major rooms. Its third floor contained a game room in the front, and in the rear were quarters for fifteen or more servants, an amount necessary to meet the needs of Mr. Hamilton's constant stream of houseguests. Hamilton spent a fortune on custom-made and imported furnishings. The main rooms had Italian marble mantles, Belgian cut-glass chandeliers surrounded by bas-relief, and hand-carved wainscoting. With such exquisite details, the Hamilton Turner

Mansion became one of the best examples of gable Baroque architecture in America.

"Because he was president of the electric company, his house was the first in Savannah to have electricity. At night the mansion was ablaze with lights—an example for all who were skeptical that electricity would replace kerosene."

She pointed up at the flat roof. "See that cupola? At night Mr. Hamilton liked to stroll on the narrow walkway around it. From there he could see for miles—over the city and out to the Savannah River. I imagine that as a former naval officer he would look out at the Savannah River shimmering in the moonlight and recall the excitement of slipping past the Yankee blockade."

"I'm sure he would. But what about the ghost?" I asked.

"I was getting to that. He used this house to display fine objects of art collected from all over the world. Because of the house's valuable contents, Hamilton decided to station a sentry on the roof to guard against intruders. One morning when the guard did not appear for breakfast, a servant climbed the narrow stairs to the roof and found the guard lying dead in a pool of blood. Someone shot him during the night, but when the murder occurred or who the murderer was would never be known. After the death, no one was eager to take the murdered guard's place. Mr. Hamilton tried to patrol the roof himself but had to abandon the practice due to poor health. He died a few months later.

"I've passed by the Hamilton Turner Mansion many times and was familiar with its history, but it wasn't until shortly after I took a job in a shop up the street that I noticed the ghost. It happened on a night I stayed at the store late to work on the books. There was a full moon that night, and as usual I passed by the mansion on my way home. As I looked at the house, a movement on the roof caught my attention. I stopped right here on the sidewalk and looked up to see what it was. The tall figure of a man, silhouetted in the moonlight, stood near the iron rail. Although it was difficult to see him clearly, I could tell he was shouldering a rifle. While I watched the figure, a cloud passed across the moon, and for a moment it was too dark to see him. When the cloud passed, I could see him again. Then he just disappeared! I was so startled I screamed and ran all the way home.

"I stayed awake most of the night and wondered if I should tell the pretty blonde lady who lived there what I had seen. But I decided it might really scare her if I told her. I've never believed in ghosts, but I don't believe people can just vanish either. I saw the figure on the roof one other time, on a similar night. I thought I might be going crazy, but I heard one of the nuns at the nearby school say something that made me think she had seen it, too. Do you think it was the spirit of James Hamilton himself coming back to protect his house? Or could it have been the murdered guard?"

"I wish I knew," I replied.

We were both silent. Then she said suddenly, "I must be going," and before I could ask more questions she rapidly walked off into the night.

Ms. Nancy Hillis, a former Miss Tennessee who appeared as the character "Mandy" in the book *Midnight in the Garden of Good and Evil,* was living in the house at the time, and agreed to speak to me about the ghost.

"What do I think about the apparition?" the attractive, blond Ms. Hillis replied when asked about the ghost. "I've heard of the figure on the roof, but I am more familiar with the ghost inside the home. Guests sometimes ask, 'Who was that gentleman in a Victorian suit sitting in a chair at the top of the stairs? He looks like he owns the place'?"

"I tell them I suppose it could only be Mr. Hamilton—or his ghost," Ms. Hills continued. "This magnificent house meant so much to him. If he enjoys visiting now and then, I have no problem with that."

THE HAMILTON TURNER HOUSE IS ON LAFAYETTE SQUARE AND IS A PRIVATE HOME AT THIS TIME. THE EXTERIOR, HOWEVER, IS WELL WORTH SEEING. THE HOME IS MENTIONED IN CHAPTER NINETEEN OF JOHN BERENDT'S BOOK, *MIDNIGHT IN THE GARDEN OF GOOD AND EVIL*.

THE GIRL THE NUNS LOVED

Tybee Island

FOR SOME YEARS CAMMIE MCCALLUM HAS HELD A RESPONSIBLE POSITION AT THE MEDICAL COLLEGE OF CHARLESTON. SHE COULD VACATION ANYWHERE IN THE WORLD, AND SOMETIMES DOES, BUT A FAVORITE PLACE OF HERS IS SAVANNAH. IN THE PAST SHE HAS TOLD THIS MACABRE STORY ONLY TO CLOSE FRIENDS, BUT NOW SHE IS WILLING TO SHARE IT WITH A LARGER AUDIENCE.

Afterward, I read stories similar to mine from other states. Wherever we live people express certain common tragedies, but that doesn't make them less valid.

I remember the summer well because mother and I just weren't getting along at all. It was the summer after my graduation from a private school in Charleston. I felt pretty grown-up, but Mother still wanted me in by midnight. It was so ridiculous!

Finally Dad said, "Cammie, would you like to visit your Aunt Mirabelle in Savannah?" Mirabelle Featherstone was his youngest sister and not nearly as stuffy as my mother.

Mother frowned but didn't say anything. "That would be all right with me," I said after a moment's hesitation, as if making a concession. There really wasn't anything I would enjoy more.

"Mirabelle and Tom will take good care of her," Dad said to Mother. "Let her go, Janice. Why don't I call Mirabelle now," and he did. He was smiling when he hung up the phone. "She said she'd love to have you."

I was elated! There was always something going on at the Featherstone's house, and I liked my first cousin, Myra. She was two years older than I and had a slew of friends. I also loved her funny older brother. He was nicknamed "Horse Feathers," but most everybody called him "Horse" for short.

I had been feeling really down since the end of school. There was nothing to look forward to, and Charleston could be so dull in the summer. My younger sister was selecting her first prom dress, and all I could think about was how great the dance had been at school with Alex. He hadn't come home from college, electing to join his folks for a summer-long trip to Europe instead. He said he would write every day, but there had been no letters so far, and he had been gone two whole weeks!

The second day I was in Savannah, Myra said, "Cammie, a crowd of us are going to a dance at the beach tonight. Want to go?"

"I'd love it," I said happily. Summer fun for Myra and her friends revolved around the beach.

"Better take a jacket then. It will be cool out there tonight over the water."

That evening we had to wait until Myra's date, Stephen Lucas, arrived from Atlanta, so it was after eight o'clock before he came by the house to pick us up. I liked him immediately. He had a direct gaze, and his friendly blue eyes gave me an approving look. We started down Interstate 80 toward Tybee Island and the beach, Myra and Stephen in front while I was in the back between Horse and his friend, Martin McLean. They were talking across me, and since I had nothing else to do, I sat in silence watching the road. I was getting irritated thinking that this Martin guy could at least say *something* to acknowledge my presence. He was so rude!

It's not far out to the island, and there's not much to see along the way except bridges and marshlands. As we approached the last bridge, the one at the north end of the island near the lighthouse, I saw a girl standing a short distance ahead of us. She was waving, trying to flag us down.

Horse saw her also because he called out, "Stephen, that girl's trying to wave someone down."

Braking, Stephen slowed to a stop. As the girl walked gracefully up to the car, I could see she was wearing a beautiful satin dress that gleamed in the dark. Long black hair framed her face.

"Need help?" Myra said to her.

"Just a ride. Do you have room for me?" she asked in a soft voice.

"Of course," said Myra opening her door. "Hop in." She slid over and the girl settled in beside her.

"I'm Myra Featherstone, this is Stephen Lucas," Myra said, and then introduced the rest of us in the backseat. The girl nodded and smiled politely as she murmured something that must have been her name, but I couldn't hear it. She said she was warm, although she was the only one not wearing anything around her, and she asked if she could lower the window. I, for one, was a little chilly, but Myra answered, "Of course." She and Myra were talking away, but because of the wind from the window, I heard only a few words. Horse leaned over the seat now and then to say something to her. I heard him compliment her on the pearls she was wearing.

"Where did you want to go?" Myra asked as we approached the place at the beach where they were having the dance.

"Nowhere in particular," the girl replied.

"Well, come on and join us."

"I would love to," she said. Horse seemed pleased.

"I didn't hear your name," he asked, trying to be casual but failing utterly.

"Laurie, Laurie White," she answered.

The band was taking a break when we went in so we found ourselves a table and then wandered out on the pier. There was quite a cool breeze coming off the water. Horse offered Laurie his jacket.

"Oh, I'm not cold. It was warm inside, and the air out here feels wonderful," she said. I had left my wrap at the table and was shivering. Martin put his coat around me. We heard the music start up and went back in to dance. Stephen was first on the dance floor with Myra. Martin asked me to dance, and I saw Horse place a drink for himself and Laurie on the table. He asked her to dance, and as she stood up I thought her white satin dress as lovely as a bride's. One fast number was followed by another, until Martin and I danced ourselves breathless.

I was perspiring when the band started into a fast-paced Latin rhythm, and we went back to the table to sit down. Horse came up with Laurie, and he was as winded as we were. He pulled out a chair for her and one for himself, and then sat as he wiped beads of perspiration from his forehead. But Laurie did not sit down. She stood at the table looking cucumber cool and staring over at Martin as if waiting for him to say something.

Finally, when she didn't sit down, Martin rose politely and asked her to dance. As he took her hand an expression of shocked surprise crossed his face, but I didn't stop to think about it until later. I watched them walk toward the dance floor and noticed Laurie's dress more than I had before. It was a heavier satin than you usually see. It looked perfect, as if it had been stuffed with tissue paper and just come out of the box—not a wrinkle on it. Some girls have all the luck. They don't wrinkle their clothes. They don't perspire like I do, and their skin is flawless and white as marble.

Each of the boys danced with Laurie once except Horse.

He danced with her several times, and when I saw her rest her forehead against his chin, he was actually blushing. I never realized my cousin was such a shy thing! The band wasn't as good for dancing as we expected, so we sat at the table and talked a lot. When we left it was a little after midnight.

"Where can we drop you off?" Stephen asked Laurie.

"Right where I got in the car," she said.

Everyone protested, but she wouldn't listen.

"When I asked you where you live, you told me over on Wren Street at North Beach," said Horse. "Let us take you there." She just shook her head, and we had to let her out at the bridge, right where we first saw her. While we were driving home, I turned to Horse and said, "A nickel for your thoughts."

"I was just thinking about how pretty Laurie was, but her hands and face were as cold as ice," he said and shivered.

Martin heard him and said, "That's exactly how it was when I took her hand to dance with her." I recalled his expression of shock when he took her hand to dance. What a strange evening it had been.

The next morning we were dressing for church when Stephen phoned. "I just went to the car and guess what I found on the floor," he said to Myra. "It's the string of pearls Laurie wore last night."

Myra told Horse, and they decided we should all drive over to the beach that afternoon and take them to her. As we drove out there that afternoon, Myra looked at the necklace. "I don't think these are real, but they're good pearls and they look just like new."

She dropped the gleaming white spheres into my hand, and I saw the knot between each of them. The gold filigree clasp opened and closed too easily. "She is lucky she didn't lose them while she was dancing," I said.

We reached North Beach and started looking for Laurie's

house. "The address she mentioned is somewhere along here," said Horse as we drove down Wren Street. Finally he told Stephen to stop. "That's it. There's the house. It's got to be."

"You must not remember correctly," said Myra. "That's not a house, it's a nursing home."

We knocked on the door, but no one there ever heard of her. Driving through town we decided to get a coke and began talking with a man in the restaurant.

"She gave you the right address all right," the man said after we told him our story. "A girl named Laurie once lived there, but that was years ago when I was a boy. That building was part of a convent. She hadn't taken her vows yet, and she slipped out to go off with a young man who wanted to marry her. Their car crashed near that bridge on the north end of the island, and she was killed. The nuns loved that girl, and they decided to bury her in a satin wedding gown. She must have had the string of pearls around her neck in the coffin."

"But why did we meet her?" Horse managed to ask. I think the rest of us were too shocked to talk.

"Perhaps it was the anniversary of the accident. Every now and then, someone reports seeing her."

"We could go back next year to return her necklace," said Martin looking at Horse.

"Not a chance," Horse replied, his face strangely white under his tan.

None of us talked much on the way home. That's been a long time ago. But sometimes on summer nights when I drive across that last bridge on the road to Tybee Beach, I think of Laurie and I feel cold all over. As far as I know Myra still has the pearls. I wonder if she ever wears them?

THE SHRIMP FACTORY HAUNTING

315 River Street, Savannah

DURING THE SUMMER, COLLEGE STUDENTS GRAVITATE TO SAVANNAH TO FIND A JOB, ENJOY THE COAST, AND MAKE NEW FRIENDS. AMONG THE MOST POPULAR PLACES TO WORK ARE THE RIVERFRONT RESTAURANTS. THE FOLLOWING ACCOUNT IS FROM A YOUNG MAN WHO WORKED IN ONE OF THESE HISTORIC RESTAURANTS FOR A SUMMER. HE DIDN'T REALIZE THAT ONE OF HIS NEW SUMMERTIME ACQUAINTANCES WOULD BE A GHOST.

For some reason, I found myself printing my name on an application for bartender at the Shrimp Factory. I had no bartending experience, but somehow I got the job. For the next few months it would be Brad Hughes, bartender.

Well, why not? It would mean fun and funds until I went to Georgia Tech in the fall and started work on my master's degree in engineering. And maybe the events of that summer were just what someone with my skeptical mechanical and scientific background needed.

The Shrimp Factory restaurant is attractive, with its stone walls, exposed beams, and bricks around the archways. I thought it would be a nice place to work, especially since I wouldn't be with my family.

"You'll probably want to make your own plans this summer, Brad," my father had told me.

That was the year all of the Hughes family, except for me, decided they wanted to spend the summer in Scotland instead of at our house in the North Carolina mountains. I wasn't interested in making the trip and thought that Savannah would be an interesting change of scenery for the summer. I could divide my time between work in Savannah and hanging out at the beach on Tybee Island.

Since I hadn't been too concerned about the art of making a good drink at college, my first week tending bar was

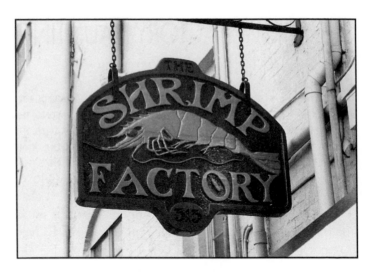

Shrimp Factory entryway

pretty hectic. I had never heard of some of the drinks the customers ordered. Tourists come to Savannah from all over the country, and their tastes are unlike those of the locals, or any of the good ol' boys.

Aside from learning all the different drinks, I also had to familiarize myself with the wine stock. Now and then some connoisseur would ask me for a wine I had never heard of, or one we didn't keep behind the bar, and that meant someone had to go after it. It happened the first day I was there.

"Ron, would you go upstairs and get me a bottle of good Merlot," I asked a waiter who seemed experienced. "One of my customers wants the best we have."

"Sorry. Too busy," he replied.

I started to snap, "You think you're the only one that's busy," but didn't. Instead I asked our manager, Terry, where to find it. Then I went upstairs and got the wine. Seeing a keg of beer leaking badly, I tightened it and came back down. I told Terry that someone left the keg with beer running out of it, and he glanced up at the ceiling toward that part of the wine room. We both saw a wet spot.

"It was probably Joe," he said. I looked puzzled, so he told me the story of how in the early days the restaurant had been a storage place for cotton, and slaves were often locked upstairs at night. Terry believed that one of the slaves, whom he called Joe, now haunted the attic.

"When I go up there, I always say, 'How're you doing today, Joe? Hope you're doing well,' just to stay on the right side of him," Terry said with a little smile.

"Are you serious?" I asked.

"Never more," Terry replied. "We've had some strange things reported, like finding beer kegs open. Sometimes people hear a strong wind howling up there when there's no wind outdoors."

I wanted Terry to tell me more, but a party of twenty guests came in, and he went off to check on their seating.

Lunch the next day was hectic, and I needed a hand. I asked a waitress named Judy if I could talk her into bringing a bottle of wine down for me. She seemed to be extra nice to me because I was new. It took awhile, but she finally brought it down. On another occasion I asked a waiter. That time I had to wait so long I was about to go myself before he finally showed up with it. I knew by now that I would have to familiarize myself with that storeroom.

The next morning I went upstairs to look around before any customers arrived. The rafters were festooned with cobwebs, and it was dark up under the eaves. It was kind of eerie up there, but I didn't think much about it. I was trying to get a read on where the various brands were kept when I heard a noise. It sounded like a groan, someone in real misery, and it startled me. I looked around, but since I didn't see a soul, I decided it was my imagination. I chose several varieties of wine that were often requested and carried them downstairs.

It was soon plain that most of the employees working at the Shrimp Factory weren't eager to go up to the storeroom at night because they thought the place was haunted. One of the waiters who was pretty friendly said, "I'll confess that I've felt a presence in this place. It's happened more than once right here in the restaurant—not just upstairs." Talk like that seemed silly to me at the time. I'd never taken much stock in ghosts.

A few weeks after I arrived, I had a date with Judy on my day off. She was a nice, down-to-earth kid who was a rising junior at the University of Georgia in Athens. We talked over dinner, and it turned out we both knew some of the same people. Before the evening was over I said, "Why does everyone make such a big fuss about going up to get wine?"

"Don't ask me," she said. I was glad she shared my opinion about ghosts.

One night a customer asked for Dom Perignon, and we didn't have any at the bar. It was about ten o'clock, and busy as I was, I knew better than to ask anyone to get it. When I went upstairs to the storeroom, I had the craziest feeling. In the first place, the light over the stairway seemed dimmer than usual. Then I touched the switch to turn on the main light and nothing happened. I went back downstairs and got a flashlight from under the bar, but the batteries must not have been fresh for the bulb inside it looked like a dying ember.

I returned to the storeroom. I knew the corner where we kept the champagne, and in the semidarkness, I found the boxes. Then I became acutely aware of shadows moving on the wall. Convinced that they were caused only by my flashlight, I turned it off and stood perfectly still in the faint glow from the bulb over the stairs. I couldn't be sure, but as I watched the shadows, they appeared to continue moving for a moment. Then they stopped. It gave me the strangest sensation. Undoubtedly my eyes were playing tricks on me.

Reassured, I continued along between the rows of boxes toward the far corner of the room. I couldn't find any Dom Perignon, so I quickly gathered up several cheaper brands. Suddenly, I saw more shadows projected on the surface of the boxes. There came a sound of rushing feet—heavy and very purposeful. And then the enormous figure of a man seemed to materialize out of nowhere. His dark face and angry eyes thrust forward close to my own. Terrified, I jumped back. Outside the wind began to howl, and above its roar I thought I could hear groans and a murmur of voices.

The shadows now appeared menacing, and the enormous man seemed to move among them. For a few seconds I stood trembling while the voices around me seemed to grow to an angry crescendo. "Doky, doky, va doky!" they called.

I don't remember how I got from the storeroom back down to the restaurant—just that it happened very quickly.

"Sorry sir! Very sorry. We are out of Dom Perignon tonight," I gasped breathlessly to the customer. "All we have is Cribari."

He nodded, looking at me strangely. My apologies and excitement probably seemed out of proportion to our not having the brand he preferred. When I poured the champagne into his glass my hands were trembling.

A week before I left to go back to college, Judy and I went to a movie. Afterward we walked along the Savannah River. She asked casually if I had ever experienced anything upstairs in the wine storage room. Some people at the restaurant had told me Judy got irritated whenever stories of the supernatural were mentioned, and I had the feeling she was testing me.

"Nothing," I replied, not about to reveal my experience to a nonbeliever.

"Well, I'm glad someone else around here besides me is normal," she said with derision. "I heard all summer about how the restaurant was once a cotton warehouse where slaves were held after they were brought from Africa, how they loaded the cotton in the daytime and were chained to the wall at night so they wouldn't jump into the river and commit suicide."

"That may have been true," I said.

"What does it have to do with me now? That's ancient history. Some people even say there are times you can hear weird noises upstairs."

"No kidding? Sounds crazy to me," I said, and Judy nodded agreement.

"I know what you mean," she said. "Unreal." It was our last talk before I went back to college.

That year I listened to a campus lecturer who spoke on the days of slavery. He said that the slaves were chained to each other with wrist cuffs or neck collars after they were first brought over. And that they continued to use words from their own language, often combining them with words from English into an almost unintelligible patois.

I was unable to forget the chant I had heard in the wine room, so I waited to talk to him after the program.

"Va doky," I asked him. "What would that mean?"

"You can't ever be sure, of course," he replied, "but in one of the more common languages doky meant 'devil,' and va . . . that meant 'to kill'."

For a moment I could hear once more the howling of the wind as I had heard it upstairs in the old warehouse, an eerie backdrop to the sound of the angry, rhythmic chant. And I could hear those voices as if it was yesterday. Who was the devil they were chanting about? Had they wanted to kill their owner? Had they wanted to kill me? I shivered. Would I go back there if I needed to work another summer?

The answer to the last question was yes. I came back, but I never went upstairs alone again. I waited until someone could go with me, explaining that I needed to carry down a number of bottles at one time.

THE OLDE PINK HOUSE

23 Abercorn Street, Savannah

The Olde Pink House in Savannah's historic district has a turbulent history. Prior to the Revolutionary War, the home was a meeting place for many who desired independence from England. In a city that was primarily loyal to the King of England, the men who met in the Pink House were forced to conceal their activities to avoid being charged with treason.

One night in January of 1776, Joseph, John, and James Habersham invited a gathering of like-minded friends to the Pink House for the first time to plot revolution from England. The men's father, James Habersham, Sr., had died the previous year. He was a fierce Loyalist, but now that he was gone, his sons had no fear of their father's connections to the crown. The conspirators could meet at the house safely.

However, Loyalists in Savannah were quick to notice the curious gatherings at the Pink House. In order to put off suspicion, the group of revolutionaries, now calling themselves the Liberty Boys, staggered their arrivals at the home. Some of the men sauntered down Abercorn Street toward the house on foot, as if on an evening stroll, not wishing to risk driving their carriages. Too many parked vehicles would raise the curiosity of Loyalists living on Reynolds Square. Others entered the house from the rear entrance, away from the watching eyes of the city.

After entering the house, the men ascended the handsome Georgian stairway and entered the second-floor room on the right. The room's beautiful ceiling cornice, interspersed with medallions, probably went unnoticed during one important meeting.

"Well, Joseph, what can we do for the benefit of King George tonight?" asked one young man sarcastically. Whether it was Button Gwinnett, George Walton, Edward Telfair, or another of the young men was hard to determine over the murmur of voices.

"We are here to plan the kidnapping of the governor of Georgia!" rang out Joseph Habersham's audacious reply, and the room was suddenly quiet.

Then John Houstoun, one of the four original organizers of the Liberty Boys, spoke. "And who will execute this daring plan?"

"I shall be the one," said Joseph boldly.

"Governor Wright was our father's friend and a frequent visitor to this house," protested the more conservative James. "Father would turn over in his grave!"

"Yes. He would have tried to protect the governor, probably," said Joseph. "Perhaps we should hold Governor Wright here so that he may feel at home while we decide how he can best serve our cause."

"But that's treason!" exclaimed his brother.

"You are right, brother. And if we do not win our freedom from England, all of us here will be hanged as traitors," said Joseph. "But if we attain it, we will be heroes!"

The room resounded with cheers for Joseph's courage. A few weeks later he walked into the governor's council meeting and said, "Sir James, you are my prisoner." The governor surrendered. This was not the only bold act of the revolution planned in the Pink House. Though the odds against these young men succeeding were almost overwhelming due to the fact Savannnah was the stronghold of Georgia's Loyalists, the Liberty Boys fought diligently for independence. Fortunately,

*The Olde
Pink House*

the American colonies were victorious, and the young men became some of Georgia's most prominent leaders after the war.

But James Habersham was not to enjoy the success of his comrades. His business fortunes declined, and much to his sorrow, he was forced to sell his beloved Pink House after the Revolutionary War. However, the home continued to play a vital role in the country's history. During the War of 1812, captured British gold was stored in one of the home's two vaults. Later, when Savannah was captured by Union troops, Brigadier General Lewis York seized the home for his headquarters following General William T. Sherman's March to the Sea. But through it all, the elegant old house survived.

The Olde Pink House is now the home of one of the city's finest restaurants, but James Habersham has not been forgotten. A special room in the home displays authentic furnishings from the time of the Habershams' residence. Through a locked metal gate, people may view the antique-filled dining room just as it was when the house belonged to Habersham in 1779.

Given the home's unique history, perhaps it is not surprising that many claim to have experienced the supernatural within it. Some of these experiences have occurred in the restored dining room. Sometimes the room's furniture is found rearranged in the morning. Other times candles are found ablaze in the room when nobody in the building had a key to the metal gate. And passersby have reported looking through the room's window and seeing people moving about in the candlelight.

On one of my recent visits to the fine tavern downstairs in the Olde Pink House, I learned a little more about some of the bizarre things that have happened there. I was sitting by the fire with a fellow guest, and what with the warmth of the fireplace and that of the after-dinner brandy cradled between his hands, he seemed eager to talk. While we sat on the comfortable leather sofa watching the flames, he began his odd story.

"Last year I attended a banquet here—excellent I must say—but during the meal I felt the strong presence of someone near me. Glancing up from my dinner, I saw no one but the man on my left, who was occupied with his food and paying me no attention. I returned to my own dinner, but the sensation was too persistent to be ignored. Again I turned my head. This time I saw a gentleman in old-fashioned attire standing to my rear and staring down at me intently. This made me quite uncomfortable. The man wore a wig of the sort common in George Washington's day. Frankly, I thought his costume was out of place for the occasion, but it was so superbly fitted that I rose slightly from my chair to tell him so. At the same moment a waiter asked me if I wanted more coffee. When I turned back to the gentleman in Colonial attire, he had disappeared. I asked the waiter for the identity of the person, but he steadfastly denied having seen anyone behind me."

A few minutes later, Rick Ellis, the manager of the tavern, took me and my husband on a tour of the house. According to Ellis, the house derives its name from the original pink stucco, which was restored and now covers the building once again. During the tour we admired many of the house's beautiful features: the entrance hall and the fan light over the front door, the staircase, said to be the finest in Georgia, and the mellow tones of the heart-of-pine floors.

Finally, when we reached the upstairs of the building, our host himself brought up the topic of the ghost. "There are guests who claim to have seen a man in Colonial dress," he said while we admired the antique furnishings.

"Have you any idea who it could be?" I asked.

"The description fits that of James Habersham, Jr.," he replied. "When you go back downstairs look at the large oil painting of Habersham in the front hall. They say the ghost looks just like that picture."

"After a party, I once had a guest inquire whether the gentleman wearing a Colonial costume was employed by the Pink House. Imagine that! Of course he wasn't," said the manager smiling, "it's enough of a challenge to keep competent help without hiring someone to scare them away!"

"Do you look upon the stories of a ghost, or ghosts, as a joke?" my husband asked.

"Not at all," Ellis said, glancing around cautiously. Then he began to share a surprising experience.

"One night after the restaurant closed and only the lounge on the ground level was still open, about twenty-six of us were in the first-floor room. Suddenly, the door to the second floor swung open with the loud squeak it always makes. All the staff looked up to see who could have gotten up there, because nobody is allowed in that part of the building after the restaurant is closed. The room we were sitting in suddenly became extremely hot, and as we stared at the staircase, we saw a white vapor descending the stairs.

"Twenty-six people dashed out of the building, leaving the safe unlocked and the cash register open. With my hands literally trembling, I made myself lock the door, and I took the key to the owner. That was the night I almost quit because of the ghost."

THE OLDE PINK HOUSE ON REYNOLDS SQUARE IS THE ONLY SURVIVING PRE-REVOLUTIONARY WAR MANSION IN SAVANNAH. IT WAS BUILT IN 1771. NOW A RESTAURANT WITH A TAVERN ON THE GROUND FLOOR, THE RESTORED HOUSE IS ADJACENT TO THE PLANTERS INN.

CELEBRATION OF SPIRITS

Bonaventure Cemetery, Savannah

Bonaventure was Savannah's most impressive plantation house. Built before the American Revolution, its beautiful gardens stretched from the house down to the edge of the Wilmington River.

The plantation was the home of John and Mary Tattnall and their two sons, John and Josiah. The older generation, loyal to King George, returned to England with their family when the war was imminent, but young Josiah's sympathies were with Georgia. Risking his life, he returned to the colonies and served under General Nathanael Greene. The young man soon rose to the rank of brigadier general. After England's defeat, Josiah Tattnall became a member of Congress. Later he was elected governor of the new state of Georgia.

In the years that followed the Revolutionary War, Bonaventure became a magnet for the most prominent families in Georgia and the South. A constant stream of wealthy and influential guests arrived at the home in fine carriages or on sloops that were docked at the river. The home grew famous for the great banquets and house parties thrown by Josiah Tattnall. Perhaps the most elaborate dinner parties hosted by the Tattnalls were the annual Bonaventure Thanksgiving Day celebrations. For these occasions, the dining room table and sideboard were laden with wild turkeys, baked hams, oyster pies, quail, and fine imported wines. The home's mantles and bannisters were festooned with greenery from the gardens, and the fireplaces burned brightly in every room to give Bonaventure a warm and welcoming appearance.

It was during one such Thanksgiving celebration in the early 1800s that tragedy befell Bonaventure. On this day, the guests were just sitting down to enjoy the meal's first course when a butler hurried into the dining room and whispered something to Mr. Tattnall in a grave tone. Josiah Tattnall rose from the table and, quite calmly, followed the butler out of the room.

In a few minutes he returned and made an announcement to his guests. "Ladies and gentleman, I apologize for this interruption. Please take your wine glasses and plates to the garden. The servants will be there with the tables momentarily. We have decided that since the weather is pleasant, it will be a treat to continue our dinner out there."

The guests murmured in surprise, then smiled at the whim of their host and followed him outdoors. Just behind them came the servants carrying the tables and chairs.

When the food had arrived and everyone was seated, Josiah Tattnall rose from his chair and once again spoke to his guests.

"My good friends," he began, "with deepest regret I must tell you that this is the last of the many celebrations we have had here together. Bonaventure has caught fire and will soon be gutted by flames." For the first time, his voice trembled. "Let me assure you, we are all quite safe, so I do not want this to become a time of sadness."

Just then a butler asked the host if the lamps and candles should be brought outside. "No," said Tattnall, "the flames from Bonaventure will soon illumine the occasion." And in the dancing light from the fire, the guests feasted.

As the dinner reached its conclusion, Tattnall rose and said, "May the memories of the joyful occasions we have shared here never end. I invite each of you who wishes to do so to offer a toast to all the happy occasions we have had in this house in the past." Sparks from the flaming mansion were now rising high into the sky. Lifting his crystal goblet to his lips, Josiah Tattnall drained the glass, then shattered it against one of the giant oaks surrounding the home. One guest after another followed suit, standing to offer toasts of gratitude for the hospitality they had enjoyed over the years, then shattering their glasses against the huge trees.

Bonaventure was never rebuilt after the fire. In the years that followed, the gardens and terraces of the plantation became a cemetery. Today, Bonaventure Cemetery, with its gnarled old oaks, moss-draped branches, and exquisite statuary, is regarded as one of the most beautiful cemeteries in America. It is said that those who chance to walk by the cemetery at night during the last week of November can sometimes hear the sounds of revelry, as if a great party was taking place somewhere on the grounds. Women's soft laughter and men's sonorous voices seem to eminate from somewhere beyond the cemetery's statues. And from the direction of the Tattnall plot, the bell-like sound of one crystal wine glass after another shattering against one of the ancient oaks wafts on the evening breeze.

BEAUTIFUL BONAVENTURE CEMETERY IS SEVEN MILES FROM SAVANNAH. TO REACH THE CEMETERY, TAKE U.S. 80 EAST FROM SAVANNAH TO DOWNING STREET. TURN LEFT ONTO DOWNING STREET AND PROCEED UNTIL IT DEAD-ENDS AT BONAVENTURE ROAD. TURN RIGHT AND CONTINUE TO THE CEMETERY. THE CEMETERY IS OPEN DAILY FROM 8:00 A.M. TO 5:00 P.M. (A WORD OF WARNING: THE GATE IS LOCKED PROMPTLY AT 5:00.)

A NIGHT IN ROOM 201

The Kehoe House, 123 Habersham Street, Savannah

For several years, my husband and I talked about spending a night in the Kehoe House. The inn has been featured in numerous magazines as a romantic place to stay. On my trips to Savannah, I have always been impressed by the imposing Gothic appearance of the home, but my interest in the house heightened when I learned Rooms 201 and 203 had a reputation for being haunted.

The house was built in 1892 by William Kehoe, an Irish immigrant. When William was nine years old, his family left the famine and oppression of Ireland and arrived in Savannah, which was known as a town where the Irish were not discriminated against. As William grew up, he developed a gift for managing finances and soon became prosperous.

When I travel to research a ghost story, I do not carry, as one magazine describes it, a "Ghostbuster's Toolkit." My only tools for hunting ghosts are my own finely honed senses which can detect a sudden heightened awareness or a stabbing chill. Instead of a psychic entourage, I often rely on eyewitness accounts to document my stories. I usually find that normal, everyday people provide more reliable and descriptive accounts of ghosts than those who claim to have some sort of special psychic ability.

The Kehoe House

During the course of my research, I have come across other ghosts that are said to reside in certain rooms in hotels or inns. I'm usually enthusiastic about trying to stay in one of these "haunted" rooms, but my husband will have nothing to do with them. "Nothing doing," he usually replies, "I'm not staying in any haunted house."

When I mentioned the Kehoe House, he surprised me by

agreeing to stay at the inn. He had seen the house on a television program titled "America's Most Romantic Inns" and was actually excited about taking me there. "It *is* absolutely beautiful," he said. "Of course you know nothing is going to happen, but you will enjoy the experience."

The room he reserved was Room 201. A confirmation of our reservation arrived via fax, along with a history of the house. I particularly liked one sentence in their description: "The Kehoe House is a place of dreams . . ."

It was early spring when we arrived in Savannah, and the tips of the azalea buds in Columbia Square were showing a delicate pink. We rang the bell of the Kehoe House and admired the sparkling Victorian glass doors while we waited. We were then led inside and discovered we were just in time for afternoon tea. Joining us was a pleasant couple on their way from Florida to visit friends in Boston.

After tea, we were shown to Room 201. It was immediately clear the Kehoe House was everything the advance information had promised. The second-floor room featured a high ceiling and warm, peach-colored walls. Each room in the house has a balcony, but the rooms share little else in common. Our bright and cheerful room had a corner bath, a handsome period wardrobe, an oriental rug, and several tall windows. Everything about the room reflected warmth and hospitality. As I hung my clothes in the wardrobe, I smiled in amusement; it was hard for me to believe that this lovely room could possibly be haunted.

While I was unpacking, my husband sniffed the room's flower displays, which were dried and had no discernible odor. He suffers from allergies, and I decided he was just checking to see if the flowers would give him problems during the night.

After we had settled in, we went to sit on the balcony. There was no door. Instead we opened one of the tall windows and walked outside to enjoy the lovely afternoon light.

We left our room at six o'clock to have cocktails downstairs. As I walked down the stairs, I admired the beautiful oak panelling and the Egyptian pyramid–style newell post on the bannister. Several couples were already enjoying a glass of wine and hors d'oeuvres. Everyone was talkative and friendly enough, although it did occur to me that the conversation was a bit hushed. About seven, we all left in different directions to enjoy Savannah's many fine gourmet restaurants. Waterfront restaurants appeal to me anytime, and that night we chose the River House.

Over dinner, my husband and I discussed the cocktail hour. I remarked that the room where we had our drinks was much longer than the little parlor where we had tea.

"Yes, the Viewing Room is much longer than the other rooms," my husband replied.

"The Viewing Room?" I inquired.

"Yes, I read in some of the brochures that the room was used as a viewing room when the house was a funeral home."

I immediately recalled the guests' tendency to talk in hushed tones during the cocktail hour and wondered if it had anything to do with the room's history. Then I quickly dismissed my slight sense of discomfort and enjoyed a fabulous dinner.

We did not return to the house that night until around 10:30. After we entered our room, my husband again made a point of sniffing around, just as he had done that afternoon. We climbed into bed, and while I was determined to sit up and wait for the appearance of a ghost, it was clear that my husband had no such plans.

"Don't tell me that after making a special effort to reserve Room 201 for us, you are going to sleep without waiting to see if something happens," I said.

"That's right," he replied sleepily.

"Well, I'm going to stay awake," I said firmly.

Placing several pillows behind my back, I propped myself

up to wait for something to happen. Finally, the day's activities proved too much for me, and I fell asleep shortly after one o'clock.

At about two that morning, I opened my eyes and briefly turned on the light. Again, I tried to stay awake but soon fell asleep. Sometime later, I heard a key slowly turning in the lock. Perhaps I was not startled because I knew the security at the Kehoe House was excellent. In any case, I was still half asleep when I heard the sound in the door. Then I heard a sharp crack, as if the door was opening, followed by the sound of the door closing with a resounding crash.

I immediately opened my eyes and sat up in bed. In the far corner of the room, I could see a tall woman with long, dark hair. The woman's floor-length gown was a luminous white. With trembling fingers, I turned on the bedside light and looked again, only to find that she was gone.

I thought of waking my husband, but since he obviously had not seen or heard anything, I knew he would scarcely be able to explain what happened. Instead, I tried to sort out my thoughts. Who was that woman? I thought. Had the door actually opened, or did I just hear the *sound* of it slamming? I lay awake until dawn fearing the woman might reappear. Finally, unable to help myself, I fell into a sound sleep and did not wake until we received our breakfast call.

As my husband and I dressed, I told him of my experience during the night. After hearing my story, he asked, "Were you able to smell roses?"

"No," I replied.

"Well, the entire time we have been in this room, I have been acutely aware of the fragrance of roses or rose water," he said. "That's why I've been sniffing around the room. I can't believe you haven't noticed the smell."

"Well, I haven't," I replied, "but I'll take your word for it. Why don't I go down to breakfast while you shave."

"Fine," he said. He started towards the corner of the room but then stopped abruptly with a puzzled expression on his face. "Nancy, before you go down come over here a moment."

I walked over to where he was standing and immediately felt a chill. "It's so cold here!" I shivered.

"I noticed this spot last night," he said. "I can feel a tremendous chill here, though it's a little less strong than it was before."

"This is right where I saw the lady in the white gown!" I exclaimed.

I was excited by the discovery, but there seemed to be nothing else to do but proceed with the day. After breakfast, I wanted to take some pictures. It was too overcast to walk, so we went directly to our car without returning to the room.

When we returned at 10:30, the maid had just finished cleaning our room. The first thing we did was walk to the place in the corner where we had felt the chill.

"The chill isn't here now," I said.

"The fragrance is gone, too," he replied.

"So it is not something they use to freshen the rooms?"

"Apparently not," he answered, "unless Lysol now smells like fresh roses." However, he was still not satisfied and walked over to Room 203, where the maid was just starting to clean, to ask her if she used any cleaning products that smelled like roses.

He returned in a few moments looking baffled. "I just felt a distinct chill in a part of that room," he said. "I wonder if strange things happen in there, too?"

"That's said to be the other haunted room," I replied.

"Let's see if it's available tonight so we can find out," he said, now eager to see the ghost for himself.

"I'm glad I got to experience at least one ghost in what may well be the world's most haunted city," I answered as I packed my bag, "but I don't feel like staying up all night to see another one."

THE KEHOE HOUSE AT 123 HABERSHAM STREET IS A LUXURY, EUROPEAN-STYLE INN. A GOURMET BREAKFAST IS SERVED EACH MORNING, AND EACH EVENING COMPLIMENTARY HORS D'OEUVRES ARE SERVED AT COCKTAIL HOUR. FOR INFORMATION AND RESERVATIONS, CALL 912-232-1020.

HEARTBREAK AT THE 17HUNDRED90 INN

The 17Hundred90 Inn,
307 East President Street, Savannah

When Anne Powell left England for the New World, it was because her sister, Elizabeth, wanted to go. Elizabeth, the adventurous one of the pair, argued that the girls had no future in Bristol since their parents had died in a typhoid epidemic and left them with very little inheritance.

"We can earn our own way when we get there," Elizabeth argued.

"And what shall we do?" asked Anne.

"We shall do what women have always done. Take care of children, sew, cook, be a lady's maid, or a companion to someone. Those things will be needed there just as they are here."

"Oh, I know you're right," said Anne, "but the very thought of doing such a thing scares me. I wish I knew how to make up my mind about something and not worry." She had grown increasingly timid and fearful since the death of her father, whom she had often relied on for advice and guidance.

"You must learn to think for yourself," Elizabeth told her often. "If we can't think for ourselves, we are like cripples."

"But you've always been different, even when father was alive," Anne would reply. "Sometimes you even dared to question his decisions."

Elizabeth's persuasion finally wore down her sister, and the two girls booked passage on a ship to Georgia with the small amount of money they had been left by their parents. Anne questioned why they were not going to New York or Philadelphia—any city where they were likely to find work—but Elizabeth assured her that Georgia was seeking new settlers and that they would receive a warm welcome there.

Elizabeth was excited as they packed their clothes in a small trunk and said their farewells to neighbors and the family priest. Father Daniel Finney gave the girls his blessing with a glint of admiration and respect in his kind blue eyes.

On the journey to Savannah, Elizabeth befriended the Holcomb family, whose children took an immediate fancy to her. She was soon teaching them games and reading to them to fill up the long days at sea.

Anne whiled away the hours sewing and doing embroidery in solitude. Though she was not outgoing, her attractive appearance and blonde hair attracted the interest of a young German sailor named Hans. The two struck up a friendship that quickly blossomed into romance. Hans was pleased by the way she deferred to his opinions and sought his advice.

When the ship reached Savannah, the Holcombs offered Elizabeth a job in Charleston and agreed to pay for her lodging in the city for the next two weeks until they were ready to make the journey up the coast. The girls each took a room at the inn on East President Street, but when Elizabeth tried to pay for Anne's room with her advance from the Holcombs, Anne refused. "Hans has agreed to pay for me," Anne said. "We shall be married within the week, and he says I will never have to worry about taking care of myself again."

Hans did make one visit to the inn, but after that night, he never returned. The next day the innkeeper asked Anne for additional money, telling Anne the sailor had paid for only the first night. Anne told the innkeeper it was a mistake, for she and the young man were to be married later that week. Elizabeth payed for Anne's room, though Anne insisted Hans would be returning any moment.

"You aren't giving him a chance to prove himself," Anne told her sister angrily. Elizabeth had her doubts about Hans, but she held her tongue.

A few days later, the two young women took a walk down by the waterfront. As they strolled along the docks, they saw several sailors sporting with some local girls. There, in full view, was Hans with a girl on his lap. Anne and Elizabeth hurriedly walked by the group, and Hans never even looked their way. When the sisters were out of sight, Anne burst into tears and ran back to the inn alone.

Elizabeth found her sister crying on the bed in her room. "Don't worry about him," said Elizabeth warmly. "You can come with me and work for the Holcomb family."

"They won't want me," Anne sobbed. "Anyway, I want to go with Hans! I love him, and he said he wanted to marry me!"

"Why Anne, you wouldn't want to marry him if he is going to act like this, would you?" Elizabeth said, trying to reason with her infatuated sister. "You're lucky to find him out."

"He wouldn't act this way if we were married. I know he wouldn't," said Anne, crying even harder.

"No. He would probably act worse!" said Elizabeth, now exasperated with her sister.

Nothing more was heard from Hans. The Holcombs paid several visits to the inn to make sure Elizabeth and her sister were comfortable, but Anne would not even come downstairs to see them. She spent most of her time embroidering. She would often get up during the night and walk the floor crying and wringing her hands in despair.

Elizabeth explained the situation to Mrs. Holcomb, who agreed to hire Anne as well, though she had no idea what skills the girl might possess. She was a kind and compassionate

The 17Hundred90 Inn

woman and felt sorry for the young girl. Elizabeth tried to reason with her sister, insisting Hans was not worth her grief.

But Anne refused to listen to reason. On the night before the Holcombs were to come for both girls, Anne Powell hugged her sleeping sister and then threw herself out the window down into the courtyard below. As she plunged to her death, she emitted a piercing scream that could be heard throughout the inn.

Today, the place where Anne Powell met her untimely death

is known as the 17Hundred90 Inn. It houses one of the finest restaurants in Savannah's historic district as well as a popular inn. On occasion, piteous sobs can be heard coming from one of the inn's upstairs rooms, and sometimes, guests at the inn hear a young woman's terrified scream piercing the night.

THE 17HUNDRED90 INN IS OPEN FOR LUNCH AND DINNER. FOR INFORMATION, CALL 916-256-7122.

THE PIRATES' HOUSE

20 East Broad Street, Savannah

The Pirates' House is a rambling, unpainted structure that has welcomed visitors with food and drink since 1753. Located only a few feet from the Savannah River, it was once an inn for seamen, many of whom drank their grog in the chamber known as the Captain's Room. Here they bragged about their exploits on the seven seas, and God help the unwary sailor who knew not the kind of men that invited him to the Pirates' House for a drink!

Treasure Island, Robert Louis Stevenson's classic book, often refers to Savannah. Some of it undoubtedly was set in the Pirates' House. Some even believe that Captain Flint died in an upstairs room, and a few go so far as to say his ghost wanders through the building on moonless nights. On these nights, it is said a man's rough voice can be heard shouting, "Get me the brandy. Get it, I say!"

Today, the building is a unique restaurant with over a dozen dining rooms. On a typical night, the restaurant, which features a pirate ambience, is full of well-dressed tourists and locals enjoying some of the finest cuisine in the city, but there was a time, not as long ago as you might think, when men as wicked as the Devil himself stayed in these rooms. Men like the murderous "Black Dog" and "Billy Bones." Pirates from as far away as Madagascar and the Red Sea swaggered about the house wearing pistols and cutlasses, their boots pounding on the wooden floors.

Evil deeds were common among these cutthroats. Many a man was killed within the home's walls, and even more were shanghaied. In those days, sailors would ply unsuspecting young men and boys with liquor. When the victims were too drunk to realize what was happening, the sailors would take them to ships waiting in the harbor. It is said that a tunnel leading from the Pirates' House to the river was used to secretly transport shanghaied sailors to the harbor. These men were forced to serve on the ships and were usually treated no better than slaves. The practice was so common that English sea captains would shanghai men as readily as pirates. And the brutality of many of these English captains was far worse than that of the pirates they hunted.

Today we wonder how such nefarious practices could go on right under the noses of local officials. However, in those days, no one asked questions about a bill of sale or how a ship in port came to have such a rich cargo. As long as the ships were bringing commerce into the city, most officials had little concern about how these sailors did their business.

One resident of Savannah had a remarkable experience during a dinner at the Pirates' House. "There was a night some years ago when I decided I wanted to learn whether the pirate ghosts still roamed through the house," the man began. "I asked myself, Why not go in search of the tunnel that is said to lead from the house to the river? A tip to one of the waiters enabled me to find it, and soon I found myself considering whether to lower myself down from the mouth of the

The Pirates' House

tunnel into its shadowy depths. I backed in cautiously, and the toes of my boots began to find some footholds. I was certainly not afraid, for I could still hear voices from the restaurant above.

"Then I found myself on the hard earth floor of a dark, musty tunnel. I was determined to walk as far as I could go, with the hope of reaching the river at the other end. I estimated that would be little more than the distance across the street. The light from my small flashlight was not as strong as I wished, but it was all I had, so I pressed forward. I carefully extended one foot at a time, all the while keeping a hand on the tunnel wall. The tunnel was increasingly damp, but on I went. So much for inebriated pirate ghosts singing in raucous voices, I thought with considerable boldness.

"Then something brushed the leg of my trousers and stepped onto my foot. It was that close. In panic, I pointed the beam of my little flashlight below me and saw an enormous cat. Our eyes met, and the beast, startled too, fled off into the blackness.

"With my heart pounding, I walked a few more feet and came upon a small door that was blocking my way. There was dirt wedged underneath it, but I managed to dig it away. The door would still not move so I put my shoulder against it and broke the rusty lock. As I pushed back the door, I stepped into ankle-deep water. Then, to my relief, the tunnel began to slope upward. I knew this short passage could only lead to the river, but it was obvious I was in a part of the tunnel that hadn't been used in years.

"Suddenly my foot struck a hard and uneven object. Again, I pointed the flashlight's beam downward, and this time it picked out something I hadn't expected to see. It was a bony hand attached to a skeleton. The bones were sprawled against one of the biggest, heaviest doors I've ever seen. Surprisingly, the skeleton did not startle me as much as the cat had. I walked up to the door and saw in an instant there was no way I could open it. However, I could hear the sound of lapping of water on the other side, along with the faint sound of a boat motor some distance away.

"After listening at the door for a few seconds, I heard the sound of a dull thud behind me, as if the door I had pushed open a moment or two before had closed. I immediately began to worry that I was trapped in the tunnel, perhaps to suffer the same fate as the skeleton in front of me. It was at that moment that I heard the sound of footsteps and the voices of men shouting and cursing.

"'And if we should find another mother's son, we'll take him too,' said a loud voice. 'And cut his gizzard out if he don't take the oath,' said another. 'I'll do it me self. What do you say, Cap'n?'

"The men were getting closer now, and you can imagine my terror. I looked desperately for some place to hide. Then I heard, 'I say when we gets to sea, we'll keel haul him, if we need to change his mind.' I believed this voice was that of Flint, and I have never heard such meanness in a voice in all my life. A chill went down my spine. I stooped and pressed myself against the wall, hoping they would pass by me in the darkness. A group of shadowy figures went by in a blast of icy air, then passed through the massive door in front of me as if it wasn't even there.

"I turned and raced back down that tunnel, finally reemerging at the entrance inside the Pirates' House. I rejoined some of my friends. They asked me what had happened—why my clothes were dirty and wet, and why I seemed so quiet—but, of course, I never told them.

"I'm not sure exactly what happened to me that night, but I do know I heard the voice of Flint and his wicked crew. I've often wondered whether I would go down in the tunnel again. It's closed now, though, and I guess it's well that it is. But I've heard people who work at the restaurant, and others, tell me that sometimes you can still hear the pirates' voices. They say it has to be a foggy, moonless night, and the restaurant must be quiet and empty. Then, and only then, can you sometimes hear them cursing and laughing their sinister laughs from the tunnel below."

THE PIRATES' HOUSE IS LOCATED AT THE INTERSECTION OF BROAD AND BAY STREETS. THE RESTAURANT HAS BEEN RECOMMENDED BY *GOURMET*, *MCCALLS*, *BETTER HOMES & GARDENS*, *SOUTHERN LIVING*, *REDBOOK*, AND MANY OTHER PUBLICATIONS. FOR INFORMATION AND RESERVATIONS, CALL 912-233-5757.

AMERICA'S MOST HAUNTED HOUSE

Hampton Lillibridge House,
507 East St. Julian Street, Savannah

Savannah's beautiful Hampton Lillibridge House looks more like a New England sea captain's home than a typical Southern house of the period. The home, built in 1796 by a wealthy planter from Rhode Island, features a gambrel roof and a widow's walk with a view of the river.

Several years ago, the home was moved from its original location by Jim Williams, a well-known resident of Savannah. Mr. Williams began plans to restore the house, but soon after these renovations were underway, workers started to describe strange events occurring inside the home. Eventually, these incidents became so common that a famous investigator dubbed the home "the most psychically possessed house in the nation."

The first supernatural event was observed just after the home had been moved to its present location. Brick masons, who had been working on the house's new foundation, ran out into the middle of the street and refused to work. The agitated foreman walked up to Jim Williams and said, "Mr. Williams, that house is full of people, and they ain't working for you! I want you to go in there."

Williams went in and heard a number of loud crashes, as if furniture was being thrown against a wall. Above him he heard the sound of people running across the floor and kicking over furniture. Williams and some of the masons investigated the house and found it was empty. Only then did the brick masons go back to work. However, this return to work was short-lived; the next day the brick masons claimed they heard whispers and laughter in the house. This time they got in their cars, left the house, and refused to come back. After this incident, the workmen who remained at the site were spending more time listening than working. "I was way behind schedule," Williams recalled, "and something had to be done."

After talking with friends, Williams decided he would have an exorcism performed on the house. An Episcopal bishop, a scientist, and all the workmen gathered for the ceremony performed by the bishop. "In the name of the Father, Son, and Holy Ghost, I ask that the evil spirits leave this place! May the holy archangels of the Lord dwell here forever," the bishop called out. Then he blessed the house.

The exorcism seemed to work, for the noises left the house, and the relieved workmen went back to their jobs. The next step was to sand and varnish the floors. One day, the contractor in charge of the work on the floors came to Mr. Williams and asked him if he had visited the house the night before.

"I went back to finish up last night and heard footsteps," the contractor said. "Someone was walking around at the foot of the stairs and on the floor down below me. I was upset because it was still wet. Thinking you might have dropped by, I took my flashlight and shone it down on the floor I had just finished varnishing. No one was there, and there were no footprints!"

Since the house did not seem haunted before the restoration

Hampton Lillibridge House

project began, it seems likely that some of the features added to the house might have brought the presence of ghosts along with them. Jim Williams was a consummate artist at restoring old homes. The bricks for this house had to be an early terra-cotta color instead of the well-known Savannah gray. He found the bricks he wanted in some old houses in middle Georgia and brought them to Savannah. Similarly, the home's weather-boards had to be similar to its original ones—hand finished with a beaded edge—while the windows were redone with old glass found at local junkyards and paneled shutters that really worked. The home's original widow's walk had been removed, and Williams rescued it from one of the city's slums. Any or all of these materials added for the restoration could have been the source of the ghosts.

Williams moved into the restored house during May of 1964. On the day he moved, workmen took bets that he would not be able to stay through the night. Yet despite his misgivings about spending the night alone on the third floor of the empty house, he slept extremely well.

However, the quiet did not last. On the second night, he heard a terrible moan followed by a the sound of four people in heavy shoes shuffling up the stairs. "I got out my German Luger that I keep beside my bed," Williams later recalled. "You can imagine how frightening this was. I waited for them to stop at my door, then come into the room, but they went right on up to the top floor. There it sounded as if they were having a square dance, screaming and hollering—behaving like a bunch of drunks."

Williams heard these exact same noises every so often. The worst incident occurred the first hot night Williams experienced in the house. The window air conditioner had not yet been installed. He awakened to the now familiar noises and sat up to discover that "the room was full of little tiny swamp mosquitoes that really sting."

Williams remembered he had a can of mosquito spray downstairs in the kitchen. He got his Luger out of the drawer and started down the steps, gun in hand. Just as he was opposite the drawing room door, he saw it open five inches. He paused, then decided to go on past it. He reached the kitchen, found the spray, and started back. This time, he saw the drawing room door close as he passed by it. Though his heart was pounding, he walked back to his room and sprayed it for mosquitoes. When he finished spraying, he went back to bed but stayed awake for the rest of the night.

One night, he woke at about 3:30 to the sound of footsteps near his bed. Assuming it was a burglar, the frightened Williams called out, "What do you want?" But there was no answer, only the sound of running feet. Williams hurried into the library and turned on the light. He could still hear the footsteps, but there was no one to be seen. On another occasion, the door between his bedroom and the adjoining morning room opened. A black figure entered the room and then, as Williams stared in disbelief, the figure vanished.

One of the strangest incidents occurred on a night when Williams was not in the house. That night, three houseguests heard strange noises upstairs. One of the three, a husky fellow, went upstairs to investigate. When he didn't return immediately, the other two guests went upstairs and found him lying on the floor trembling with fear. The man claimed that when he had walked into one of the rooms, he had the sensation of stepping into a lake of cold water. The man found himself fighting a mysterious force that seemed to pull him toward a thirty-foot chimney shaft at the side of the room. The guests decided to go to the apartment of a neighbor across the street and wait for Williams to return from work. Before they could close the door of the apartment, they heard a woman scream twice. They ran out into the street and looked over at the house. Standing at a third-floor window was a man wearing a white shirt and black bow tie. This time, the trio did not investigate.

By now, Jim Williams was ready to seek further assistance in ridding the house of its ghosts. The man he called was Dr. William G. Roll of the American Psychical Research Foundation. Dr. Roll stayed in the house for four nights while trying to find evidence of caverns, underground streams, antimagnetic waves, or other circumstances that could cause the phenomena. Dr. Roll eventually concluded the incidents were caused by "emotional waves," or vibrations given off by a human being after severe trauma or death. It was this research that led Roll to dub the home "the most psychically possessed house in the nation."

Jim Williams finally moved out of the house several years later. Since then, the house on Julian Street has changed hands twice. The present owners say that if there are any spirits in the old house, they have been friendly ones, though some puzzling events have occurred. "There have been times when I have had the feeling that I was not alone," recalled one of the present owners, "and twice I have heard a sound like that of furniture being moved across the floor overhead, although the house was empty."

Right after this couple moved in, the woman found herself unable to close the door to a small storage area Mr. Williams had installed in the house. She called the previous owner for assistance. The previous owner came over and locked the door "tighter than a drum" with a combination lock. The interior of the house was being painted, and the next morning the painters found the door to the storage area wide open!

These incidents would lead one to believe that ghosts still reside in America's most haunted house.

THE HAMPTON LILLIBRIDGE HOUSE IS NOT OPEN TO THE PUBLIC; PLEASE RESPECT THE PRIVACY OF ITS OWNERS.

SAVANNAH'S FAVORITE GHOST

Elba Island Lighthouse, Savannah Harbor

It was 1950, and Patrick Shannon was finally returning to Savannah. The city had been his home until 1930, when he was forced to leave it abruptly. Patrick was a lifelong sailor, and even the majority of his years in Savannah had been spent aboard a boat. As he sailed down the coast, his mind flashed back to all the times he had entered Savannah's harbor as a boy. In those days, the one thing you could be certain of as you sailed through the harbor was that Florence Martus would wave to you as you passed by Elba Island. Florence had been the sister of Elba Island's lighthouse keeper and was famous for waving to each ship from her front lawn as it entered the harbor. The story went that, many years ago, Florence had promised her heart to a young sailor and made a vow that she would be there to greet him when he returned. Through the years, Florence greeted each ship, hoping that it was finally bringing home her true love.

Patrick remembered the joy he had felt each time the woman waved her apron or flashed a lantern at night as he sailed past her home into the harbor. But that joy disappeared after the accident that took the life of his best friend. Patrick had narrowly escaped death himself that dark night, and afterwards, he had been consumed by guilt. Though he didn't know for sure, he felt the accident had been his fault. And even if it wasn't, he knew there was more he could have done to save his friend's life. Patrick's guilt had intensified when an official inquiry was called into the accident. Part of Patrick desperately wanted to stay and find out the truth about what happened, but part feared that if he did, he might wind up facing time in jail, or worse.

In the end, fear won out, and he sailed away from Savannah, vowing never to return.

Now, after twenty years "on the run," Patrick decided to return to the city he once called home and find out what happened at the inquiry. But first he decided to stop at Charleston. The Coast Guard records would be stored either there or in Washington, and he wanted to see what they revealed about the inquiry.

The clerk in the Coast Guard's record room was helpful, but the records were not there. "You need to look in Washington," said the clerk. "Everything's been sent there."

Pat's face must have reflected his disappointment, for as he closed the file drawer, the clerk said, "You probably have a pretty good idea about the date of the inquiry you're researching. When you get to Savannah, why not go to the library and start searching the microfilms of the newspaper?"

"It's worth a try," said Pat. "Thanks."

On the trip from Charleston down to Savannah, Pat Shannon thought about the people he might meet on the streets. After twenty years would he recognize any of his friends? Would they know him? Would they condemn him?

Soon his boat was entering Savannah harbor. He stared at all the ships and noted how the city appeared so different from the sleepy town of his past. Much of it was new, but there were old landmarks, too. Like Florence Martus waving from the island. Who would have believed it after all these years? She had taken off her apron and was waving it at him just as she had always done. It was amazing how little her appearance had changed. He waved back to her with his hand and sounded a salute on the ship's horn. This had to be a good omen, he thought.

He started searching the newspaper microfilms later that day. He searched for hours and soon his eyes grew tired. The next day was Sunday, and he went to mass. On Monday, he was at the library when the doors opened. He searched throughout the morning, took a quick break for lunch, then went right back to work.

He thought he was near the probable date of the inquiry, but there was no way to tell for sure. The Coast Guard was notorious for changing inquiry dates. Plus, the paper may not have covered it, or he could have already passed over the article by mistake. His eyes were getting tired again. He got up from the hard oak chair and walked around for a few minutes. He stared out a window, then devoted himself once again to his task.

Again, he started poring through the microfilm. By 4:30, there was only one possible roll of film left. He was tempted to go back to his boat but decided it would be foolish to leave just one roll unchecked. He threaded the film through the machine and started scanning the headlines.

A half-hour later, a headline leapt out at him. As he read the opening paragraph, he realized he had found it! The story was only about three-inches long, and he shuddered to think how easy it would have been to miss it. With his heart pounding, he read the rest of the story, finally finding the information he sought in the last paragraph: "Pat Shannon, who was injured in the boating accident, was not available to testify. However, due to the committee's unanimous decision that there had been a freak engine malfunction, Shannon was exonerated of blame."

With these words, the years of guilt and doubt at last came to a close for Patrick Shannon. That night, he treated himself to a nice dinner in a restaurant on River Street. To his surprise, he recognized the manager as an old boyhood chum. His old friend was overjoyed to see him, and the two talked for hours.

"Well, Savannah's changed," said Shannon, as the evening drew to a close. "The only thing that is always the same is the woman who waves at me from Elba Island."

His friend looked puzzled. "You don't mean Florence Martus?"

"I certainly do. She greeted me as I came in the harbor just the way she used to do."

"Pat, Florence Martus died back in the early 1940s. You couldn't possibly have seen her—unless it was her ghost that greeted you!"

FLORENCE MARTUS, THE WAVING GIRL OF SAVANNAH, WAS BORN IN 1869 AND DIED IN 1943. IT IS SAID THAT SHE SOMETIMES STILL WAVES AT PASSING SHIPS FROM THE FRONT LAWN OF HER FORMER HOME ON ELBA ISLAND. IN 1971, A STATUE WAS ERECTED IN HER HONOR ON RIVER STREET.

THE ISLAND AND LIGHTHOUSE ARE LOCATED IN SAVANNAH HARBOR, SEVEN-AND-A-HALF MILES SOUTH OF THE CITY. FOR MORE INFORMATION ON THE LIGHTHOUSE, CONTACT THE SAVANNAH VISITOR CENTER AT 912-944-0460.

COLONIAL COAST AND GOLDEN ISLES: ST. SIMONS ISLAND

THE HAUNTED LIGHTHOUSE

St. Simons Lighthouse, St. Simons Island

Clump, clump, clump went the heavy footsteps on the cast-iron stairs of the lighthouse. They reached the second platform, then the third. "Clump, clump, clump, clump, clump." John Stevens, the new keeper of the St. Simons Lighthouse, knew who those footsteps belonged to, and he knew he would hear them for the rest of his life.

Working atop the lighthouse, Stevens recalled his arrival two years ago to apply for the position of assistant keeper. Prior to his interview, he stood and admired the impressive white tower silhouetted against the blue sky. As he gazed upon the structure, he thought the palm trees surrounding the buildings made a beautiful setting for the classic red-brick house beneath the tower.

Before applying he had learned all about the unfortunate history of the St. Simons Lighthouse. The tower and all the outbuildings were first destroyed by the Confederates in 1862, and when the rebuilding began several years later, one member of

St. Simons Lighthouse

the work crew after another was stricken with a mysterious illness. The contractor himself fell sick and died. Work halted until one of the bondsmen restarted the job, hoping to protect his investment. But after only a brief time, he was dead too. The work was not completed until the summer of 1872, and the lighthouse finally began operation on the first day of September that year.

Several years later, Keeper Fred Osborne decided that he needed an assistant. Osborne had a reputation for being difficult, and there had been few applicants by the time he interviewed the young John Stevens.

When Stevens arrived for his interview, the keeper was on his way to the top of the tower with extra kerosene for the lamp. Stevens carried it for him, and they talked as Mr. Osborne went about his duties.

"What experience do you have?" Osborne asked him.

"Not much, sir, but I assisted in the Charleston lighthouse on Morris Island when the regular assistant was ill."

"You would have a lot to learn, Mr. Stevens," said the keeper.

"I know that, sir. I would be glad to follow your instructions."

Osborne looked out to sea for a few minutes in silence. Finally he said, "Do you know anything about the weather or the behavior of storms?"

"A little, sir."

Although word had circulated among lighthouses along the coast that an assistant was needed at St. Simons, Fred Osborne was growing discouraged in his search for an experienced man. Since the old keeper believed Stevens genuinely wanted to learn, he decided to take him on and train him.

At the start, the attitude of both men exhibited a reasonable degree of goodwill. However, as Osborne instructed Stevens in some of the minor duties that fell to a keeper's assistant, it was obvious that he treated the tower's Fresnel light with fanatical pride.

"Each face of this light is surrounded by a ring of triangular prisms, which reflect and magnify the light's intensity," he explained to Stevens as he gently rubbed the spotless surface with his cloth. "The lenses revolve around the kerosene lamp and are powered by a clock mechanism. Of course, it's important never to run out of kerosene for it."

He pointed out the manner in which weights were pulled to the top of the lighthouse and then made a timed descent to the bottom. This timing was necessary in order to produce exactly one flash per minute. Although Stevens already knew it, Osborne went on to explain how each light along the coast had its own distinctive pattern, and according to the number and timing of the flashes, mariners at sea were able to identify the lighthouse and know their ship's location.

"It's also important to oil the lamp regularly," continued the keeper, showing exactly where to put the oil in the mechanism. Stevens nodded eagerly, trying to show Osborne he was an attentive student.

"Now some keepers may think it doesn't matter, but I always keep these lighthouse windows sparkling. Look. Not a fingerprint on them," said Osborne proudly.

"That is so the light will be brighter when it shines through them?" said Stevens, trying to show that he knew how imperative this was.

"Yes, but not entirely," the keeper answered gruffly. "It also means that I am better able to see out of them. I might spot a ship in trouble sooner, or be able to judge the weather a little more accurately. Do you understand, Mr. Stevens?"

"Yes, sir."

Osborne turned and fixed him with an intent stare. "I believe the most important part of this job is the *appearance* of the lighthouse windows. By them I can tell what kind of a keeper a man is."

"I see, sir," Stevens replied, slightly taken aback by the keeper's harsh tone.

"And if a U.S. Lighthouse Service inspector should pay us one of his surprise visits, he would look at those windows, too, and judge us by them." As if to prove his point, Osborne whipped out his handkerchief to rub at what might have been a fly speck in the corner of a window.

"How far can the St. Simons light be seen at sea, sir?" asked Stevens.

"About eighteen miles. That is if we have carried out our duties to *perfection*," Osborne said.

This was one of the first of many such lessons, and as Fred Osborne continued educating the new assistant keeper in his duties, friction developed between the two men. Stevens came to resent his superior more and more, and rumors soon reached the islanders that there were problems at the lighthouse. This was not a surprise, since disagreements might be expected when two people work closely together. However, no one realized how serious the bitterness had grown between Osborne and Stevens. They soon would.

March of 1880 arrived with a sense of foreboding. On Sunday morning, when Fred Osborne came to relieve his assistant, the sky was overcast. Clouds covered the sun, and the sea was rising fast.

"I thought you were to polish the prisms on the light last night," said the keeper accusingly.

"I did," said John Stevens, trying to control his anger.

"In the same way you did the windows, I suppose," said Osborne. He inspected a tiny smear on one of the windows with the candle flashlight he used to mount the stairs. "You must have put your fingers on the glass when you looked out," he said sarcastically.

"Why you old cuss!" Stevens blurted, unable to stand the

keeper's insults any longer.

"How dare you speak to me like that!" said Osborne. There was a peal of thunder in the distance. "Don't you know a storm is on the way? By afternoon the weather will probably be so thick that ships will be lucky to see this light. If they don't, it will be your fault!"

"What an old Jonah you are," Stevens accused.

"No!" Osborne exclaimed, his anger reaching fever pitch. "I'm sick and tired of your sloppy ways. We're going to settle this once and for all. Let's go outside." He hurried down the spiral stairs with Stevens following behind at a distance. When Stevens finally got outside, he saw Osborne standing about a hundred feet away. Assuming Osborne wanted to fight, and more than happy to oblige, he began walking toward the angry keeper.

"Don't get any closer!," Osborne shouted, drawing a pistol.

Ducking down, Stevens ran back into the house and seized his double-barreled shotgun, which was loaded with buckshot for deer hunting. He went back outside and stood by the door of the lighthouse, waiting for Osborne to make a move. Osborne then walked toward him along the path near the fence, and when the keeper was about a hundred feet away, Stevens fired. Buckshot struck Osborne in the abdomen in four places. With blood gushing through his clothing, the keeper fell to the ground.

Shocked by what he had done, Stevens took Osborne to the hospital in Brunswick, reporting the incident as "an accident." Then he returned to the lighthouse.

On Wednesday, after several days of severe pain, Fred Osborne died, and the sheriff took Stevens into custody. The harbingers of bad weather that had instigated the shooting on Sunday went unfulfilled until the latter part of the week, when a violent storm began battering the coast. In Brunswick a decision had to be made quickly whether to hold John Stevens and leave the lighthouse unattended, or let a possible murderer free and risk his escape.

No other keeper was available, and after much debate the sheriff and his deputies decided that the safety of ships at sea was paramount. There could be no interruption of the lighthouse operation, so they took Stevens back to serve as keeper until he was tried. When the storm was over, the sheriff found him still at the lighthouse. At the trial Stevens claimed self-defense, and since there were no other witnesses to give evidence, he was acquitted.

But the experience left John Stevens a different man. He often complained of hearing strange sounds. Rather than startle the skittish keeper half to death, visitors soon formed the habit of hailing him before they climbed to the top of the tower. "Ahoy, Stevens!" they would call from the first of the five landings before mounting the spiral stairs. "It's Bill Williams bringin' you fish and wantin' to pass the time of day," a friend might sing out as he climbed.

But John Stevens was obviously troubled. During particularly vicious storms, he often heard the heavy *clump, clump, clump* of footsteps. They would reach the second platform—*clump, clump, clump, clump*—then the third, and the fourth, and finally, the fifth and last.

"Who's there?" Stevens would call with a terrified voice. Then, getting no answer, he would jump from his chair and rush out to the metal platform to stare down the dark spiral of stairs, shouting again and again, "Who's there? Who's there!" His voice, reflecting the agony of his fear, echoed eerily down the stairwell.

Until the day he died, John Stevens was convinced that he heard the spectral footsteps of the dead keeper dragging himself painfully up the stairs.

A later keeper, Carl Svendsen, and his wife also heard the tread of a man's feet on the stairs many times during the forty years they lived at the lighthouse. Although the lighthouse is no longer in operation, visitors still sometimes report hearing heavy footsteps in the old tower, and many vow they smell the kerosene of an old-fashioned lamp as they climb the cast-iron stairs.

ST. SIMONS LIGHTHOUSE IS ON THE EASTERN TIP OF THE ISLAND. TO REACH IT, CROSS THE CAUSEWAY TO THE ISLAND EAST FROM BRUNSWICK AND TAKE KINGS WAY TO THE END OF THE ROAD. THE 106-FOOT-TALL WHITE TOWER PROVIDES A SPECTACULAR VIEW OF THE ISLAND, AND IT IS CONSIDERED AN UNUSUALLY FINE EXAMPLE OF AMERICAN LIGHTHOUSE ARCHITECTURE. THE MUSEUM OF COASTAL HISTORY IS NOW HOUSED IN WHAT WAS ONCE THE KEEPER'S QUARTERS. A SMALL ADMISSION COVERS BOTH MUSEUM AND LIGHTHOUSE. THEY MAY BE TOURED DAILY EXCEPT MONDAY AND ON CERTAIN HOLIDAYS. FOR INFORMATION, CALL 912-638-4666.

EBO LANDING

St. Simons Island

Every spring break the group of friends was eager to get home to St. Simons Island from their colleges on the mainland. Jimmy Ford was already sitting in Poor Richard's Restaurant with his frosted glass of beer when Jeff Morton walked in fresh from the University of Florida at Gainesville. Minutes later they were joined by Lou Freeman, home from Yale.

"What's happening?" Jeff asked Lou.

"Oh, not much. I saw Jerry and Marshall Edwards at the camera store a few minutes ago and said something to them about meeting us tonight." Jerry and Marshall Edwards were black, and all of the young men had grown up fishing, hunting, and playing ball together. Now they were attending different schools, but the bonds of friendship were still strong.

"Good," said Jeff, picking up his menu. "And do what?"

"Let's go out to Ebo Landing," said Jimmy.

"You mean Dunbar Point don't you? Isn't that what it's called nowadays?" said Jeff. "There's nothing there. What do you guys think is going to happen."

"Who knows? Maybe something weird," said Jimmy. "Folks say you can sometimes hear a chanting if you sit out there late at night."

"Kids probably say that," said Jeff. He grinned. "Well . . . at least it will give us a chance to catch up."

After dinner and a few beers, they called Jerry and Marshall Edwards, telling them where to meet, and headed out to Dunbar Point around ten o'clock. They rambled on for an hour talking about basketball, girls, and summer jobs. The murmur of their voices and a chorus of frogs were all that broke the stillness around them.

Finally Lou began to get restless. "What are we supposed to hear at this place?" he said.

"Voices," said Jimmy.

"Yeah, so do crazy people," said Lou. "I'm getting tired of waiting for something to happen. You and Jimmy want to stay, Jeff?"

"I've got nothing else to do," said Jeff.

There was a long silence and then Lou got up, yawned, and stretched. "I'm going, guys," he said. Jimmy Ford joined him.

"But what about Jerry and Marshall?" Jeff asked.

"They should be along soon," said Jimmy.

"Okay. You two go ahead," said Jeff. "I might as well wait and go back with them."

"They'll be here before eleven," said Lou. Then the two young men disappeared into the night.

Jeff had bought some hamburgers on the way to the landing, eaten one on the way over, and now went back to his car to get another. Returning to the stream, he leaned back against a palm tree and munched his burger.

Finally he saw the lights of a car. The car pulled up and only Jerry emerged. Jerry joined Jeff by the stream, and the two friends caught up on their activities since their last meeting. Jerry talked as if he might have to drop out of college for a semester and take a job until he could earn enough to go back. After awhile the conversation died out and Jerry fell asleep. As Jeff listened to his friend's even breathing he thought it was crazy to wait like this. He was ready to wake Jerry and leave, but for some reason he didn't. Why not wait until midnight, he thought, wasn't that supposed to be the witching hour?

The quiet was intense, only broken by the buzz of the mosquitoes. Then despite himself, Jeff started to feel a strange sense of expectancy. He glanced at the luminous dial on his watch. Only a few minutes before twelve. Standing up, he stretched and walked slowly along the creek. As he looked down at it, he saw a remarkable sight. It was as if Dunbar Creek was actually wider than when he first arrived earlier that night. But that was ridiculous. He stooped to give it a closer look, then suddenly leapt back for it appeared the water was rising steadily toward him.

It was then that he heard the first sound. Nothing loud. Just water lapping up against the bank. But it was as if something was just around the bend in the creek, ready to appear at any moment. It made him think of the sound a large launch makes as it glides through the water—but gliding very quietly, as if its motor was cut off.

It was a bright, moonlit night, and Jeff waited for the boat to appear around the bend. Was it a smuggler's boat? he wondered. No, that was crazy, smugglers wouldn't be on Dunbar Creek. He moved behind a clump of bushes to watch. He could now see that the creek was indeed much wider. It was up over the edge of the bank. His heart beating rapidly, he hurried back to Jerry's side.

"Jerry, Jerry!" he whispered, shaking his friend softly. "Wake up! We've got to hide."

Jeff could sense the ship that was causing the waves was approaching. He felt a breeze coming off the water, and at the same time became aware of a sickening stench in the air. He wondered what cargo the ship could possibly be carrying.

"Whatsa matter?" Jerry said, stirring sleepily.

"Get up and get behind the bushes."

"What's the hurry."

"Shut up!" Jeff whispered urgently.

Jerry started to reply angrily, but then he stopped, for he did see. They both did, and it was no launch.

There before the two young men was a clipper ship with a sharp bow and a lean, rakish hull. The masts were tall and billowing. Her lower yards were greater in length than half the deck, and the head spars were enormous for the size of the craft. The moon shown full upon her. She was beautiful, but at the same time there was something savage about her. And from her direction came the vile odor.

Every foot of her deck swarmed with cargo—black men, women, and children. The ankles of each attached by chains to the wrists of another. The leg irons of the men were secured to a great chain that ran along the bulwarks on both sides of the ship, while the women and children stood in the middle.

Jerry was now wide awake. He and Jeff watched while someone thumped a kettle and sailors wielding cat-o'-nine-tails forced the people to dance. There were screams of pain as the lashes caused them to leap into the air.

"That's a slave ship, isn't it?" Jeff whispered to Jerry.

"Yeah," Jerry responded. "The sailors are making them dance to show buyers on shore what lively condition they're in," he whispered.

Very slowly the ship glided past and anchored some distance away. Still chained together, but forced to form in a rank, a line of men marched off the clipper ship onto the bank. Then, chanting as they went, they made a mad dash for the river and plunged into the water. One head after another disappeared below the surface, and the weight of the chains was so great that none could be saved. The chant seemed to go on and on and linger in the two friends' ears, even after the water had closed over the men's heads. As the sound faded, Jerry and Jeff trembled with shock and fear.

Then the vessel and its suffering cargo began to fade and was soon gone. Once more the night was peaceful and the moon shone brightly above the empty bank.

"What were they saying?" Jeff asked before he realized Jerry couldn't understand the chant any better than he could.

"I don't have a clue," Jerry answered. "You've probably heard the story about how the captured Africans brought here were Eboes. They couldn't understand our language and didn't understand what was happening to them. Some even thought they would be eaten. They chose death instead, marching into the water chanting in their own language, 'The water brought us and the water will take us away'."

Finally, not knowing what else to do, Jeff put his hand on his friend's shoulder. "You know Jerry, I feel guilty that my race did something like that."

Jerry shrugged. "Don't. I'm sorry to say that selling people into slavery was also an old African custom. After raids, leaders of the winning tribe often made their prisoners into slaves. And they sold the slaves not just to whites, but to other tribes, too." There was no anger in his voice, only deep sadness.

Now the stench of blood and human excrement that had hung over them like an evil spell was gone. And the size of the creek? Its waters had retreated. Jeff placed his hand on the ground. The sandy soil extending several feet beyond the bank was still wet.

"The amazing thing," Jeff wondered, "is figuring out what could have produced that scene tonight."

"I've heard of all sorts of events out of the past being reenacted. Maybe that's what happened," Jerry said, obviously shaken. "But please remember one thing, I don't want to be the one to tell anybody we saw it."

Afterwards, the two friends rarely spoke about what they had seen. The great cypress trees standing knee-deep in the water and marshlands of St. Simons Island offer no hints about the origin of the strange ghost ship. Jerry and Jeff suspect they never will.

MARY THE WANDERER

St. Simons Island

Angus and Martha MacRae's hope of a safe voyage from Glasgow to the New World was short-lived, for the MacRaes and their two children were not long at sea before tragedy struck.

It began when a passenger on the ship *Anne*, carrying immigrants from Scotland to Savannah, came down with the disease every ship feared—the deadly smallpox. Angus MacRae was among the first to suffer the aches and fever, followed by an outbreak of painful sores over his entire body. Within a few days he died.

Some days later he was joined in death by his only son, Stuart. Soon the entire ship was ravaged by disease. Out of the family of four, only thirteen-year-old Mary and her mother were not taken. Then Mrs. MacRae began to show the first signs of the horrible disease. As Martha MacRae tossed with fever, Mary nursed her and prayed desperately. For awhile

Martha seemed to rally, then as the epidemic reached its height, she died in her daughter's arms. Mary wept as her mother's body, along with others, was tossed overboard unceremoniously by crew members on the verge of death themselves.

When the ship finally reached harbor in the New World, one in every three of the passengers and crew was dead. Mary, having lost her parents and brother, was alone in the world.

A young couple named Jeremy and Amelia Grant took pity on Mary. She was a lovely, titian-haired girl, but in many ways she was still a child in need of comforting and protection.

"We're newlyweds and don't have much to offer you," Jeremy said apologetically. "Little more than a roof over your head. In Savannah last year, I met a man named Marston with a large stable, and since he had no sons of his own, he wished to take me on. Our future is there."

"You're welcome to share whatever we have," added Amelia, with a quick, warm smile. Mary took an instant liking to the kind couple, and she gratefully accepted their offer.

The Grants' quarters were attached to the stable. They made a bed in the loft where Mary could sleep, and it was there that she quietly sobbed out her grief over the loss of her family.

As time passed, the girl overcame her sadness. She grew to enjoy the fragrance of clean hay, the pungent odor of horses, and the mist of the animals' warm breath curling upward in the brisk morning air. She helped Amelia with the children in the great house, and sometimes at night she would hold the lantern while Jeremy treated a sick stallion or a mare giving birth to a colt. Two years passed happily.

One evening Jeremy came into the small kitchen for supper, his face flushed with excitement.

"A cotton planter from St. Simons Island brought his horses to be stabled. The Marstons invited him to stay at their home," he said.

"He must be the older gentleman I met before I left to-night," said Mary. "As I went through the hall with the children, the Marstons called us into the library and introduced us."

"Did he have a large head with thick white hair, a red waist-coat and a gold-headed cane?" inquired Jeremy.

"Aye. That he did."

"That was him—Mr. Demere from St. Simons."

"Is he a wealthy man, Jeremy?" asked Amelia.

"Yes. And he wants to take our Mary home with him."

"Home with him! He doesn't even know me!" Mary exclaimed. "Why?"

"Out of the goodness of his heart, I suppose," said Jeremy. "After he heard about the loss of your family and how you came to be here with us, he told Marston he would like for you to become his ward."

"But what if I don't want to go?"

"Why shouldn't Mary just stay on with us, Jeremy?" asked Amelia. She and Mary were now like sisters.

"This man has a large cotton plantation on St. Simons Island," said Jeremy. "We can't even give her a dowry when the time comes. We ought to do what Mary's parents would have wanted for her own good." Although neither the Grants nor Mary wanted to part, they knew that Jeremy's argument was correct, and they agreed that she should go.

Thoughts of the impending separation made them all gloomy at the evening meal until Amelia, putting an arm around the girl, said "Don't be sad, Mary. Living with people like the Demeres will be like a fairy tale."

And that is how Mary MacRae came to arrive at the Demeres' plantation, known as The Grove. She soon moved into the big brick house known as Mulberry Hall. Her new home was on the south end of St. Simons Island, with a bed-room overlooking the sea.

Mary was introduced to Mr. Demere's wife, Anne, and the

Demere's boys, Joseph and Raymond, Jr. Joseph was a serious young man who would be leaving soon. His father was giving him Harrington Plantation for his own. Raymond, Jr., would be given another of the Demeres' plantations when he came of age. He was intelligent, enjoyed being outdoors, rode well, sailed, and drew people to him like a magnet. The slaves worshiped the tall, athletic "Mistuh Raymond," as they called Raymond, Jr.

Although it often happened that white children played with slave children as they grew up, this usually stopped as they grew older. But Raymond, Jr., with his tousled black hair and ready smile, was still closer to some of his black childhood friends than his father liked.

"I hope he will grow out of that," his father would say disapprovingly to his wife after catching Raymond, Jr., exchanging a joke or some reference to past adventures with one of the slaves.

"Well, people of both races are drawn to Raymond. They sense that he is kind and decent," she said.

"He's easygoing," his father snapped. "I wish he could be a soldier for awhile; it would make him a better disciplinarian. A soldier knows how to command respect."

"The servants will respect him, but they will also love him," said Anne Demere. She looked at her husband and sighed; he was a harsh man.

Mrs. Demere was kind to Mary, but she was more than twenty years older than the girl and not a companion for her. Mary's thoughts often returned to Amelia. She missed the little house in Savannah and the horses in the stable.

Mr. Demere could be very generous, and one day he gave Mary a beautiful bay horse of her own. Filled with delight by her new gift, she lost track of time and rode until after dusk. She hurried to the supper table and apologized for being late.

"Where have you been, Mary?" Mr. Demere asked irritably.

"I'm afraid I rode farther than I realized, sir."

"You are not an experienced rider, and we were afraid you might have been thrown," said Mr. Demere.

"I'm sorry, sir." Mary's face flushed.

Demere's voice softened as he reached over and patted her hand. "That's all right. But don't worry us like this again. I can teach you to become a fine rider. Tomorrow we shall—"

"Tomorrow I shall instruct her in the finer points of riding and show her the island trails," Raymond, Jr., interrupted. His father glared at him.

Under the tutelage of Raymond, with Mr. Demere sometimes accompanying them, they rode over the sandy cotton fields of the plantation. Drawing the silky threads of the sea island cotton between her thumb and index finger, Mary learned the value of the long fibers and how to judge the grade. It was the basis of the island's economy, and The Grove was known to grow some of the finest cotton along the coast.

Father and son were amazed at Mary's intelligent questions about running the plantation, and Mary found herself enjoying her rides with them as they inspected the crops. She loved the sound of the surf and the calls of the sea birds overhead.

When Mrs. Demere was not caring for the health of the plantation's servants, supervising the household staff, or compiling lists of purchases for her husband and son to make on their trips to Savannah, she would show Mary how to work the tiny stitches on the sampler she had given her. Mary often nodded over her needle and found the verse depressing, but she finally finished the sampler. As she added the last stitches, she sat back to peruse her handiwork. Not until then did she appreciate the truth in the sampler's words.

The rising morning can't assure
That we shall end the day!

For death stands ready at the door
To take our lives away.

Thinking of her parents, a tear slid down her cheek. She wiped it away quickly and held the finished sampler out for Mrs. Demere to inspect.

"I should have found something more cheerful for you to work on, my dear," said Anne Demere as she stared down at the words.

"Aye. The verse is sad," said Mary.

"At the time I chose the pattern for it, I was downcast over the loss of our infant son who died when he was less than a month old. Perhaps the verse saddened you, and that is why it has taken you so long to complete it."

Guiltily, Mary realized that another reason the sampler had proceeded so slowly was because young Raymond had been more on her mind than mastering the intricate needlework. Blushing, she glanced over at Mrs. Demere, thinking the older woman must surely see into her heart, but Anne Demere continued to talk with no idea of the girl's inner turmoil.

One evening the family decided to go for a picnic supper beside the ocean, and they lingered until the still air was resounding with the piercing cries of petrels, gulls, and other sea birds.

"There are so many birds, and they all seem to be heading toward the island," said Mary looking out over the water.

"They do that before a storm," said Raymond. "I don't like the look of those clouds on the horizon." The clouds were black, and their skirts were tinged with a coppery hue. "A hurricane may be on the way."

"Yes," agreed his father. "Raymond, take your mother back to the house. I'll help you repack the basket, Mary." Mary was surprised at Mr. Demere's effort to help her for he was often aloof towards her.

Before Mary could speak, Raymond said curtly, "There's

no need for that, sir. I'll help Mary." His father's mouth tightened. He seemed about to speak, but instead he turned and set out for the house.

Alone now, Mary and Raymond placed the dishes, glasses, and remains of the ham biscuits and lemon trifle back into the basket. Gusts of wind tugged at Mary's auburn hair. Raymond appeared to be in no hurry as he adjusted the straps on his horse.

"Do you realize we have known each other for almost two years," he said as they stood close together.

"I feel as if I've always known you," said Mary.

Raymond gave the strap a final tug, securing the basket, and then reached over and drew her to him. "Mary, I love you. Do you know that?"

She looked up at him wide eyed, unable to speak.

"So much that I want you for my wife."

She gasped.

"Please don't say no!"

Finally able to find her voice, Mary said, "I'm not, Raymond. I'm . . . I'm just surprised."

"Do you love me?"

"Oh, yes, Raymond," she replied, looking earnestly into his eyes. "I love you very much!"

"Then I shall tell my father that I want to marry you, Mary," he said. He bent down and kissed her. Rain was beginning to fall, and the drops of moisture caught in her hair and were wet against his cheek.

Returning to the house, they entered the drawing room hand in hand. Raymond's father, his back toward them, stood with the ramrod straight stance of a military man as he stared into the fire.

"Sir," said Raymond.

Demere turned, and as he saw their clasped hands, he stiffened even more.

"We have come to tell you that Mary and I love each other and want to marry."

Demere's face reddened and his eyes blazed. "You aren't ready for marriage, Raymond," he said abruptly. "You're just a boy."

"I'm a year older than you were when you married mother."

"You're not the man I was at that age. If you were more like me—"

"Perhaps I don't want to be like you, father," said Raymond, cutting him short.

"Why you young puppy! You aren't good enough for that girl!" Just then a blast of wind struck the side of the house and rattled the drawing room windows. The storm was beginning. "What Mary needs is a *real* man," said Mr. Demere, crossing over to his ward and putting his arm around her waist. His voice softened. "A man who can take care of her."

"Don't touch her, you old fool!" Raymond burst out angrily.

"You aren't going to marry this girl. I'll tell you that." His father's face was livid. "And if you do, you won't receive an acre of land from me!"

Raymond raised his fist as if to strike his father. Instead he lowered it and rushed from the room. Mary knew he went off in his boat when he was upset or wanted to think, but surely not tonight! Not when a hurricane was on the way. She was after him in an instant and caught him at the back door.

"Where are you going?"

"To Brunswick—perhaps Darien."

"Please . . . don't go!"

He held her tightly for a moment. "I can't stay here."

"Then let me go too!"

"I'll come back for you, Mary. I promise," he said. Then he disappeared into the storm.

Closing the door Mary hurried toward her room. In the hall she felt Mr. Demere's hand grasp her arm. She jerked herself free, but not before she saw his angry face. She rushed into her room and bolted the door. With a splinter of kindling, she lit a lantern from the embers in her bedroom fireplace, threw a cloak about her, and again entered the dark hall. The flame flared up brightly. What if she met Mr. Demere again? She knew he would certainly try to stop her. Shielding the glow of the lantern with her cloak, she hurried quietly down the stairs, past the closed drawing room door, and through the long hall to the back of the house.

Outside the wind tore at her slim form and whipped the branches of the mulberry trees. Needles of rain raked her face. Spanish moss, as wild as a witch's hair, blew in the wind.

As she reached the dock, she saw the rope used by Raymond to tie his boat laying where he had hurriedly thrown it.

"Raymond . . . Raymond . . . Ray-mond!" she screamed desperately. There was no answer. How far could he go in the darkness with his boat tossed by mountainous waves? The sea would break his small craft to bits and toss it back upon the beach. Had he been carried up along the shore near Hamilton Plantation and hurled against the foot of the bluff? Holding the lantern high, her eyes searched the edge of the foaming water. She thrust her body, a frail adversary against the force of the storm, forward and made her way close to the foaming water.

Then, as she waded in the churning water along the edge of a small inlet, the hungry water sucked at her foot, removing a slipper. Lowering the lantern and looking down, she shrieked as she recognized part of Raymond's shattered boat. She knew his body must be out there somewhere among the black, violently tossing waves.

To her left loomed the bluff overlooking the treacherous currents where the Frederica River joined the sound. It could have been here that Mary decided to end her life, or perhaps she was swept out to sea in the water that sometimes engulfs the island at the height of a storm. In any event, after several days of searching, the Demeres were forced to assume that both Mary and Raymond were dead. Their bodies were never found.

The words embroidered on the sampler were prophetic.

> For death stands ready at the door
> To take our lives away.

But neither death nor time have been able to erase the mysterious phenomena seen over the years near The Grove plantation. Ever since that savage hurricane, island folk have reported a light bobbing along near the water's edge on stormy nights. To glimpse it you must brave the gale and the spray, and go to the south end of St. Simons Island.

And on such a night, look sharp around you. You may see a luminous figure, lantern held high, hurrying through the mist. That light will be Mary the Wanderer searching for her lost sweetheart.

THE DOCTOR'S GHOST

Crescent (Near Darien)

When Jack d'Antignac looks out from the dormer windows of his home, he can see past the coastal marshes to the ocean. From its perch on a high bluff, the home affords views of Creighton Island to the left; Sapelo Island, with its wildlife and giant oaks, in the distance; and the legendary Blackbeard Island on the horizon.

"My grandfather bought the house," recalled the sixty-two-year-old Jack. "Prior to that, a Dr. Brewster lived here until the day he died in the big bedroom upstairs." Jack paused and took one more look out over the water. "I grew up in this place."

Jack is a tall man, whose brown hair still has only a tinge of gray. He attended Georgia Tech for two years, with a goal of becoming an engineer. "But the call of the sea brought me home," said the muscular outdoorsman. Today, Jack d'Antignac is in the seafood business, combining a life of hard physical labor with the more cerebral duties of running a business. Each day, Jack spends time unloading his boats at the dock before heading to the office to handle the day's administrative duties.

As someone in the seafood industry, Jack d'Antignac has accommodated himself to a life in tune with the rhythms of the sea and the seasons; as the owner of a haunted house, he has accommodated himself to the supernatural. In fact, he even let CNN do a Halloween special about the house several years ago.

According to Jack, one of the first supernatural experiences in the home happened to his uncle many years ago. "One summer a short time before I was born, my uncle was staying here by himself for the weekend," Jack recalled. "It was dusk, and he was sitting on the porch when he noticed a gentleman with gray hair coming across the yard. My uncle saw the man was wearing a long coat with tails and a bat-wing collar. Then, to his horror, he saw that the man had no visible legs from the knee down.

"The figure drifted up the porch steps and right through the front door. My frightened uncle ran next door to the home of Tavy Hopkins. That gentlemen got his shotgun, and the two came back and completely searched the house. It was empty. My uncle was only about twenty at the time, and he asked Tavy if he might spend the night at the Hopkins home.

"That night, there was a bad storm with hurricane-force

The d'Antignac House

winds. The wind blew over a large tree that fell through the roof of the room where my uncle had planned to spend the night. A heavy limb plunged into the bed where he would have slept. The limb could have killed him or seriously injured him. After that, my uncle decided the ghost had appeared to him not as a threat, but as a warning."

Jack said the family came to believe the strange man was actually the ghost of Dr. Brewster, who had lived in the house before Jack's grandfather. Jack was too young to remember his first experience with the home's ghost, though he heard about it from his parents.

"I was only four or five at the time and slept in a large crib-type bed in my parents' room," Jack began. "Years later, Mother told me what happened. She said she was awakened one night by a tapping on her shoulder. She looked up sleepily into the face of a man beside her bed. The man was beckoning to her and saying in a gentle but persistent voice, 'Someone is ill in the back room. Come with me.' My parents had a number of guests in the house that night. Though she was only half awake, she thought this man must be one of her guests so she followed him down the hall.

"When she reached the dining room, the man walked right through the table. Still drowsy, my mother tried to follow him and slammed into the edge of the table. The pain snapped her wide awake, and it finally dawned on her that the man was not one of her guests. Before the man disappeared, she noticed his strange coat with the same long tails and batwing collar my uncle had described.

"My father came rushing into the room and helped my mother back to the bedroom. When they got there, they found a large black widow spider on her pillow. If the man had not led my mother out of bed and into the dining room that night, the spider might have gone undiscovered and fatally bitten her. Both of my parents believed this was another good deed on the part of the ghost of Dr. Brewster."

As Jack grew older, many other mysterious events happened around the house. One time, the family heard knocking and slamming sounds they could not identify. "With the help of the servants," Jack recalled, "the knocking noises and sounds of slamming doors were pinned down to an empty room. At times, guests refused to sleep in the adjacent room and had to be given another room."

The benevolent Dr. Brewster may even be responsible for saving the house. Jack recalled the winter they closed the house and went to live in Fort Myers, Florida, for the winter. "That spring, we returned to discover there had been a fire in our master bedroom. The ceiling light had burst into flames, but oddly enough, the fire went out by itself. At that time, the ceiling was heart-pine, and the electrician was amazed that it didn't continue to burn. We think that putting out the fire was the work of Dr. Brewster."

One night some years later, Mrs. d'Artignac and her sister heard heavy footsteps on the upper floor. Certain that they had a burglar, they called their neighbor, Tavy Hopkins, who was now accustomed to being called upon. Tavy hurried over, pointed his loaded shotgun up toward the landing, and shouted, "Come down or I'll shoot!" They all heard the sound of pounding feet in the upstairs hall approaching the stairs. Whoever it was seemed to come down two stairs, hesitate, then run back to the second floor. Mr. Hopkins and the two women searched the entire upstairs but could not find a living soul.

"They finally concluded it had to be our ghost," said Jack. "I have heard noises from up there all my life, and I suppose I always will."

THE D'ANTIGNAC HOUSE WAS BUILT IN THE 1790S AND IS ON THE NA-TIONAL REGISTER OF HISTORIC PLACES. IT IS A PRIVATE HOME AND NOT OPEN TO THE PUBLIC.

COLONIAL COAST
AND GOLDEN ISLES:
ST. MARYS AND
CUMBERLAND ISLAND

THE RIVERVIEW HOTEL PHANTOM

Riverview Hotel, 105 Osborne Street, St. Marys

The Riverview Hotel was constructed in 1916. The hotel, overlooking the St. Marys River, is near the ferry which goes to Cumberland Island. When the hotel was first constructed, there were few other places to stay in St. Marys, and many men who came to work in the city or on Cumberland Island made the hotel their second home.

Jerry Brandon, the owner of the hotel, is a distinguished man in his fifties. Brandon lived in the hotel as a child during the 1950s, at a time when it was closed to the public. The Brandon family occupied the downstairs. Jerry Brandon's mother did not allow him and his sister, Sally, to play upstairs, because that portion of the hotel had been closed off for a number of years. However, Jerry and Sally's curiosity was incessant, and the childrens' mother finally gave up on her losing battle to keep them from playing on the second floor.

Jerry recalled one particular incident told to him by Sally. Sally and her friend Jeanie Porter were playing in one of the dimly lit second-floor halls. As the children chased each other down the long hall, they screamed in changing voices, producing weird echoes. Whenever they found an unlocked door, they would run inside the empty room and make hollow, moaning sounds to try to scare one another.

Later, after Sally and Jeanie had played this version of hide-and-seek for awhile, the girls started playing with their dolls. "I've never been in the second-floor hall of the north wing," Sally said, as they combed their dolls' hair. "Let's go see what's there." Jeanie, a bit more timid than her good friend Sally, was eventually persuaded to go.

As they walked through the hall of the north wing, they began to read off the room numbers. "Room number one, room number two," Sally counted, "and that's room number—." Sally stopped suddenly and clutched her friend's arm. Standing in front of the third room was the figure of a man wearing a black felt hat and a long black coat. He was standing with his back to the girls and slowly turned to look at them. As he did, the girls could see his face was the color of beef tallow and his eyes were a dull, dead black. Both girls ran until they got outside.

"What did you think he had on?" Jeanie asked.

"A broad-brimmed black hat with a wide ribbon band around it," said Sally Brandon.

"Yes!" agreed Jeanie, "and a long black coat."

"What did you think about his eyes?" asked Sally.

"They were scary!" Jeanie exclaimed. "I didn't like them."

"He was dreadful. Not like a real person at all."

The girls did not mention the incident to their parents, but Sally eventually told Jerry. "It really worried me," Jerry remembered, "but at least it kept us from ever playing up in the north wing again."

Jerry recalled another supernatural incident that happened in the hotel. "There was one room that was really haunted.

That was room number nine. When we remodeled and enlarged the rooms, it became part of room number eight."

According to Jerry, a semipermanent guest who worked at the bag plant was staying in that room. One day a friend of the guest came to visit. The guest hadn't come in yet, so the desk clerk gave his friend a key to the room. The friend went upstairs to wait.

After the man had been upstairs only a short time, the hotel staff saw him running down the stairs. The man's face was as white as his shirt. The man said he had been taking a nap and woke up because something seemed to be jerking his leg and trying to pull him out of the bed.

"That wasn't the only time it happened either," Jerry continued. He then went on to tell how one night a group of men were having a business meeting at the Riverview and staying overnight so they could go fishing the next morning.

The next morning, one of the men was missing at breakfast. He finally came in during the middle of the meal and said, "Something tried to pull me out of bed in the middle of the night!" The man was late for breakfast, he said, because after the incident, he threw on his clothes and went to another hotel.

"He was just the nervous type, I guess," Jerry Brandon said as he finished his story. "Most of our guests don't mind a ghost or two."

RIVERVIEW HOTEL IS LOCATED IN ST. MARYS HISTORIC DISTRICT. THE HOTEL IS KNOWN FOR ITS PICNIC LUNCHES, COMPLETE WITH BASKET AND CHECKED TABLE CLOTH, THAT VISITORS CAN TAKE ON TRIPS TO CUMBERLAND ISLAND. FOR MORE INFORMATION ON THE HOTEL, CALL 912-882-3242.

"BABY JANE" OF ORANGE HALL

Orange Hall, 303 Osborne Street, St. Marys

When the Reverend Horace Pratt arrived in the coastal community of St. Marys in 1821, he found its mild climate and proximity to water delightful but its "religion in a low and languishing state." The churches that had been established soon after the town was founded had lost their zeal. Pratt, an energetic and intellectual Presbyterian minister from Connecticut, immediately began to remedy this situation.

Just over a year after his arrival, he became the pastor of St. Marys's new Presbyterian church and married a lovely girl named Jane Wood. The marriage was a fruitful one; in its first four years Jane Wood Pratt produced four children, two of whom died. In 1829, after six years of marriage, Jane also died.

Horace Pratt pored himself into his work after his wife's death. His Presbyterian church flourished, as did an African Church that Horace paid for with his own money before dontating the church to the Black community.

About three years after Jane's death, Horace married again, this time to a woman named Isabel Drysdale. Isabel was Horace Pratt's first cousin and had been a beloved friend of Jane Wood Pratt. The couple named their first child Jane in her honor.

When the little girl was two, the Pratt's moved into pala-tial Orange Hall. The house had been built by Jane Wood Pratt's father and given to the couple as a present. Baby Jane delighted in romping though the great house, which was the most magnificent home in St. Marys. Jane was a delightful child who took an intense joy in everything she did. She would carry on long conversations with her dolls, hug or reprove them, and often give them rides on the bannister of the grand

Orange Hall

staircase. If guests were present, she might receive a frown from her mother when she reached the bottom of the stairs with her dolls, but if her mother was away at a meeting, Jane might even slide down the rail herself.

Baby Jane's room was the large front bedroom on the left side of the house. Through the windows of her room, Jane would watch with great interest everything that happened on the street. One morning the servants told her that Acadians had moored their ship at the St. Marys dock. They were emigrating from Nova Scotia to Louisiana and had stopped at St. Marys on the way. Without asking whether she might go down to see them or not, Jane slipped out and was soon at the waterfront. The dark-haired, French-speaking Acadian women made a great fuss over the pretty child and her yellow curls, even though Jane was unable to speak a word of their language.

But the ship bearing these friendly visitors also brought a deadly disease to St. Marys. About two weeks later, Jane woke up with a fever and a headache.

"Mama, I feel dizzy and I hurt all over," the child said. When the Pratts called the doctor, he examined the child and determined she had yellow fever. By now a number of people in St. Marys were ill, and the disease was beginning to reach epidemic proportions. Horace Pratt prayed fervently for Jane and felt that his prayers had been rewarded when her fever dropped. However, it quickly rose again, and by now Jane exhibited the yellow skin and bleeding gums that indicated the disease was entering its final phase.

"My darling, Baby Jane," cried her father, "with God's help you will get well."

"Father, am I going to die?" the child asked.

"Don't say that. Of course you are not going to die!" her distraught father answered.

In private, he asked the doctor if his daughter had a chance.

"There is always a chance, sir," said the doctor.

"How much of a one?" persisted her father.

"I can make no promises," the doctor replied.

The next day, Baby Jane was delirious. Her mother tenderly wiped the blood from the poor child's bleeding mouth. Jane tossed and turned and tried to get out of bed. Soon, she was unable to recognize her mother. Finally, late that afternoon, the delirium passed and six-year-old Jane seemed to be herself again. She looked up and said, "I love you, mother." Then turning to her father, she said, "Please, daddy. Don't worry. Some of the most beautiful angels have been sent by my heavenly Father. He loves me, too, and if I should die, those angels promised to take care of me until you and mother get there."

Her father knelt beside her bed, tears streaming down his cheeks. "I'm not afraid, daddy," she said, stroking his hair.

That night the child lapsed into a coma that is characteristic of the last stages of yellow fever and is usually followed by death. Her mother stayed at her bedside all night. Toward dawn, the little girl's sweet face became peaceful. As the morning light streamed through the window of her room, Baby Jane's spirit departed to join that of the angels and her Father above.

Today, the home is open for tours, and Baby Jane's room has been preserved with her dolls, toys, and tiny, child-sized furniture. As visitors tour this beautiful old house, someone will occasionally ask about the pretty little girl who just passed them on the stairs. Others have seen a girl in a white dress with blue ribbons in her hair skipping up the walk or playing in Jane's room. Recently one tourist said, "I didn't think you allowed anyone in Baby Jane's room, but a child is sitting in a chair in there looking out the window toward Wheeler Street. Is that all right?" The tour guides checked the room, but there was no child in the room, nor were there any children anywhere in the house.

Many think this mysterious child is the apparition of Baby Jane. In fact, sightings of the ghost are apparently becoming more common. One hostess said, "More and more visitors are asking about, and seeing, the ghost of Baby Jane." Perhaps it makes sense for this happy, sweet young girl to return to Orange Hall—the place where she knew such joy as a child.

ORANGE HALL, LOCATED IN THE HEART OF ST. MARYS, IS NOW THE CITY'S VISITOR CENTER. IT MAY BE TOURED EVERY DAY EXCEPT THANKSGIVING, CHRISTMAS, AND NEW YEAR'S DAY. FOR INFORMATION, CALL 912-882-4000.

THE POLO PLAYER OF CUMBERLAND ISLAND

Cumberland Island

SHEILA WILLIS IS A NATURALIST AND GENERAL ORNITHOLOGIST WHO
WORKS FOR THE NATIONAL PARK SERVICE ON CUMBERLAND ISLAND. THE
ISLAND, LOCATED JUST OFF THE GEORGIA COAST FROM THE TOWN OF ST.
MARYS, WAS ONCE A PICTURESQUE RETREAT FOR THE WEALTHY. IT WAS
DONATED TO THE NATIONAL PARK SERVICE IN 1972. EACH YEAR, THOU-
SANDS OF VISITORS TAKE THE FORTY-FIVE-MINUTE FERRY RIDE FROM ST.
MARYS TO ENJOY THE EIGHTEEN-MILE-LONG ISLAND'S WILD NATURAL
BEAUTY. WILLIS CONDUCTS PROGRAMS AND BIRDING EXPEDITIONS FOR
SOME OF THESE VISITORS, AND THE FOLLOWING ACCOUNT IS FROM ONE
SUCH EXPEDITION.

My trip started out in a perfectly ordinary way. It was a
normal fall weekend. When I took the ferry over on Friday, I
was looking forward to meeting the "birders" who would be
arriving on the island. I felt I would probably already know
some of these birders, but others would be new to me and
new to birding. I always enjoy watching people's reaction the
first time they meet me and realize I'm part Native American.
My dark eyes and straight black hair give me away. People say
my keen powers of observation probably come from my ancestors—people who were accustomed to recognizing different varieties of birds, plants, and animals as part of their daily
life. I don't know if that's true or not.

I do know that Native Americans were the first to appreciate the beauty of this place, long before wealthy people like
the Carnegies made the island an exclusive retreat. Four or
five centuries ago, the Timucuan Indians lived on this island
inside palisaded villages. They raised grain here and took only
what they needed from the natural bounty of the island and

the ocean. Whenever I see their many burial mounds on the island, I wonder whether the Timucuans are among my own ancestors.

On Cumberland Island, a group of us may sight as many as a hundred varieties of birds in the course of one fall day, and Friday, we saw some rare ones. That evening, I sat in the living room of the park's staff quarters and wondered what the weather would be like for the expedition the next day.

After I made my supper in the staff quarters' communal kitchen, I took my food into the living room where I joined two friends from the park service who were also spending the night. As we talked, I watched a man descend the stairs from the second floor. He wore polo clothes and riding boots that reached his knees. Without speaking, the man walked through the hall and out the front door.

"Who in the world was that?" I asked.

"Who do you mean?" one of my friends replied. "We are the only ones here tonight."

"What about the man who just came down the stairs? From the way he was dressed, he was probably headed toward the polo field."

Both of my friends looked at me strangely. "If you really saw someone dressed in polo clothes, I doubt if you'll see him come back," one of them said.

"Why not?" I inquired.

"The polo field isn't in use. What you may have seen is the ghost of the dead polo player."

"Good heavens!" I said, remembering how white the fellow's face had appeared.

"The man apparently broke his neck during a polo game years ago and died," my friend said. "I've heard he's been seen here at the staff-quarters house by a number of people. Others claim to have seen a man astride a fine polo pony galloping past the ruins of Dungeness in the moonlight."

Plum Orchard Mansion
PHOTO BY BRENDA BARBER

Dungeness was the name of the home of Lucy Coleman Carnegie and her husband, Thomas, who was the brother of Andrew Carnegie. The home burned to the ground in 1959 and was never rebuilt. The ruins of the house remain on the island, and though they are eerie, I had never experienced anything strange there before.

I tried to remain calm, considering I had just seen a ghost. Then we all began telling stories of strange things that had happened to us on the island. I recalled the night I was out here during a storm. A crash of thunder woke me. I happened to glance through the bedroom window and saw a bright red light shining a short distance away. I couldn't understand where the light was coming from. I wanted to call someone to look at it with me, but I was alone in the staff quarters that night. Afterwards, I explained the light to several people, but no one has ever been able to tell me what it was.

My friends agreed that was odd, but one of them had an

even stranger story. "How would you like to be in the Plum Orchard house when you know it's empty and suddenly hear something you know can't be happening?" he asked.

We stared at him. "Like what?" asked my other friend.

"Like hearing the dumbwaiter rise from the kitchen to the upstairs, stop several times in different rooms, return to the kitchen, and then go back upstairs all over again," he said.

My other friend and I speculated about how it would feel to be alone in the Plum Orchard house with the phantom dumbwaiter; we agreed we would be scared. Then I thought of another strange story. "Do either of you remember the old caretaker who used to work at Stafford Cemetery?" I asked, referring to one of the island's two cemeteries. Both of my friends nodded.

"He told me quite a story before he died. At the time, I didn't believe him, but now I'm not so sure. He said that sometimes at night, he would see a lady in a red dress standing beside the cemetery's gate. She always seemed very upset. At times she would grasp the caretaker's arm and plead with him to take her to the other cemetery. 'I am buried in the wrong graveyard, sir,' she would say to him. Each time the caretaker saw her, he would ask for her name, but she would shake her head and refuse to reply.

"He told me he knew she was one of the ladies of the evening the Carnegies brought out by boat to visit the servants," I continued. "Somehow, she died out here on the island. Whenever the caretaker saw this tragic woman trying to leave her grave and get to the other cemetery, it made him upset. He ended his story by saying, 'And I've never felt such a freezing cold hand on my arm as hers.'"

After I finished this story, neither of my friends spoke. Perhaps they were thinking about how this poor woman came to die on the island. I was more concerned about the polo player I had seen earlier. I waited up half the night for him to return from his "match." He never did. The next day I led my birding expedition as usual, and nothing else unusual happened for the rest of the weekend. But I will never forget the figure I saw strolling through the staff quarters, nor the stories we shared that night.

THE FERRY SCHEDULE FROM THE TOWN OF ST. MARYS TO CUMBERLAND ISLAND VARIES ACCORDING TO THE TIME OF YEAR. FERRY RESERVATIONS ARE LIMITED. FOR INFORMATION AND RESERVATIONS, CALL 912-882-4335. FERRY RESERVATIONS MAY BE MADE UP TO ELEVEN MONTHS IN ADVANCE. THE ISLAND IS THE HOME OF THE TINY BAPTIST CHURCH OF HALFMOON BLUFF, WHERE JOHN F. KENNEDY, JR., AND CAROLYN BESSETTE WERE MARRIED. IT IS ALSO HOME TO THE STATELY GREYFIELD INN, WHERE THE KENNEDY-BESSETTE WEDDING RECEPTION WAS HELD.

MAGNOLIA MIDLANDS

THE SURRENCY HOUSE

Surrency

Many ghosts have been well documented, but perhaps no ghost has been witnessed by as many people as the one that haunted the Surrency House. It has been estimated that over thirty thousand people traveled to the small town of Surrency, located in south Georgia close to Jessup, to catch a glimpse of the ghost. At the height of the ghost's fame, the local rail line ran a special train for people wishing to view the ghost. The rail line even used the ghost in its advertising.

Allen Surrency and his family were prominent, respected citizens in the community, which bore the family's name. Allen Surrency's extensive business interests in the area positioned him as a leader of the small town. The family's home served as a type of informal hotel—housing relatives, friends, and passing visitors—and the family was well known for its hospitality and kindness.

On the day of the ghost's first appearance in 1872, Allen Surrency had gone to Macon to buy supplies. That night, a minister was a guest in the Surrency home. The minister was chatting with one of the older Surrency boys when the pair heard thudding sounds on the front porch. The boy went out to investigate. When he returned, he told the minister, "There are hot bricks falling on the porch."

Clem, the Surrency's married daughter, was visiting that night. She decided to go wait for the evening train in case her father was on it. When she reached the railroad tracks at the station, she saw a bright light coming down the tracks. The light grew larger and brighter, but there was no sound of a train. The young woman watched in horror as the light continued to bear down upon her. She turned and ran back home as fast as she could. As she opened the front door, hot bricks began to shower the porch behind her.

Clem told the family and their guest what had happened. As she did so, the minister threw a stick of wood on the fire blazing in the family's fireplace. The stick was immediately hurled out of the fireplace onto the floor. Again the minister placed the stick on the fire, and again it was hurled onto the floor. At the same time, a whatnot stand in the corner toppled over. China ornaments that had been on the stand were slammed to the floor and broken into small pieces. Then, the tongs beside the fireplace seem to take on a life of their own and could not be returned to the rack.

The ghost seemed to be everywhere. A pair of irons flew from a shelf towards the minister's head. The minister jumped out of his chair, narrowly dodging the irons. To add to the mayhem, a clock on the mantel began striking the hour, then continued to chime several hundred times despite many efforts to stop it. Matters were made worse when the home's windows refused to stay closed. Mrs. Surrency called on the minister to help her close them. He managed to get one closed, but as soon as he released it, the window shot open then slammed shut with a thunderous bang, completely shattering the glass.

The minister gave up on the windows. Hearing weird noises outside, he quickly went over and closed the door. But when he took his hand off the knob, the door was thrown open so violently that it slammed against the wall and shook the whole house. This was repeated several times.

When Mr. Surrency arrived on the morning train, he found a crowd waiting to meet him. Several friends told him about the mysterious events as the crowd walked toward the house. He was followed by the train crew and all the passengers. Instead of its normal five-minute stop in Surrency, the train ending up staying in the small town for over an hour.

Surrency hurried into his home to ask his wife what was happening. The woman tried to explain but could scarcely find the words. Surrency locked some nails, clothes hooks, and other small articles he had purchased on his trip in a drawer and went back outside to try to find a reasonable explanation for the strange events among the horde of onlookers. As he spoke with some friends, he glanced down and saw the nails and clothes hooks lying on the ground at his feet. As he stooped to pick them up, a nearby stack of wood started flying through the air.

Surrency went back inside to eat breakfast with his family. As they ate, the dishes slid from the table to the floor. When the cook placed a dish of ham and biscuits on the table, it went flying out the window. The ghost repeated this trick many times in the days that followed.

These events became a source of constant humiliation for the Surrency family. At first Mr. Surrency thought they might be the object of a joke by some friend or neighbor who intended no harm, but they quickly discounted that possibility.

The ghost seemed especially interested in playing pranks with the family's food. The cook would often fill a frying pan with meat and place it on the stove, only to have the pan turned upside down whenever she turned away for a moment.

It became easier to live on canned food. Even cheese and crackers posed a danger, for often the crackers would end up sailing across the room while the cheese would end up smashed against the wall. The ghost ended up breaking so many dishes that Mr. Surrency bought tinware.

A favorite prank of the ghost was to hide shoes and items of clothing. The items would stay gone until their owners had worn themselves out looking for them, then they would appear in some obvious corner. On one occasion, Mr. Surrency took his clothing to a small storage building and locked it up to protect it from the ghost. When he returned to the house, he found the clothing in a heap on the floor. Guests would often find a hat or a shoe missing. One school teacher, fearing the ghost would hide her shoes to embarrass her, tucked them between her two mattresses before she went to sleep. When she woke up the next morning, they were both gone.

Among Mr. Surrency's possessions was an exceptionally beautiful pair of cut-glass wine decanters that had been presented to him by a hunting club in Savannah. Fearing they would be broken, too, he took them out in the middle of the night and buried them in the garden. After he got up the next morning, he went out to see if they were safe. The decanters were lying on top of the ground smashed into small bits. Within three days, each piece of chinaware and glassware in the house was broken, as well as all the mirrors.

On one occasion, two train passengers sat talking while the train was making its normal stop in Surrency. The window was open beside them. Suddenly, a huge crosstie rose from a pile in front of Surrency's home and hurled itself toward the train. The flying crosstie whizzed into the railroad car through the open window and narrowly missed the two passengers.

Incident after harrowing incident took place in the home. Eventually, news of the mischievous ghost spread throughout the South. Scientists investigated the home and tried to solve the mystery without success. People started to visit the little town just to catch a glimpse of the ghost, and many were not disappointed. During a period of five years, it is estimated that thirty thousand people visited the Surrency home in hopes of seeing the ghost. Mr. Surrency, however, did not profit from the ghost. The hospitality extended to visitors, together with the cost of replacing all that was destroyed, almost ruined him financially.

He was eventually forced to move his family to a house several miles out in the country. The ghost followed the family to their new home, though its activities did settle down a bit.

One day the strange incidents ceased as abruptly as they had started. The Surrency house burned about a half-century later, but the Surrency ghost will never be forgotten.

THE SCREVEN LIGHT

Screven

A carload of young men and women sat crammed in a Chevrolet station wagon on a secluded dirt road near the tracks of the old Seaboard Coast Line between Screven and Jessup. They had often heard stories about the mysterious "ghost light" at Milligan's Crossing, and tonight they had decided to see it for themselves.

The night air was quiet as they eagerly watched and waited. It was approaching midnight, and the desolate countryside was pitch black. It was an unusually warm October night. Janet Royal was growing hot in the overcrowded car. Now and then, with a flick of her handkerchief, she would wipe her steamy breath off the car windows.

Janet thought back to earlier that evening when she had told her mother she was going out in search of the ghost with her friends.

Her mother had laughed. "You're going to Milligan's Crossing? Well, don't let the ghost get you," she had teased.

Now Janet was growing anxious. It had just rained, which was "the best possible time to see the light" according to one of her companions in the car. Janet finally rolled down the window and let in the humid night air. Her friends were joking and laughing around her in the car, but Janet kept her eyes glued out the window. She heard the light always came from the direction of Jessup, so she looked that way into the thick night.

The girl beside Janet suddenly screamed. All talk stopped. Now everyone was rolling down the foggy windows, leaning across each other, and staring out. At first Janet could not see it. She continually scanned the blackness until she saw the distant flicker in the distance. The light seemed to be on the railroad track.

"That's it! That's the ghost light!" a young man whispered. Janet felt the hairs rise on her arms. Janet and her friends got out of the car and walked up to the track. A few minutes later, the light was almost upon them. Some of the girls screamed as they scrambled back into the car. Then, to their astonishment, the light passed right over them and disappeared.

"I will never forget that night," remembered Janet Royal, who is now an assistant principal at Oak Vista School in Jessup. "The light was a glowing, clear white ball, sometimes dim and sometimes very bright. It swung from side to side as it floated along the tracks."

Many people in this area have seen this light, and there are numerous stories about how it started. According to one story, a flagman was struck by a train near the crossing as he walked along swinging his lantern. According to the story, the impact severed the man's head from his body. The bobbing light that is seen along the track is carried by the ghost of the flagman, who is still searching for his head. However, few people in the area take this story seriously.

Accounts of the eerie light actually date back as far as the Civil War. Through the years, its presence has become so familiar that it is now an accepted part of the community. Generations of Screven residents have made the light a source of entertainment and chills. Some years, local churches took hayrides to the crossing to watch for the light. Several attempts have been made to give the light a scientific explanation, but no one has ever offered a convincing reason why the light appears to hover down the tracks. Many have proposed a theory that the light is caused by swamp gas floating near the tracks, but even that explanation does not explain all of its characteristics.

No one really knows what causes the light, but as one resident said, "There is definitely something here, and we've learned to live with it."

Janet Royal's interest in the light has remained since that dark and humid night. Today she has no better explanation for it than she did years ago, though she discounts the local stories. "I believe the Screven light existed way back in time, prior to all the legends we hear today."

THE LIGHT MAY BE SEEN AT MILLIGAN'S RAILROAD CROSSING ON BENNETT ROAD (GA 38) OUTSIDE OF SCREVEN. IT IS USUALLY SIGHTED LATE AT NIGHT.

ATLANTA METRO

THE HAUNTED COURTHOUSE

DeKalb County Courthouse, 101 East Court Square,
Decatur

When L.L. Kitchens, Jr., left his home to give his weekly tours of the DeKalb County Courthouse on the morning of Friday, January 13, 1995, little did he expect what was in store for him that day. He did notice the date as he walked out the door, but Kitchens always felt the superstitions about Friday the Thirteenth were silly. Kitchens loved history and volunteered his time every Friday to guide tours through the Courthouse on the Square Museum, located inside the old courthouse in downtown Decatur. Why should this Friday be different just because of the date? he thought. As far as he was concerned, it wasn't.

Kitchens knew some people got spooked in the courthouse no matter what the date. There were employees who refused to be in the building by themselves. And he had heard work crews and janitors tell of "phantom footsteps" or "presences" in the building. But Kitchens was more interested in history than ghost stories. He was an eloquent tour guide, with a rich store of knowledge about the courthouse's past.

The Bowdon Inn (see story on page 155)

On this cold afternoon, the courthouse was virtually empty. About 3:30, Kitchens was ready to call it a day. "I was thinking there would be no more tours for the day when this gentleman came in with two ladies," he recalled.

Reverend David Venator of Pilgrim Trinitarian Congregational Church in Boston was on his way home after a conference in Orlando and had decided to stop to visit former parishioners in Atlanta. The minister's friends, remembering his interest in history, decided to take him over to the museum in Decatur's old courthouse to see the collection of Civil War relics.

"There are three rooms on the main floor," Kitchens said, remembering the day. "I was showing them the first room when Reverend Venator walked to the wall where Stephen Decatur's sword was displayed. He stopped in front of the sword and said, 'I feel a hard chill at this spot. Someone is standing on the other side of this wall'."

According to Kitchens, Venator claimed he was psychic and this "chill" meant someone was trying to contact him. Venator then pulled a chain with a small white triangle from his pocket and waved it in front of the wall. Kitchens knew that an old, unrestored stairway was behind the wall. The stairway leads to a basement that was once the location of a holding cell where prisoners who were on trial were kept. The stairway is accessible through a door near the museum's entrance, but the door is never mentioned on the tour since the basement is not on the tour. Kitchens and the rest of the staff of the historical association are convinced that Venator couldn't have known of the passage.

"When I explained to him that there was an old stairwell behind the wall where he was standing, he asked if he might see it," Kitchens remembered. "I opened the door. The minister took a few steps down the stairs and said, 'There's a spirit down here'."

Then, as if he were hearing something and repeating what

he heard, the reverend said in a slow voice, "I was tried and found guilty of a crime I did not commit." Venator then seemed to come out of his trance-like state and said, "The man is crying. I sense a spirit on the stairs a few feet away from me. There is a negative energy down here."

Venator took a tiny gold chain with a plumb bob from his pocket. He told the group he used the chain sometimes for dowsing. Then, holding it between his thumb and forefinger, he moved it around in a circle. Kitchens recalled that after Venator was finished swinging the chain, "He looked up and said to me, 'This stairwell is haunted'."

Though Venator returned to Massachusetts, though he was still very interested in the spirits at the courthouse. According to a story by David Joyner in the *Atlanta Journal-Constitution*, Venator was able to "revisit" the courthouse from his office in Boston by using the dowsing chain. The story reported that Venator discovered several ghosts in the stairwell, and that some of these spirits were still bound in chains.

Of course, prisoners that are considered dangerous are often taken to the courtroom in chains, in case they attempt an escape; but it makes one wonder if the ghosts the New England minister sensed are those of people who received death sentences in this building since the courthouse has only been in use since 1898 and Venator's account seems to indicate much older spirits.

Leon Kitchens regarded the visit of the psychic minister as interesting, but the strange event was not enough to change his opinion of silly superstitions. "I'm not one to fear ghosts, nor have I ever had any uneasiness about being in the courthouse, alone or otherwise," he said. "The visit by that minister from Boston just made Friday the Thirteenth a more interesting day."

FOR INFORMATION ON THE OLD COURTHOUSE ON THE SQUARE MUSEUM, CALL 404-373-1088.

SUICIDE HOUSE

Campbell Road, Lawrenceville

CINDY COLLINS HAS BLONDE HAIR, TANNED SKIN, AND BLUE EYES WITH A FARAWAY LOOK IN THEM. SHE IS WEARING THE BLUE JEANS AND LONG-SLEEVED SHIRT SHE USUALLY WEARS WHEN SHE'S OUT DIGGING OR WEEDING IN HER GARDEN. WHEN SHE IS ASKED ABOUT A CERTAIN HOUSE WHERE SHE ONCE LIVED, THE RECOLLECTION SEEMS TO MAKE HER SHIVER. FOR A MOMENT SHE IS SO DISTANT IT SEEMS SHE IS RELIVING A PERIOD OF HER LIFE, BUT FINALLY SHE TELLS HER TALE.

It was a pretty house, but people never stayed. They moved in, but before long they always moved out. It had a white frame with a gable on each side, a green roof, and a wide, screened-in front porch. Red crepe myrtle trees grew across the front—pretty in the summer. Before we moved in a man named Craig shot himself there with a double-barreled shotgun. Did it while his family was at church. I never did understand why my husband wanted to buy that house. He knew Mr. Craig killed himself in it, and our children heard it as soon as we moved into the neighborhood.

"Momma, why'd daddy want to buy the house that man shot himself in?" the children asked me. I didn't know what to say except you couldn't always avoid buying a place where something bad had happened.

Even before it happened, you could feel a presence there. I wondered later whether my husband felt it, too, and whether it worked on him.

One day, our oldest son saw his father hold a pistol to his head and take his own life in that house. I don't guess my son will ever get over that. I'm just glad his little boy, Bobby, wasn't there to see it. Bobby's mother had him at the store that day, and when she came home, it was all over and the body gone. We tried, but we couldn't keep the way he died from Bobby, or anybody else either. The whole family knew it. Of course, we moved out after that. There was too much pain in that house, and I didn't want anything to do with it.

When he was ten, Bobby said the strangest thing to me one day. "I can see Grandpop," he said, like my husband was standing right in front of him. It was broad daylight, and there was obviously nobody there, but he definitely saw a figure. It was enough to spook you.

"But I'm not afraid of him," the boy continued. "He says he's sorry now that he did it. He's missed seeing me and his other grandchildren."

Then Bobby tugged at my arm and said, "Grandma, can't you see him? Grandpop's right there in front of you. I don't know why you can't see him. He's got blond hair and blue eyes, and his face looks like he's been out in the sun."

I didn't know how to respond to this. Finally I said, "What do you think he's wearing, Bobby?"

"Why he's wearing a green shirt and blue pants, and he's got on work boots," Bobby answered, not hesitating for a moment. My husband was a supervisor at a construction site, and boots and blue jeans were exactly what he wore to work every day.

"Mr. Craig's spirit is the cause of it all, Grandma," Bobby said. "You know what Mr. Craig's spirit tried to do to Mr. Murphy, but it didn't work."

Mr. Murphy had moved into the house after we moved out. He also tried to commit suicide, but he wasn't successful. His wife was at home, and she sent for an ambulance. They saved him in spite of himself, and it wasn't long after that before they moved out. I knew all of this from the paper and from local gossip, but I don't see any way Bobby could have known it.

Nothing else strange happened for the next couple of years, and I gradually put the incident with Bobby out of my mind.

Then one summer day, my son Michael was over that way and decided to stop and look in the house. Nobody was living there, and he just wanted to look around. It was a hot day outside, but Michael said that when he opened the door, it was cold as ice inside the house. "It was Dad," he told me later. "I know he was there."

Then one day after Christmas that year, Bobby said to me, "Granpop's buried over at Ebenezer Cemetery, isn't he?" I said yes, although I was startled because Bobby had never been to his grandfather's grave and nobody in the family ever mentioned it to the children. By now Bobby was thirteen, and a lot more aware of our family's history.

At Easter Bobby went out there for the first time, and he walked right to the grave as if he'd always known where it was. He stood there, staring down at it for awhile like he was off in another world. Then he sat on the ground. Reaching out, he put his left hand on his grandfather's gravestone and his right hand, palm down, on the grave. He didn't say a word, but his eyes looked like he was in a trance.

I said, "Bobby why are you putting your hand there like that?"

"Because Grandpop hasn't gone anywhere, Grandma. He's close to us right now. I can tell by the way his grave feels," Bobby replied.

"By the way it feels!"

"Oh yes. He's still in there."

"His spirit isn't there now, Bobby."

"Something is. I feel it moving right under that sod, grandma. Rest your hand here," said Bobby, but I didn't want to do it.

"I feel it," Bobby said again. He stared down at his hand, which seemed to tremble.

"That's impossible, Bobby," I said.

"No, Grandma. It's not," he said, looking up at me with a serious expression on his face. "I wish I could help him. He needs to go home."

When he said that, memories of my husband's tortured, unhappy life flooded over me, and I wanted to just cry and cry. Home, I thought, what is home for somebody who was always as miserable as he was? Where do people like that go? Lord only knows!

Then Bobby put his head down against the grave. "Listen. I hear a deep voice like his. It says people who die a violent death can't rest. Help him, Grandma, help him," he pleaded. His eyes were big and dark with anguish, and as he spoke the wind began to blow leaves across the grave.

Maybe it was the wind, or maybe it was something else, but there was suddenly an icy chill in the air. "Come on. It's time for us to go, Bobby," I said. At first it seemed like he didn't hear me. I was halfway to the car by the time he rose from the grave.

I don't know if Bobby really heard my husband's voice or felt him at the grave. The incident upset me so much I never asked Bobby about it again, and if Bobby has ever experienced it again, then he didn't mention it to me. But last winter something made me drive out to the house that had seen so much tragedy. First time in over a year I'd been past it. It was a cold, drizzly day, and I don't know what made me go out there. I went the way I always used to go: driving down Highway 21, turning right when I reached Sweet Gum Road. Like I always did, I began to look over to the left after the turn. I knew I would see the old place soon. And all at once, there it was. It stood empty in the midst of a treeless, weed-stubbled lot, paint peeling, windows glaring at me like red, evil eyes as they reflected the late afternoon sun. I looked toward the room where my husband died, and I was sure I saw a face at the window. I pulled off the road onto the shoulder. And then my foot must have slipped off the clutch because the car stalled.

An unreasoning panic shot through me. After repeated

attempts to restart the car, the motor finally shuddered to life, and I accelerated with a jerk. I've never thought of myself as easily frightened, but that was my last trip to see the old place. Still, I can't stop wondering how a house—or a presence in it—could effect people in such a deadly way.

THIS HOUSE IS NOT OPEN TO THE PUBLIC; PLEASE RESPECT THE OWNER'S PRIVACY.

RETURN OF "DOC" HOLLIDAY

The Holliday, Dorsey Fife House,
140 West Lanier Avenue, Fayetteville

As the police officer watched the figure standing in front of the historic John Stiles Holliday House, he noticed something incongruous and mysterious about the man. The officer could tell the man wore a broad-brimmed hat, well-worn boots, and out-of-date clothing, though his face was partly concealed by the shadows of the late November dusk. As the officer studied the figure more closely, he thought he saw a gun belt under the man's jacket. Alarmed by the belt, the officer approached the man cautiously, half expecting him to pull out a six-shooter. He called out to the mysterious figure, asking him what he was doing there, but as soon as he spoke, the man disappeared.

This policeman is not the only person who believes he has seen an apparition of the legendary "Doc" Holliday in front of the John Stiles Holliday House. Many others have had similar experiences, all noting the appearance of the strange man who appears to be from the old West.

Victoria Wilcox, an acknowledged authority on John Henry

"Doc" Holliday, may be able to shed some light on why the legendary gunfighter has been spotted in front of the John Stiles Holliday house. According to Wilcox, incidents that occurred at the house may be the reason Doc Holliday left Georgia for the West in 1873.

John Stiles Holliday was a prominent physician in Fayetteville, the first member of his family to get a college degree. John Henry Holliday was named after John Stiles, his uncle, and as a boy, John Henry often visited his uncle's beautiful home for family gatherings. It was on these occasions that something more than friendship developed between John Henry and his uncle's daughter, Martha Anne Holliday. Mattie, as everyone called Martha, was a lovely gentle girl. It's interesting to note that Margaret Mitchell, Mattie's cousin, modeled the character of Melanie in *Gone with the Wind* after her.

During the frequent family gatherings of this extended Irish family, Mattie and John Henry were constant playmates and companions. He would often meet her under the trees in the yard, and they would share secrets as they walked together or sat beside the Greek columns on the front veranda.

In 1867, the year he was sixteen and she was eighteen, John Henry spent the summer with Mattie's family. It is entirely possible that summer was when John Henry and Mattie discovered their love for each other.

In the following years, John Henry attended a dental school in Philadelphia. After graduating in 1872 at the age of twenty-one, he returned to Georgia. He worked in a dental office in Atlanta and visited Mattie frequently. Late that same summer, he inherited a building in Griffin, Georgia, from his father and opened an office there in November. This practice lasted barely three months. In January of 1873, Doc suddenly closed his office, sold the building he had just inherited, and left Georgia for Texas.

In the West, he developed a reputation as a man who was

Holliday House
PHOTO BY LISA M. HART

touchy when drinking and quick to use his revolver. From Dallas, he drifted to Denver, and from Denver to Dodge City, where he gambled and rode in the posses of Wyatt Earp. He followed Earp to Tombstone, killing three men on the journey. During those years in the West, Doc wrote letter after letter to Mattie and never married.

In 1883, Mattie Holiday became a nun. She took the name "Melanie" for Saint Melanie, who took the veil after marrying a kinsman. Obviously, Mattie chose a namesake saint whose life had parallels to her own.

Doc continued to write letters to Mattie in the convent, proving the strength of the bond between them. We have no way of knowing what these letters contained, for Mattie burned them. It is said that she later regretted this action, but the act itself makes the story of their romance all the more credible.

"I don't think Doc Holliday ever wanted to be a gunfighter," Wilcox said. "He started out satisfied to be a dentist in a sleepy southern town." Without Mattie's letters, it's impossible to know what truly happened, but it is quite possible Doc left Georgia with a broken heart.

Since the girl's beautiful old home in Fayetteville has been open to the public, people occasionally ask about the young man in boots and a broad-brimmed hat seen walking under the trees or leaning against one of the veranda's great columns in the moonlight. If, indeed, an apparition is there, who else could it be other than Mattie's suitor and confidant, the legendary Doc Holliday?

VICTORIA WILCOX IS CURRENTLY WORKING ON BOOK ABOUT JOHN HENRY "DOC" HOLLIDAY. THE HOLLIDAY, DORSEY FIFE HOUSE IN FAYETTEVILLE IS OPEN TO THE PUBLIC. FOR INFORMATION, CALL 770-460-6322.

THE GHOSTS OF DUNWOODY HOUSE

Dunwoody House, Chamblee-Dunwoody Road, Atlanta

Linda and David Chesnut are an attractive, intelligent couple in their mid-fifties. Linda has two masters degrees from Georgia State—one in interior design and one in preservation—and David is a graduate of Oglethorpe University and Emory University's law school. By all appearances they are a normal, happy couple, and not at all the kind of people you would expect to find living in one of Georgia's most haunted houses.

When asked to tell about some of the things that have

happened in the house, Linda begins her story in a calm voice. There is no indication of fear at all, though the events she tells of are enough to send a shiver down the spine of almost anyone.

"Our daughter, Caroline, was ten when we first looked at the house on Chamblee-Dunwoody Road," Linda begins. "Caroline had a pony, and the property had a barn. That was one reason we were interested in seeing it.

"We looked at the house in February. Over a century old, the main portion of the house was built during the Reconstruction era in a style called Piedmont Plain. Behind the house is a cemetery with graves of some of the Donaldson family, who built the house and originally lived in it. Some of the Donaldsons buried there were victims of a smallpox epidemic in the late 1800s. Ironically, no ghosts have been seen there.

"We first visited the house on a very cold day. When we went in, I couldn't even turn on a light because the electricity was off. But something attracted us to the home immediately. Although it was unheated, the house had such warmth and appeal that we knew it was for us.

"That's not to say the home was perfect. My mother came out with me later, and when she saw all the plaster falling off the walls, she actually cried. 'How can you consider it!' she said. 'This old place looks so dreadful compared to the lovely home you have just built.'

"But something about the house was irresistible to us. We moved into it in 1975, and we started noticing some strange things right away. To our amazement, whenever a new guest came for dinner the lights in the dining room would flicker off and on. One electrician who came to look at the problem on several occasions finally refused to go back under house. He said, 'It's just not possible for this to happen. There isn't any wiring problem'."

Soon the flickering lights would be the least of the

Chesnuts' concerns about the house. In the middle of one night, a cousin saw the apparition of a lady with long brown hair in one of the bedrooms. Another morning, in this same room, Mrs. Chesnut also saw this long-haired ghost.

People driving up to the house, as well as the Chesnuts themselves, have been greeted by the face of a woman staring out the window of the bedroom. Her hair is severely pulled back, and the outline of her dress suggests a high collar and leg-of-mutton sleeves, indicating she is a lady of the 1890s.

Speculation about the origin of this ghost has centered around the family of the home's builder, William J. Donaldson. Donaldson was a captain in the Confederacy who had a total of three wives before he died in 1900. "David grew up with some of the descendants of William J. Donaldson, and he asked them if they knew anything unusual about the house. They all confirmed that the right front bedroom—the room where the woman has been seen—was the birthing room. For many years it was the custom to set aside a special room in the house for a mother with a new baby."

According to Linda, none of the Donaldson descendants could think of a reason why the woman's ghost would return to the room, though some recalled a shooting which may have occurred there. The story goes that a man insulted one of Donaldson's daughters. Donaldson, who was of the old school of chivalry, fired a pistol at the man. The man returned fire, but no one was killed. Could violence that flared in the room be the reason the woman returns to it?

Several other unusual things have occurred at the house. Linda recalls that in the early morning hours some overnight guests have heard the sound of slamming doors followed by a chorus of voices that sound similar to the Mormon Tabernacle Choir.

"One of my cousins had a furnace go out during an ice storm, and we invited them to come and stay with us," Linda says. "Repair problems turned what we all thought would be a few days into four weeks. The couple slept in the room where the woman had appeared—the birthing room. After a few nights they asked if my daughter's radio was playing church music in the middle of the night. Neither David nor I have ever heard the music, but they heard it many times."

The Chesnuts' pets are not immune to the ghosts. "In various rooms in the house, I have seen our animals react even when I saw nothing," says Linda. "The dogs' hair stands on end, and they act as if someone is in the room with us, even though it is empty."

In recent years the most dramatic incident in the home involves an old edition of the New Testament. Published in 1884, the testament belonged to a relative of David's stepmother.

"I was reading the newspaper one day," says Linda, "when out of the corner of my eye I saw the testament rise several inches off the table. Needless to say, I was shocked. Then I saw it do the same thing on another occasion." When she told her husband about it, he gave her a skeptical grin. Then one day the same thing occurred while he was watching a football game on television. As he stared at the Bible in astonishment, it moved slightly on the table, then rose very slowly into the air." Even when the Chesnuts do not see the book move, it is seldom found in the same position where it was left.

"But of all the things that have happened, nothing has ever seemed unfriendly," says Linda. "My first impression was that these events were due to the curiosity of loved ones. For instance, an uncle and I were very close. There will be times when something happens in the house that is like something he might have done. It's a confirmation that there is a life after death."

It is fortunate for their spirit guests that the Chesnuts' appreciation of history extends to sharing their home with residents from the past.

THE PINK LADY

Atlanta

THERE ARE MORE PEOPLE THAN WE REALIZE WHO AT SOME TIME IN THEIR LIVES HAVE LIVED IN THE SAME HOUSE WITH A GHOST. THE LADY WHO TELLS THE FOLLOWING STORY WAS ONE OF THEM. OFTEN, AS MRS. ROBERT GORDON AND HER HUSBAND DROVE DOWN MOREHEAD AVENUE IN ATLANTA, SHE WOULD TOUCH HIS ARM SAYING, "LOOK OVER THERE, ROBERT. THAT HOUSE ON THE HILL IS THE ONE THAT HAD THE GHOST. THE ONE WITH THE PORCH ACROSS THE FRONT." MRS. GORDON DIED SEVERAL YEARS AGO, BUT WE ARE FORTUNATE SHE COMMITTED HER STORY TO WRITING. SHE REMAINS DEAR TO THE HEART OF HER HUSBAND, AND ROBERT GORDON SAID HE THOUGHT SHE WOULD BE PLEASED FOR THE FOLLOWING ACCOUNT OF HER SUPERNATURAL EXPERIENCE TO APPEAR IN THIS BOOK.

When I was in my early teens, we moved into a big old house in the Little Five Points section of Atlanta. It was an old-fashioned place built with a large hall that ran from the front porch to the back porch. On the left were three bedrooms and a bath, and on the right were the living room, dining room, and kitchen. The rooms were spacious and high-ceilinged, and I fell in love with it at once.

The first night, as I sat at the kitchen table talking with mother who was cooking at the stove, I had the feeling you get when someone is staring at you. Thinking the girl from next door must have quietly entered the back of our house, I turned to greet her, but instead found myself staring into the face of a young girl I had never seen before. There she stood in strange flowing garments of the palest pink. Although her features were indistinct, I had the feeling she was quite young. In my astonishment I could neither move nor speak, and before I could recover myself, she was gone.

Mother turned to see why I had suddenly fallen silent and gave me a curiously speculative stare. "You look as if you had just seen a ghost," said she.

I gulped and replied, "I think I have, and she was wearing the most beautiful pink dress I've ever seen."

That night at supper everyone teased me about my "Pink Lady," but I didn't care. I knew it had actually happened. Afterward, as mother and I stood out in the yard talking to the people next door, mother was telling our neighbors about what I had seen. We were standing in a place bare of grass or weeds, and there were no small animals about. Suddenly, as she talked about my experience, something gave the hem of her dress a sharp tug. This startled mother so that she jumped, and our neighbor's daughter, standing near her, was so terrified that she ran home.

My next odd experience occurred inside the house. It was a sensation of being followed, or it would be more accurate to say *accompanied*. This would begin at night when I entered the front hall. Only when I had walked the length of it and reached the kitchen door did I feel alone once more. My mother experienced this many times, but we were the only two members of the family to whom it happened. It became common for each of us, but though we sensed the lady's presence, we did not see her.

I actually saw my "Pink Lady" again only once. One night a girl friend and I were on a date with two brothers. When the four of us returned to the house, my family had gone out. My date and I sat down at the piano. The other couple stood in the curve of the baby grand, listening as I taught my friend how to play a tune called "Love in Bloom."

He was doing rather well with a one-finger version when I

distinctly felt someone standing in the doorway watching us. Since the other couple was beside the piano with us, I thought my mother and father had come home. I said, "He's doing pretty well, isn't he?" as I turned my head.

There in the archway, between the living room and dining room, stood the Pink Lady. For a moment I was too startled to move. Then my hands came crashing down on the keyboard, and my face must certainly have been a picture of shock. Rising quickly from the piano bench, I rushed into the dining room, then the kitchen, and finally, the hall. I told my friends what I had seen, and we all searched together until we finally convinced ourselves that the house was empty. They were still reluctant to leave me by myself. When mother and dad returned a few minutes later, they found four very uneasy young people.

During our first years in that house, my brother was just a baby, and some evenings after he had been put to bed, we would hear crying that seemed to come from his bedroom. I would go in to check on him, only to find him sleeping peacefully. No sooner would I return to the living room and begin again on my homework than the crying would start once more. Mother would go into his room the second time, just to be certain nothing was the matter, and there he would be, quiet as a lamb. Then there were the times when he would be right in the same room with us, and we would hear the crying begin elsewhere in the house. We never found out what room it came from.

Several times mother mentioned hearing this crying to the family next door, who had no small children. She asked if, perhaps, they had guests the evening before who might have brought a baby with them.

"We had no guests last night," they would invariably reply, so the sound we continued to hear of a child's crying could not be explained.

After my little brother learned to walk, he began to wake up in the middle of the night screaming at the top of his voice. Unless we could get there in time, he would tear out of his room through two bedrooms, the hall, and the dining room to beat on the kitchen door. If we arrived before this happened, we would find him sitting up in bed, wild-eyed, staring at one particular corner of the room. Mother and I discussed all sorts of possible explanations, but what was carefully left unsaid between us was the thought that he had either seen or sensed the presence of the Pink Lady.

When we moved to the new two-story house, my brother's "nightmares" ceased. He did not get out of bed after he was tucked in, nor did he wake screaming a single night.

In spite of the strange happenings there, mother and I loved the old house and were brokenhearted when it was sold. The rest of the family was glad to go—especially my sisters, for they, too, had heard the crying baby.

But I could hardly bear to leave, for I knew I would never forget the Pink Lady.

TWO YOUNG LOVERS

The Public House, 605 Atlanta Street, Roswell

Roswell, Georgia, looks just the way you would expect—that is, if your only image of the South is from *Gone With the Wind*. Though only a short distance from the heart of modern Atlanta, Roswell's beautiful, columned homes transport visitors to the 1860s. One less-than-idyllic remnant of this era is the old company store of a local mill. More than a century after the Civil War, the store has managed to shed its distasteful past and become a gourmet restaurant called The

Public House. It is also a place where guests may get a taste of the supernatural.

Located directly behind the Public House's present-day location loomed the huge building of the Roswell Manufacturing Company. This mill manufactured thread, cotton, and woolen goods, while monopolizing trade in all types of merchandise. The Public House's main dining area was originally the third and final store built for the mill's workers. In those days, it was common for a mill to run a general store where the workers could purchase whatever they needed.

The mill extended credit to mill employees and paid them in mill-issued script. All this seemed a convenience until the workers realized they were being overcharged at the company store. However, by this time, the unsuspecting workers were often over their heads in debt. This situation grew even darker during the final days of the Civil War, when workers desperate for food and goods found themselves unable to pay the store's outrageous prices. It was during this grim period that a young woman named Cathy found herself working at the store to pay off her father's debts.

It was July of 1864, and despair and gloom hung over the mill village. Cathy knew these were bad times for people, and it didn't help that the weather was steamy hot. On her way to work one morning, Cathy got the feeling that something dreadful was about to happen, but she didn't know what. The situation had grown even worse since the Union troops entered Roswell on their way through Georgia. People knew the war was drawing to an end, but along with the relief that the fighting would soon be over, came a fear of what the future would hold. If it wasn't for Michael saying he would take care of her, she—but she shouldn't even think of him. It was disloyal!

When she arrived at work, there was already a long line of people waiting for the store doors to open. It made her feel sad just to look at them. As she walked past the crowd that morning, a friend stopped her. "Cathy, couldn't you get them to sell me some meat and maybe a little wood," her friend begged. "I could pay part now and part later when mama gets her money from the mill?"

"I don't think the store will do that. I'm sorry, Rosie." She could see tears start in the girl's eyes. Cathy knew her friend's family probably didn't have much food or anything to cook it with at home.

"They'll sell me some cornmeal and fatback, won't they, Miss Cathy?" said an old man, reaching out and catching her arm pleadingly.

"I don't know whether we have it yet, Mr. O'Dell," she replied. "We were out of fatback yesterday, but someone may bring some in. Do you have anything to buy it with, sir?" He held out a handful of Confederate currency.

Cathy shook her head at the sight of it and said, "I'm real sorry, sir, but we can only take things like chickens, meat, eggs, grits, or produce in payment." She hated the fact that the mill had ordered them not to accept the Confederate currency since the Yankees had arrived, but there was nothing she could do.

"But it's all I have!" cried out the old fellow, who was so crippled with arthritis he could hardly walk.

Some women overheard and shouted, "There's no script left after we pay the mill rent for our houses. You mean your store won't take his Confederate money?"

With these words, the crowd grew angry. "Confederate money ain't good enough for the mill owners, that's what," shouted a feisty old lady. "They know we're 'bout to lose the war and done traded theirs in fer gold a long time ago."

The old man's face turned white. "Ma'am, we ain't got nothing to eat at home 'cept some cow peas. Would you take them in trade for meal and meat? They's this year's crop," he said hopefully.

"Yes. If you could go back and get them, sir," Cathy replied. The crowd continued to make ugly noises as the man left on a mule so decrepit that there was no danger any Union soldiers would steal it.

Cathy opened the door with her key while the crowd waited outside. "You're supposed to be here at 6:45 Cathy, not 6:55," said the manager.

"I'm sorry, sir."

"And don't go giving nobody thread on credit today," he continued. "Remember, they has to pay cash! And only one skein per customer."

"Yes, sir."

All that day, Cathy took in whatever the mill people had managed to hide from the Yankees—tomatoes, turnip greens, potatoes, freshly killed meat, dried sausage, even hambones with only a little meat left clinging to their sides. All the while, she thought of Michael.

It began after the young Union soldier started coming in the store. He was a cash customer and the manager had said to her, "Keep a civil tongue in your head, when you speak to that boy. Understand?" She despised the Yankees, but the boy had a certain kindness that melted her disdain. Cathy often closed the store alone, and one day, Michael was waiting for her in the evening. They soon began meeting in the loft at the back of the store, after the manager had left for the day. She only dared meet with him for a few minutes, but the few minutes they shared were precious.

Michael was so young, she thought. At seventeen, he was only a year older than she was. Yet whenever she looked into his gray eyes, with their long, black lashes, she saw something in them she could trust.

Cathy's daydream was broken by a woman with a dozen-and-a-half eggs. "Isn't that enough for a bag of cornmeal?" she asked.

The manager was standing nearby and spoke up before

Cathy could reply. "No, ma'am. It takes three dozen for a bag of cornmeal. When you bring in the rest, you'll get your meal."

This went on all day. By late afternoon, Cathy's spirits were at a low point, though they quickly rose as the dashing Yankee soldier entered the store. It was Michael!

Customers shrank to one side as they always did, making it a point to ignore the hated Yankee soldier. Michael bought a handkerchief from Cathy, and when he paid for it with cash, there was an envious murmur of voices as the people near him saw the money. The purchase was extravagant, even for a Union soldier, and Cathy could tell Michael was trying to tell her something. However, she could not translate his body language. Finally, he blurted, "Miss. Could you please show me the road to Atlanta."

"Why. It's right out there. You'll see it," she stammered.

"Come outside and point it to me," Michael said.

"Do it, Cathy," the manager commanded. She followed Michael out to the front of the store and walked a few paces down the road toward Atlanta with him.

"Why did you want me to—"

"Cathy," he interrupted. "You must make some excuse— anything—and come with me. I have a horse hidden and there's a place where you'll be safe until I come back for you."

"But why?"

"The men have orders to burn the mills tonight. I heard an officer say that all the workers are going to be charged with treason and sent up north. It won't be safe for you here, Cathy."

"They're going to send the women and children, too?" she asked, shocked at what she was hearing.

"These mills were making material for Confederate uniforms. I'm sorry Cathy. Listen. I've got relatives up in the mountains. They'd keep you until this mess is all over, Cathy."

"I can't leave my papa and the only home I've ever had?" she explained desperately.

"But I love you, Cathy. I want to marry you!"

She began crying. "I hate Yankees . . . all of you!" she blurted, running from him back to the store. Before she went in, she stopped to dab at her eyes. A terrible panic overwhelmed her, and she wondered whether she would ever see Michael again.

That was a long, long time ago, and nobody knows what happened to the girl named Cathy and her young soldier named Michael. That night, Union soldiers burned all the mills in the area, creating billowing smoke that was so thick you could hardly breath. The next morning, only heaps of smoldering embers marked the sight of once-thriving industry.

While Cathy and Michael's fate is unknown, an interesting story has spread. The loft of the old store, where the two youngsters met and planned their future, now serves as a piano bar for The Public House. Guests in the loft have occasionally mentioned seeing a couple in costume. According to accounts, the two young sweethearts appear to be in deep conversation. However, the couple disappears as mysteriously as they appear. The Public House's staff also claims to have seen the young couple. Apparently, a seventeen-year-old Union soldier named Michael and his young love Cathy reunite in the loft at night, after the restaurant has closed. They have been known to dance through the loft late at night, sit in the high back chairs overlooking Roswell Square, and sometimes play mischievous tricks on The Public House employees.

THE PUBLIC HOUSE IS LOCATED ON HISTORIC ROSWELL SQUARE. THE RESTAURANT HAS BRICK WALLS, CANDLELIGHT, AND GOURMET FOOD. FOR INFORMATION, CALL 770-992-4646.

THE GOLDEN-HAIRED CHILD

ART Station, 5384 Manor Drive,
Stone Mountain Village

The Atlanta Rapid Transit station at Stone Mountain Village was crowded with families and business people traveling to and from Atlanta. Since Atlanta is just fifteen miles east of the picturesque village, the trip was an easy commute by train. Business people, having just arrived from the office, read the evening newspaper as they waited for the trolley that would carry them from the station. It was the Christmas season, so the platform was dotted with parents holding the hands of small children while trying to hold the packages stuffed under their arms. Exhausted from a long day of shopping, they, too, waited for the trolley.

The shadows of an early winter dusk were already blurring the outlines of the waiting people when snow began to fall. Children broke free from their mothers to touch the falling snow near the tracks. Some of them turned their faces upward in delight; others stuck out their tongues to catch the fluffy white flakes.

About the time the snow began to fall, the shiny green trolley approached the station. A small, golden-haired boy named Kenny pulled away from his mother, causing her to drop her packages. Anna Collins bent over to pick up her packages, and as she did, she heard the sound of steel wheels grinding on steel tracks. The crowd heard the sound too and surged toward it.

She looked for her child and saw him running towards the trolley track. Suddenly, he seemed to lose his footing and fall down right in the path of the oncoming train.

"Kenny," Anna Collins shrieked. She tried to push her way through the crowd which was positioning itself to board the trolley. The bell on the approaching trolley started ringing furiously, while the operator began to blow his shrill whislte.

"Kenny! Get off that track!" yelled his mother. This time the boy heard his mother and looked back over his shoulder to see the approaching train. He tried to get up but fell once more and let out a horrible scream. The train came bearing down upon him, and the operator, despite a heroic effort, was unable to stop the trolley in time.

Most people near the tracks now saw what was happening. They saw the beautiful, innocent child's face and heard his scream of terror. Then it all was over. The crowd stood silently as the green trolley finally pulled to a stop and the two horrified crewmen leaped down to see if anything could be done. The only thing that could be heard was the terrible sobs of Anna Collins.

A short time later, men who serviced the trolleys said that the ghost of a small, golden-haired boy had been seen near the trolley barn at the station. Commuters occasionally heard a mysterious scream, causing more than one startled parent to grab a child who had wandered too close to the track.

All of this happened a long time ago. The old trolley barn is still there, but the electric trolleys are gone. What was once the Atlanta Rapid Transit station has become a beautiful contemporary arts center featuring live professional theatre, an art gallery, and an arts-and-crafts gift shop.

Though the golden-haired boy died more than half-a-century ago, the scream of Kenny Collins still echoes down through the years. Gift shop employees tell of being at the arts center after dark and hearing a child's scream. One person has seen an angelic little golden-haired boy playing in the shop, while sometimes, employees find some of the store's gifts moved to bizarre places. The items they are most likely to find tucked away are those that would appeal to a small boy.

STONE MOUNTAIN VILLAGE IS LOCATED IN DEKALB COUNTY, ABOUT FIF-
TEEN MILES EAST OF ATLANTA AND JUST OUTSIDE THE WEST GATE OF STONE
MOUNTAIN PARK. FOR INFORMATION ON THE ART STATION AND SOME OF
THE EXHIBITS AND PERFORMANCES HELD THERE, CALL 770-469-1105.

A GHOST IN THE "UNCLE REMUS" HOUSE

The Wren's Nest, 1050 Ralph D. Abernathy
Boulevard, S.W., Atlanta

For those fortunate enough to be familiar with the Uncle
Remus tales, a visit to the Wren's Nest brings back visions of
Brer Fox, Brer Rabbit, and Brer Bear. The stories were written
by Atlanta writer Joel Chandler Harris, who used the Afri-
can-American folklore he heard growing up in rural Georgia
as the basis for his work. The characters in many of the Uncle
Remus tales are animals, but animals with such human characteristics that readers can't help identifying with them. The
stories often have a moral, but one that is underscored by
hilarious humor, giving readers no sense of being lectured.
Perhaps the most familiar Uncle Remus tale is the "The Wonderful Tar Baby," which was dramatized in the Walt Disney
movie *Song of the South.*

A visit to Joel Chandler Harris's home, the Wren's Nest, is
an opportunity to know the unusual man behind these stories
more intimately. Though the newspaper writer is often called
"Georgia's Aesop," Harris was a shy, reserved man who rarely
recognized the fame bestowed on him by the Uncle Remus
tales and his other books.

Entering the front hall of the Wren's Nest is like stepping back into the early 1900s. The wallpaper in the front hall, a striped pattern with an iridescent look, is typical of that period, while the flowered carpet with a dark red background was also common at the time. A picture of Mildred, the youngest daughter of Joel and Esther Harris, hangs on the wall to the left. A hall tree near the front door was where the Chandlers and their guests placed umbrellas and canes. The room to the right features a mantlepiece of burled oak; a cuckoo clock in the center of the mantlepiece announces the hour.

Since this a five-room house—Joel Chandler Harris was a journalist and not a man of wealth—some of Harris's sons slept in the small hall at the back of the entrance hall. Along the wall on the right of the hall is a narrow staircase, with an oak bannister, ascending to a landing. The stairs take a right turn at the landing and continue just a few steps to the second floor. It is easy to imagine the clatter of feet as children scampered up and down the stairs, particularly as visitors learn more about Harris's life and family.

Joel was born near Eatonton, Georgia, on December 9, 1848. The child was the product of a romance that his mother's family bitterly opposed, and the boy's father disappeared shortly after his birth. Joel's mother took care of her young son with income from sewing. The community of Eatonton accepted her and the boy with kindness, but young Joel's life was one of hardship.

As a child, Joel detested textbooks, but he loved to read, and with his mother's encouragement, he often composed stories. Joel once said, "My desire to express my thoughts in words grew out of hearing my mother reading to me from *The Vicar of Wakefield*." The book later seemed to provide the pattern for his own family life.

When he wasn't reading, he loved to roam the woods, ride horses on the farm where he worked with black youths, and raid peach orchards and watermelon patches. At night, he would sit by the fire in the cabin of a local storyteller, an old black man named "Uncle George," and listen to him tell fables about Brer Rabbit and Brer Fox.

At thirteen, Joel became a printer's devil on the local weekly newspaper, which led to a job at the *Savannah Morning News*. While in Savannah, he met and fell in love with Esther du Pont LaRose, the lovely daughter of a French-Canadian sea captain. Joel was so shy that he courted Esther through poems, unable to voice his desire to marry her.

Eventually, Joel accepted a position at the *Atlanta Constitution*. It was only after he had left Savannah for his new job on the paper in Atlanta that he proposed to Esther by mail. Esther accepted, and the two soon married and started a family.

As a man who never even knew the name of his own father, Harris had no male role model for marriage and parenting, yet he became a loving husband and father. His numerous letters to his wife and nine children are a touching record of his steadfast love and concern for his family. He enjoyed his family so much that he wrote at home as much as he could, rather than spending all of his time at the newspaper.

It was unusual to find a nineteenth-century man involved in child raising. Perhaps because he had no father as a role model, he and Esther parented as partners, though as a father, he wasn't much of a disciplinarian. One day Esther, upset about the children's behavior, asked Joel to speak to them. And he did. "Good morning, children!" he said.

In 1883, Joel bought a five-room farmhouse in the midst of five acres on Atlanta's west side. The Harris family had lots of animals—fancy chickens, guinea pigs, cats, and dogs. Harris also enjoyed growing fruits and vegetables.

It was while writing a column for the *Constitution* that Harris began telling the Uncle Remus stories. The stories soon became so popular newspapers from coast to coast reprinted

The Wren's Nest

PHOTO BY VAN JONES MARTIN

the column. The columns were followed by immensely successful books, which are said to have influenced writers like Rudyard Kipling and Beatrix Potter.

Harris called his homestead "Snap Bean Farm," and as he became more famous, it became his refuge from the world. Atlantans would walk down the street hoping to catch a glimpse of the famous man while he tended his many roses or wrote on the front porch.

Harris's children loved hearing the Uncle Remus stories as much as he had during his own boyhood. Harris's fifth son, Linton, was particularly fond of listening to his father's stories. With Chandler's fame well established, his working conditions at the paper allowed him to do more of his writing at home. He saw much of Linton and loved him deeply.

On September 15, 1890, Harris wrote to his oldest son Julian, who was in Canada going to college, telling him that seven-year-old Linton had been ill with a sore throat but was improving. Seven days later, he wrote Julian again, this time with a much sadder letter. The letter read, in part:

> [To Julian]
> My Darling Boy:
>
> In my grief and despair I can scarcely summon courage enough to write you of the death of Linton . . . though his throat was improving . . . his heart was affected. . . . He was very bright Friday looking at his cigarette pictures and talking about you. . . . Sunday morning he died without a struggle like a tired baby going to sleep. It is a great blow to us as it must be to you. I have always fancied that you cared more about him than for the rest—perhaps it was only a fancy.
>
> Of such dispensations as this, we have to make the best. So I am told. But I should like somebody to tell me how. . . . I hardly know what I have written. Your Mother sends her dearest love and we both bless you, and trust that heaven may guard you safely.
>
> > Your affectionate
> > Papa [1]

Over the years, the ghost of a child has been reported in the Wren's Nest, most often on the stairs in the front hall. According to reports, the ghost is a little boy about seven-years old dressed in turn-of-the-century clothes. While three of Harris's children died in their youth, the apparent age of the ghost is closest to that of Linton at the time of his death. If visitors are sensitive to the spirits of people who once lived

---

1. Keenan, Hugh T., editor, *Dearest Chums and Partners* (University of Georgia Press).

in a house, they should glance now and then at the front hall. The little boy on the stairs in 1890s attire may be Linton. But even if Linton should return from the hereafter for a few seconds to gaze at Wren's Nest visitors, it is reassuring to know he will soon return to the world beyond to hear the wonderful stories of his loving father.

THE WREN'S NEST IS ATLANTA'S OLDEST HOUSE MUSEUM. THE RESTORED HOME FEATURES GUIDED TOURS, HARRIS FAMILY FURNISHINGS, AND A DI-ORAMA FROM THE MOVIE *SONG OF THE SOUTH*. THERE ARE STORYTELLING SESSIONS AND PICNIC SITES. ADMISSION IS CHARGED. FOR HOURS AND INFORMATION, PHONE 404-753-7735.

CITY OF THE DEAD

Oakland Cemetery, 248 Oakland Avenue, S.E., Atlanta

Oakland Cemetery, founded in 1850, sits on six acres. Crowded with monuments and mausoleums, the cemetery resembles a small city within a city. Some have called it a city of the dead. The cemetery is the final resting place of Atlantans from all different walks of life. Its residents include four Georgia governors, many slaves, prominent citizens like Margaret Mitchell, and thousands of Civil War soldiers from both sides.

On one December afternoon, the cemetery was just another historic site on Norman Nawrocky's tour of Atlanta. He had first visited Atlanta during the Olympics, and now he was back to really see the city. When he arrived at the cemetery, he entered through the main gates, went past the watch house, and turned left at the hitching post. He then continued along the western edge of one of the sections until he found the right turn that led him to the Confederate soldiers' burial ground. Above their resting place towered a thirty-thousand-

Monument in Oakland Cemetery
PHOTO COURTESY OF OAKLAND CEMETERY

pound marble lion with a seventeen-foot-high monument at its base.

Though he'd read about the "Lion of Atlanta" and how it marks the place of an undetermined number of Confederate soldiers who were piled in hastily dug trenches during the last hours of the attack on Atlanta, he was still awestruck by the immense memorial.

Nawrocky noticed that the lion was depicted as having suffered a mortal wound—a spear protrudes from just above the heart of the dying animal, while drops of blood flow down from the wound. In his agony, the lion grasps and attempts to draw close to him the battle flag of the Confederacy.

The afternoon light was dimming, and as he stood alone in that part of the cemetery, he could almost feel the presence of the Confederate dead lying in the ground around him. Seven hundred of these men were buried in the final three months before Sherman's army swept into the city. This does not include those buried after they died fighting in the city's final defense.

As a student of history, Nawrocky knew something of the devastation Atlanta suffered after Sherman's attack. In July of 1864, the city had a population of twenty thousand. By November, after it had been attacked and set on fire, it had a little more than one thousand residents.

He thought about the grim descriptions of what was left of the cemetery: The surrounding chimneys sprouted up surrealistically from barren ground, while horses belonging to Federal troops grazed on the grass and shrubbery amid overturned mausoleums and broken grave stones. Coffins were scattered about from looted vaults and graves—the bodies of soldiers and townspeople alike jolted brutally out of their resting places to be replaced with Federal dead. After the final skirmishes and Sherman's departure southward, the last of the Confederate dead were brought into town. Although no one knew their exact resting place, they were all buried here at Oakland.

As Nawrocky stood thinking about those horrible times, he heard the rustle of leaves around him. He turned his head toward the sound and saw shadows swiftly shifting upon the ground and regathering among the trees. As the shadows rose, they seemed to take the form of men. There was the rattle of weaponry, and to Nawrocky's astonishment, he heard the loud and clear notes of a flute-like instrument cutting through the December air. And was that the sound of a drum? Yes! They were playing for roll call.

And then a voice began to speak. "Abraham Alford," it called in a harsh tone.

"Heah," said a voice borne on the wind.

"Ira Allen."

"Present," replied the groaning voice of a wounded man.

"Hiram Beard."

"Here," came the answer in a hoarse whisper.

"Mark Davis . . ."

Nawrocky's heart pounded in time to the drum as he listened to the roll call. These were voices straight from the grave! On and on it went, the hollow tones of the roll caller summoning a response from one dead Confederate soldier after another.

". . . Wilbur Glover," the voice intoned, "Herman Harber." And then . . . "Jim Nawrocky."

Good Lord! thought Norman Nawrocky. His own surname was being called. Nawrocky would never know if there was an answer, for he did not wait to hear the reply. He dashed back toward the watch house and quickly found himself outside the cemetery gates.

The next day, Nawrocky phoned the cemetery to ask for a list of the Confederate soldiers buried there. In a pleasant voice, the receptionist told him, "As yet, no record of the men buried here has been compiled. But we would be happy to take your address and send you one when it does become available."

"Yes. I'll expect it on Judgement Day," Nawrocky replied.

THE ROLL CALL OF THE DEAD IS MOST OFTEN HEARD AT OAKLAND CEMETERY DURING THE MONTHS OF NOVEMBER AND DECEMBER, PERHAPS BECAUSE IT WAS DURING THESE MONTHS IN 1864 THAT AN ENORMOUS NUMBER OF CONFEDERATE SOLDIERS WERE BURIED IN THE AREA. NO MATTER WHAT TIME OF YEAR, JUST BEING AT THIS IMMENSE SHRINE AT DUSK IS AN EERIE, OTHERWORLDLY EXPERIENCE—EVEN MORE SO FOR ONE WHO HEARS HIS OWN NAME CALLED!

THE CEMETERY IS OPEN DAILY FOR VISITORS. FOR HOURS AND INFORMATION, CALL 404-688-2107.

WHERE TIME RUNS BACKWARD

1848 House Restaurant, 428 South Cobb Drive, Marietta

Have you ever wanted an enjoyable evening to last, if not forever, at least twice as long? Carla Foster and Robert Harrington found a place where this could happen. This strange evening occurred during an unscheduled stop just outside of Marietta, when Carla and Robert were on their way to announce their wedding plans to her family.

"Instead of driving on and having dinner in the city, let's go somewhere quaint before we reach Atlanta," Carla suggested that night. "Mother and Dad won't expect us until at least 7:30."

"Where were you thinking about eating?" asked Robert.

"Remember that sign we've seen for a place called the 1848 House Restaurant?" replied Carla.

"The one that looks like a plantation house?"

"Yes. That's it. I've always wanted to go there," Carla exclaimed.

"It's not much out of our way. Let's try it," agreed Robert. As they approached Marietta, they saw the sign for the restaurant announcing its four-diamond rating by the AAA automobile club and its listing on the National Register of Historic Places. "Looks great," Robert said brightly, though he wondered how much the evening was going to cost.

Several miles from the sign, Robert braked his Volvo and spun into the drive that led up to a magnificent Greek Revival–style home with Doric columns, a structure that was obviously the former manor house of a great plantation.

Robert and Carla walked into the home and were greeted by an 1850s-style interior decor. It was still early, before five, and they were able to get a table right away.

"The Battle of Bushy Park occurred here," said Carla, reading the historic information about the house on the menu.

"On this very ground, ma'am," said a waiter who appeared behind them.

"How interesting," Robert said.

"In fact," the waiter continued, "the house was used as a Civil War hospital. This is one of our ten dining rooms; we call it the Scarlett Room because of the wall color. During the days when the house was a hospital, this was the operating room."

The waiter took their drink orders and left, while Carla and Robert looked over the menu. "The food looks intriguing, doesn't it?" said Carla.

"We call it contemporary southern," said a young woman who also seemed to appear out of nowhere and began filling their water glasses and lighting the small lamp at their table. "Since you are early, you might like to go upstairs and see our collection of artifacts and pictures on the second floor. The collection tells the history of this area from the days of the Cherokees to the present."

After touring the museum, the couple sat down at their table. "This house is like another world," said Robert.

"I know," Carla agreed.

"There is something very relaxing about it," said Robert, sipping his wine.

"And you're hoping you will feel the same way around my parents after we tell them about our marriage?" Carla teased.

"Well, isn't it normal for me to feel that way? What do you think they will say when you tell them we want to get married in two months?"

"They will accept it graciously, I'm sure," said Carla, but she looked a little apprehensive. Just then, the waiter reappeared to take their order. "Is it OK to look around some more," Carla asked the waiter, as if to avoid thinking about the impending meeting with her parents. "There is such a lovely view from the front porch. Can we just sit out there in the rockers for a few minutes?"

The waiter agreed. Carla and Robert once more left their table and walked to the porch, where they sat holding hands and enjoying the view.

Then, suddenly, Robert clenched Carla's hand until it hurt. "Ow!" she exclaimed.

"Shhhh!" Robert whispered. "Look over at that last rocker. Do you see anything?"

"A rocker," Carla replied

"Watch it, honey," said Robert urgently.

"It's moving. It's rocking but no one is in it!"

"That's what I thought."

Just then, the hostess called them to say their food was ready and they rose.

"It has to be the wind. A breeze is springing up," said Robert.

"Of course. That's all it could be," agreed Carla.

When they walked into the dining room, Carla felt a chill in the air she hadn't noticed when they ordered. She pulled her coat around her shoulders and ignored the chill until it passed. Dinner was excellent, and there was so much to think about, so many decisions to make, that they lingered over their dessert and coffee until Carla finally excused herself to repair her lipstick. On the way, she passed a clock, noting the time was 6:30. "Good, there's still plenty of time," she thought.

When she returned to the table, Robert said, "We probably need to hurry. Do you want to call your parents?"

"Why? It's only 6:30."

"No. It's 8:30."

"But I just passed a clock! I'll show you." They rose and walked into the room that contained the clock.

"See," she said, pointing at the clock. "There it is. I told you . . ." She paused. "Robert! The hands say 6:20 now. That's ten minutes earlier than when I looked at it a few minutes ago!"

"Ma'am, Ma'am," said a comforting voice beside them. They both turned to see another waiter, this one much older than the first. "Don't let that clock upset you. These things often happen here. The clocks may run backward. Or sometimes the chandeliers in one of the dining rooms swing back and forth, and I don't mean they just vibrate either," the kindly old man said.

"And do the old rockers on the front porch rock when no one is sitting in them?" asked Robert.

"Why yes, sir. Sometimes they do," the waiter replied. "Lots of funny things happen around here. Take the room you had dinner in tonight. People have seen red lights move across that room like laser pointers."

A waitress overheard the old waiter and said to Carla, "Don't let him spook you ma'am. These things don't really happen all that often. Not enough to make people uncomfortable." She paused, as if reconsidering, then added, "But I'll never forget the way a man looked last summer when the flower arrangement on his table was pulled right out of the vase in front of him!"

With this, the two waitpersons scurried back to work, and Robert and Carla scurried to Atlanta to announce their plans. Robert was so fascinated by what happened that night, he decided to hold his bachelor party there before his and Carla's wedding. On the night of the party, a swinging chandelier was noticed by a couple of guests!

THE 1848 HOUSE IS OWNED BY WILLIAM B. DUNAWAY. DUNAWAY REPORTS THAT, DESPITE THE UNUSUAL PHENOMENA, NO VISIBLE GHOST WAS EVER REPORTED UNTIL THE FALL OF 1996. "RECENTLY WE HAD A GUEST WHO SAW A WOMAN IN A LONG, OLD-FASHIONED WHITE DRESS WITH A

HANDKERCHIEF TUCKED IN HER SLEEVE. NO ONE HAS ANY IDEA WHO SHE COULD HAVE BEEN."

MR. DUNAWAY IS A FORMER PHARMACIST WHO OWNED A CHAIN OF DRUGSTORES. HE DECIDED TO SELL THEM AND RETIRE, THOUGH HIS RETIRE-MENT LASTED ONLY BRIEFLY. "I SUPPOSE I WANTED SOMETHING WITH WORSE HOURS," HE SAYS, SMILING WRYLY. HE HAS OWNED THE RESTAU-RANT FOR THE PAST FIVE YEARS; HIS WIFE DOT AND DAUGHTER, DAWN, WORK WITH HIM. THE 1848 HOUSE IS NOT ONLY NOTED FOR FINE FOOD, BUT HAS ALSO RECEIVED AN AWARD FROM THE MARIETTA HISTORICAL SOCIETY FOR ITS AUTHENTIC 1850S DECOR.

THE 1848 HOUSE IS OPEN TUESDAY THROUGH SATURDAY NIGHTS FOR DINNER AND FOR A "JAZZ BRUNCH" ON SUNDAY. FOR INFORMATION, CALL 770-428-1848.

THE SPIRITS OF KENNESAW HOUSE

The Kennesaw House and the Marietta Museum of History, 1 Depot Street, N.W., Marietta

"I once read an old newspaper article that said there were seven hundred ghosts in this building," said Dan Cox, execu-tive director of the Marietta Museum of History, with a smile. Though it was late and almost time to close for the day, I found the enthusiastic museum director more than willing to discuss the ghosts that seem to inhabit his building. "I don't know who did the count or how they managed it."

The museum is located in the Kennesaw House, which was the most famous hotel in the area around the time of the Civil War. Today, there is a restaurant on the ground floor, while the museum occupies the building's second floor. "We have exhibits from Creek Indian days, through the wars, and on up to the present," said Cox, who has worked for years to build the museum's collection. "We're continuously expanding."

The enormous, L-shaped hotel building was constructed of red brick on the site of an early stagecoach stop. At one time, it was also a cotton warehouse. Before the Civil War, this three-story hotel was in the heart of a booming summer retreat inhabited by Sea Island planters escaping the malaria epidemics of the coast. During the Battle of Kennesaw Mountain, the house became a Civil War hospital and morgue, first for the Confederates, then for the Federal troops. Today, the building is located on the edge of Kennesaw Mountain National Battlefield Park.

Cox boasted of the building's proud heritage, then quickly returned to the subject of ghosts. "The first thing that happened to me," he recalled, "occurred one afternoon when I was standing in my office talking with two other gentlemen. We all heard a tapping sound that started on the ground floor and began to ascend the stairs. It was as if someone wearing a wedding band on their hand was moving along the iron stair rail, their ring clicking rhythmically against the rail while they climbed.

"I told my guests, 'Just a minute. I'll see who that is.' I opened the door and stood out in the hall, but no one was there. Shaking my head, I went back in my office and closed the door. We went on with our talk. A few minutes later, we heard it again. But when I opened the door, it stopped. This happened exactly four times!"

Cox then mentioned how the building's old elevator may be haunted. According to Cox, the elevator rises by itself, the doors open and close at the top floors, then the elevator returns to the ground level. Cox said this occurs only when the building—other than his office—is empty.

"One winter afternoon as my wife and I stood talking in front of the elevator, I happened to turn my head and see a gentleman standing right beside me," Cox continued. "He ignored me. I could see he was wearing a flat, black-felt hat and a cream-colored coat that struck him about mid-calf. Something about the fellow reminded me of a medical doctor, but he disappeared so quickly that, to save my life, I couldn't tell you whether he was carrying a medical bag or not."

Cox never saw the man again, but he had his suspicions about his identity. "This building was owned by a man named Dix Fletcher who moved down here from Massachusetts. Of course, he was a Union sympathizer, even had a nephew who was a Union officer and a doctor. Dr. Wilder, I believe was the name of the nephew. During the Federal occupation here, Wilder looked up the Fletcher family and treated them. It's said that Fletcher's connection with the doctor was the reason this building was not burned by the Union troops. I've sometimes wondered if the man I saw near the elevator that afternoon was Dr. Wilder.

"Incidentally, I'm not the only one who has seen the man in the black hat and cream coat. An employee of mine was working late one afternoon when he heard a noise in the hall. Thinking someone had wandered in by mistake, he opened the office door and stepped out to ask if he could help whomever it was. A gentleman in a coat and hat passed right by him, then disappeared. From his description, the man he saw that day was the same man who appeared to me.

"Of course, we've had perfect strangers visit the museum or eat in the restaurant, then later write us letters explaining how they felt presences during their visit. I'm sure I don't know the explanation." As he finished talking, he glanced at his watch. "Well, it's closing time for the museum, four o'clock."

As we got ready to leave, the sound of the elevator could be heard from above. It paused at the second floor, and we could hear the noise of the doors opening and closing. Then, the elevator proceeded down to the first floor, and the doors

Kennesaw House

opened again. It was empty! As the elevator doors began to close again, there was a jerk, as if someone stopped the doors from closing by blocking them with a firm, restraining hand. The doors paused briefly, then closed, and the elevator creaked upwards.

We walked over and stared at the closed panel in front of the elevator shaft. We heard the doors open on the second floor, and then the elevator stopped.

"That elevator may or may not be on the second floor tomorrow morning," said Cox, as he locked the building for the night. "I already mentioned it sometimes goes up or down by itself. One of our seven hundred ghosts playing a prank, I suppose," he said.

FOR INFORMATION ON THE KENNESAW HOUSE AND THE MARIETTA MU-
SEUM OF HISTORY, CALL 770-528-0430.

THE PRESENCE AT
THE BOWDON INN

The Bowdon Inn, Main Street, Bowdon
(near Carrollton)

The Bowdon Inn, located on Main Street in Bowdon, is one of the town's most unusual Victorian homes. The inn is owned and operated by Diana Henson, whose warm, attractive smile radiates hospitality. The house was built in 1877 by a man who was a licensed Baptist minister, architect, and medical doctor. With such an unusual builder, along with such a bright and cheerful proprietor, the inn is obviously not your average abode, and this can also be said of the home's resident apparition.

"A real character" is how Diana described the inn's ghost "He," as the family named the spirit, has made a light fixture swing and moved a puppy in a box from one room to another. On one occasion, He moved the sofa from side to side, while the family sat on it! Another time, He moved a picture from one side to the other, as if trying to decide if it was straight, before finally dropping it to one side. "I didn't hang it back in that spot," said Diana, "in case the ghost was trying to make a point." Another picture—a photograph of the house taken in 1891—flew off the wall for no reason. "It was a heavy picture. We heard the crash from outdoors and ran into the house. The nail was still right there in the wall!"

Apparently, the inn's well-known apparition doesn't affect local residents since the house is a focal point for Bowdon community life. Locals hold special events here, gather at the inn for reunions, and make the inn their headquarters when family members return home to celebrate holidays.

Diana and her family first became aware of their ghost in

1984, when they were remodeling the home. After the Henson's moved in, they renovated the house themselves to turn it from a private home into an inn. Many ghost experts have noted that renovations in older homes can, and often do, precipitate ghostly activity.

Diana said, "It may have been the changes we were making that upset the ghost, or perhaps our decorating didn't suit his taste. During the work on the house, we would often leave our tools beside whatever project we were working on when we went out for a meal. When we came back, we would find the tools had been moved. In fact, they would be somewhere else in the house!"

One of the strangest events, which Diana calls the "Swinging Light Incident," took place in the den hallway. "We had been talking about taking down this light—just moving it and placing it somewhere else," she began, pointing out the huge, heavy iron chandelier. "We had company one night, and after we said goodbye to our guests, my ex-husband came back in and sat in the den while I went to the kitchen. When I returned to the den, that light was swinging back and forth for all it was worth. My ex-husband was going to try to stop it, but I told him it would probably stop in a little while, and it did. When the chandelier was tested later, it was determined there was no way to make it swing the way it did that night."

Diana said she doesn't know who the ghost could be. "There have been two deaths—one in the den, the room in which most of the incidents have happened, and one in the room above the den. A man died there in the early 1900s of natural causes, and there was also a suicide. Both incidents occurred years ago when the home was a boarding house."

Diana recalled only one incident when she was truly scared by the ghost. "I was working in the kitchen right after lunch when I heard the sound of a man's footsteps on the hardwood floor upstairs. My ex-husband had been working upstairs earlier, so I called up to him but received no answer. I didn't think much about it until I heard the footsteps again. Then I glanced out the kitchen window and happened to notice that my ex-husband's truck was gone. I checked the back door and the front and noticed the bolts were shut. I was convinced I was alone in that house, yet once more I heard someone walking across the floor upstairs. I pulled back the bolt on the kitchen door and ran out just in time to see my ex-husband's truck pulling into the driveway.

"He saw by my face that something was wrong. When I blurted out what had happened, he ran inside and grabbed an old shotgun that he wasn't even sure worked. He raced up the stairs, and I was right behind him. Each time we opened a door into a room or a closet, we were scared to look. We searched everywhere possible; there was nothing up there, nor were any of our things disturbed."

According to Diana, some of the ghost's activities may be an effort to voice its dissatisfaction. "The first night we moved into the renovated upstairs bedroom, we heard something in the middle of the night like a sonic boom. The next day, we couldn't find anyone who had heard the same sound. We wondered if the ghost was trying to make us leave the room, but we didn't move back downstairs."

After several years, Diana has come to accept the permanent "guest" at her inn. "I suppose that we came to regard him as just part of the life of the house," said Diana. "A lot of people don't believe these things, and I certainly can't explain them. All I can do is share the details. Everything is much quieter now than during those early months of the renovation. I think He has settled down now and is content that the house is a nice place with someone who looks after it."

BOWDON IS LOCATED NOT FAR FROM CAROLLTON. FOR INFORMATION ON THE BOWDON INN, CALL 770-258-9808.

PRESIDENTIAL PATHWAYS

Bonnie Castle

MISS MARY

Bonnie Castle, 2 Post Street, Grantville

The town of Grantville is only a few miles from Newnan, but as we entered the town and drove slowly by the quaint homes and old, brick storefronts, it seemed as if we had parted a beaded curtain separating the present from a Victorian past.

We came to a stop beside a young man climbing on his bicycle.

"What's your name?" my husband asked.

"Ben."

"Is that Bonnie Castle down at the end of the street?" I inquired, pointing towards a grand, two-story Victorian house.

He paused with one foot on the ground and the other on a pedal. "Reckon it is. Why?"

"Because we wanted to find it. Think we'll like it there?"

He gave us a long look. "Can't tell," he said before speeding off in the opposite direction.

We drove down to the end of the street toward the house and quickly recognized Bonnie Castle from the picture in the brochure. Today, the historic Romanesque Greek Revival home is operated as a bed-and-breakfast, and we had come here to spend the weekend. We tried ringing the doorbell, but no one answered. Then I happened to see an overall-clad figure ambling at a deliberate pace across the yard toward us. The tall, thin man continued up to the door and extended his hand toward us cordially. "I'm Darwin Palmer," he said. "Come in."

After a brief introduction, Mr. Palmer gave us a tour of the house. The five-thousand-square-foot home is covered with antiques. Art, glassware, and fine furniture inhabit just about every shelf, wall, and corner. The home's gilded ceiling and stained-glass windows are truly impressive, while an unusual exhibit of rare quilts displayed as wall hangings completes the home's exquisite interior.

As Mr. Palmer showed us around the house, he told us something of its history. Bonnie Castle once belonged to the Colley family. The Colleys' many business interests included owning the Bank of Grantville, co-owning the Grantville Hosiery Mill, and operating five farms in the region. Over the years, Franklin D. Roosevelt and many other famous people stayed in the home as guests of Itura and J.W. Colley.

After complimenting him on the house, I said, "Your literature about Bonnie Castle mentions that it is haunted. Tell us about it."

"It's no secret," replied Palmer. "The realtor who showed us the house told us right off about an incident that happened to him. Apparently, he dropped by the house and saw the cleaning lady standing under the stained-glass window at the landing of the grand staircase. He heard her talking as though she was having a conversation, but he knew she was alone. When he asked her whom she was talking to, she replied, 'Oh, I'm just visiting with Miss Mary.'"

"And where was Miss Mary?" I asked.

"The cleaning lady told the realtor Miss Mary was sitting

right where she often sat—on the prayer bench at the landing. But there was obviously no one there."

When I asked Mr. Palmer about the identity of Miss Mary, he said it was probably the daughter-in-law of banker J.W. Colley. Mr. Palmer went on to tell us that even in life, Miss Mary was a bit eccentric, often playing macabre practical jokes on visitors and passersby.

Many of these stories involve the mannequins created by Mary's mother-in-law, Itura. Itura was an intelligent, talented woman renowned for her realistic, life-size mannequins. One such story involves the home's prophet room—a guest room set aside for visiting ministers since hotels were not common at that time.

"On this occasion, there was advance warning that a minister would be staying at the Colley house," Mr. Palmer began. "Miss Mary prepared the prophet room for his arrival. As they mounted the stairs, she said, 'I hope you don't mind sharing your room with a dead person.' The minister thought this was simply a crude joke, but on entering the room, he glanced over at the bed to find it already occupied by a lovely young lady in a white dress. At first, he thought she was asleep. Stepping closer, he saw that her hands were crossed upon her breast like those of a corpse awaiting burial. With a wild shriek, the clergyman dashed out of the room and down the stairs. When the minister finally returned, Mary embarrassed the gentleman by saying, 'I find it curious that a man of the cloth should show such a fear of death'."

Itura's skill at crafting lifelike replicas of children, housewives, babies, and even soldiers killed in battle earned her a worldwide reputation with museum directors. Mary helped Itura with her business. Since orders for the mannequins could be sizable, Mary often placed them in front of the house's windows to get them out of the way. Passersby would often comment on the grim faces staring out at them from the home.

The more ignorant believed Itura and Miss Mary could only capture such graphic detail in their mannequins by frequenting morgues and stealing the facial expressions of the dead. A few people went further, claiming that certain mannequins bore a shocking resemblance to a deceased relative or friend. One woman came back from a trip to a museum in Atlanta maintaining, "That woman has stolen my dead brother's face! I saw it on a Confederate soldier in the battle of Atlanta."

After Miss Mary died, people began having strange experiences in the home. One night, an elderly resident of Grantville who was having car trouble knocked at the door of the Colley house to see if he could get some help. The lady living there at the time answered the door. The gentleman told her about his car trouble, so she invited him in and went to get her husband. As the man turned to enter the sitting room on his right, he was confronted by a heavyset figure with dark hair and a peculiar pallor on her face. He was sure it was none other that Miss Mary! The man bolted out of the house, not even waiting for the woman and her husband to return.

Miss Mary seems fond of playing with the electricity. In the late 1970s, a house-sitter and his wife were staying in the house at a time when the electricity was disconnected. The couple was startled to hear the window air conditioner switch on in a first-floor bedroom. Running downstairs to investigate, they found the room's lights on and its air-conditioner humming. Both went off seconds after they entered the room.

The Palmers, too, have experienced trouble with the electricity. "We've had a few incidents where the electricity worked even though it was disconnected," Mr. Palmer said. The Palmers have also experienced sudden pungent odors of such strength they were forced to leave a room, as well as intensely cold spots at various places in the house.

Apparently, Miss Mary is not the only ghost inhabiting Bonnie Castle. According to Mr. Palmer, the ghost of Miss

Mary's father-in-law, J.W. Colley, has also made at least one appearance at the house. The incident occurred one day when some friends of the Palmers were visiting. During the visit, the friends' daughter, Tess, sat on the front steps eating blueberries. Suddenly, Tess stood up and started waving and calling to someone. "Come over here!" she called out, though there was obviously no one there.

"Who are you calling?" asked her mother.

"That man near the gate," replied Tess.

"I don't see a soul," her mother said. "What does he look like?"

"Well, there he is, Mother," Tess called. "He's old, and he's got on a yellow shirt with suspenders and a funny straw hat."

The girl clearly saw someone, but the Palmers and the girl's parents saw nothing. Later, Mrs. Palmer was astounded to find an old picture of Mr. Colley wearing a straw hat and suspenders. In the picture, J.W. Colley appeared exactly the way Tess had described him, though the child had never before been in the house or seen the photograph.

Though Miss Mary has been dead these many years, many in Grantville still believe the superstitious stories about her and Bonnie Castle. Children never ring the home's doorbell on Halloween, and tradesmen make it a point to call at the house before dark.

Despite the rumors and the strange incidents, the Palmers are proud of their bed-and-breakfast, as they should be. After showing us to our room, Mr. Palmer suggested a restaurant where we could find a good meal after a long day of travel. We returned to the car and drove down the main street toward the restaurant. As we drove, we saw Ben once more and stopped.

"Ben, have you ever been inside Bonnie Castle?" I asked.

"No ma'am," he replied. "Don't want to."

"It's a beautiful place and there are many interesting things to see."

"I seen enough." He looked over his shoulder.

"Like what?"

"Lots a things. But mostly people lookin' out at night. In my opinion, they're people wantin' to get out!"

"How could that be?" I asked, though I recognized he was probably just repeating the rumor about Itura's mannequins that had been handed down by the townsfolk for generations.

"I don't know. But there's been lots of 'em. A Civil War soldier, a baby in a casket, a pretty girl—but not me."

"What do you mean, not you?" As I said this, I noticed there was something strange about the boy's bike. It was an old model, like the one my grandfather gave me for Christmas when I was nine.

"Nothin'." The boy was getting on his bike now.

"Who were they?"

"Miss Mary's people." His eyes would not meet mine, and he quickly pedaled away. As we restarted the car, I looked in the mirror and saw that Ben was gone. However, I still had a fine view of Bonnie Castle.

FOR INFORMATION ABOUT RESERVATIONS AT BONNIE CASTLE, CALL 770-583-3090.

THE HAUNTED SOLOMON HOUSE

103 North 13th Street, Griffin

When Latrelle Stockton, Yvonne Melvin, and Phyllis Brinson decided they wanted to buy a large house to convert into an antique shop, they visualized the antiques in an old Victorian home. They were immediately drawn to the white, two-story Solomon House. The rambling old home with a wraparound porch was built in 1908 and seemed to have a welcoming and homey atmosphere.

There had always been talk in Griffin about the history of the house—how two deaths had occurred there—but people in small towns often build bizarre legends around events that would not be commented on in larger cities. The three women were not superstitious. They purchased the house and converted it into an antique mall, renting out separate rooms to a wide variety of antique dealers. Their idea turned out to be a good one; since its opening in May of 1994, the house has attracted a steady stream of both tourists and locals shopping for antiques.

Eventually, though, some of the tenants and customers began having unusual experiences in the home. One such experience happened to an antique dealer who rented a room on the second floor. She usually kept her two dogs with her, and one day she noticed the dogs were acting strangely. They were normally well-behaved animals, but on this day they kept running back and forth on the stairs and could not be controlled. It was almost as if they were racing towards something, though no one had any idea what that something could be.

A customer who had lived in the house for a short time several years before happened to be shopping in the house that day. This customer looked over at the stairs in the empty hall and said to one of the house's owners, "Do you think those dogs are seeing the child? You know how people credit animals with the ability to sense and see things we don't."

The owner asked the woman what she was talking about. "When I lived here," the woman replied, "there were days when I would see a little girl run up and down the stairs right past me, as if she was playing with someone." The woman went on to describe the girl as being about five years old with golden-brown curls that touched the top of her shoulders. She always wore a long white dress and thick stockings in the style of the

1920s or 1930s. "At first I disliked the idea of this mysterious child running up and down the stairs, but she always seemed so happy I started not to mind at all."

Customers, too, have had strange experiences in the house. During one summer, a woman hurried out of a front room and complained to one of the owners. "I want to shop in there," said the shivering woman, "but the air conditioner will have to be turned off first. It's the only room in the house that is just too cold for me." The owner tried to explain to the woman that the air conditioner was not on.

A friend of the owners has also experienced a chill in the front room. "I have only felt the oppressive chill in that bedroom a time or two," the woman explained. "The house is bright and cheerful on the whole, and I enjoy being in it. But some people are more sensitive than others."

Most people never experience anything out of the ordinary at the Solomon House, but now and then sightings of the little girl are reported. And there are still occasional customers who complain of the mysterious chill in the front room.

SOLOMON HOUSE IS AT THE CORNER OF THIRTEENTH AND SOLOMON STREETS IN GRIFFIN.

THE PHANTOM OF ANDERSONVILLE

Andersonville National Historic Site, Andersonville

It was dusk as Robert Berry walked the grounds of the Andersonville National Historic Site. He soon found himself wandering down Pecan Lane, the old road leading from the town of Andersonville to the infamous prison for Union soldiers.

He had run into few visitors since beginning his tour, so he was surprised to see a tall figure walking some distance ahead of him. Something about the man appeared odd to Robert, and he couldn't help inspecting him more closely. He quickened his steps to gain a better perspective. As he did so, he could see the man had an unusually large head, a short body, and long arms that hung down almost to his knees. The man was dressed in black clothing, and although it was not raining, he held an umbrella over his head.

Berry slowed his pace once again, hoping the odd fellow hadn't noticed him. Berry just wasn't in a mood to talk. He relished this rare opportunity to experience the historic site in thoughtful solitude.

As he walked, his thoughts turned to the prisoners at the camp. In fact, Berry knew a great deal about the conditions at the camp. He wrote his master's thesis on that very topic, though this was a rare visit to the actual site. He knew that prisoners were at the bottom of the priority list for both North and South near the end of the Civil War. The guards at the prison camps were usually the dregs of what was left after the other men had gone to war. Near the end of the war, conditions grew even worse. For many, only the hope of exchange kept them alive. Little did they know Union General H.W. Halleck had ordered an end to all prisoner exchanges, causing prison populations to swell on both sides. Here at Andersonville, thousands of prisoners were crammed into a facility that was designed to hold a tenth of that number. Men slept on the ground and often awoke covered with vermin and even maggots. Though he tried to put it out of his mind, the terrible suffering that occurred in this overcrowded, unhealthy prison depressed him.

At that moment, he began to smell the most abominable

odor. Looking around him, he did not see anything that could have produced such a horrible scent, no garbage or livestock. The only thing in sight was the strange man, still walking a good distance ahead of him. The smell must be his imagination, he told himself.

As he continued down the road, all that research from years ago flooded back to him. He remembered reading how the prisoners weren't even issued eating utensils. Some prisoners who didn't want to eat out of their caps or shoes carved spoons out of wood or twisted scrap tin into crude utensils. Many of the prisoners were industrious. One carved chess pieces from roots; others tended gardens, about three inches wide, around the sides of their tents. Some drew with ink made from rust, while several spent their time reading the few precious Bibles and other books on hand.

But Berry knew the prisoners spent most of their time dying of diseases like scurvy, diarrhea, and dysentery. In fact, to escape disease was considered a miracle since one stream was used for the men's latrine, drinking water, cooking, and washing. Many also died from starvation. During the last year of the war, there wasn't enough food for the Confederate army, much less its prisoners.

Berry's thoughts were interrupted when he saw the black-clad figure, still a good deal ahead, drop to his knees at the side of the road as if he was looking for something. Berry found the behavior unusual, but he was determined not to let the odd man disrupt his tour of this solemn place. Berry walked on and hoped the man would find whatever he was searching for by the time Berry came upon him.

Berry's thoughts quickly drifted back to the conditions at Andersonville. For some reason, his thoughts turned to Father Whelan, the priest who had come to the camp near the end of the war. Berry was a devout Roman Catholic, and during his research he had been fascinated by Whelan's story. For a long time, the prison didn't even have a chaplain. A Macon pastor, visiting nearby Americus, accidentally came upon the camp and learned that there was no priest to minister to the many Roman Catholic prisoners. He wrote to the bishop of Savannah, informing him of the situation, and Whelan was soon assigned to the camp. Prior to coming to Andersonville, Whelan had served with the Confederates at Fort Pulaski. When Fort Pulaski fell, Whelan was sent north to prison with the other captured Confederates. He was eventually exchanged and was awaiting an assignment when the Macon pastor's letter arrived.

On June 16, 1864, in the darkest days of the end of the war, Whelan arrived at the nightmare of Andersonville. He found most of the prisoners were without proper clothing, many entirely naked. He had to receive the confessions of the sick in the midst of the crowded stockade. The sight of death was all around him, and with it, the most horrible stench imaginable.

Whelan lived in a four-by-eight-foot hut about a mile from the prison. He rose each day at dawn, had a scanty breakfast, said his prayers, and then walked the hot dusty path to spend the day at the prison.

Many times each day, Whelan would creep into the improvised tents or burrows of the dying prisoners and attempt to give them some comfort. Each day, as Whelan proceeded to the hospital area from the tents, he passed the Dead House—where row after row of corpses were placed on the ground to await the wagons that would carry them away for burial. With conditions worsening, Whelan called upon the bishop in Savannah to send help. Three priests came but didn't stay. One grew sick from continual vomiting. The other two worked for a couple of weeks and left. Berry knew that though Whelan's courage was not the kind written about in history books, he was one of the true heroes of the Civil War.

Once more, Berry's thoughts were broken by the overpowering stench. It seemed to surround him now, but still he could see nothing that might cause it. Apparently the man in black couldn't take the smell either, because he had now disappeared. Berry now ran along the road, trying to escape the horrible smell.

Finally, Berry stopped and tried to catch his breath. "My dear man," a strong voice said from behind him. Startled, Berry quickly turned to face the direction of the voice and found himself face to face with the man in black. "I'm ready to hear your confession." Berry could now see the pants the man wore were far too short for his legs and revealed his ash-colored shoes. His hair was uncombed, his face coarse, and he held the umbrella with a large, rough hand. "I am ready to give you the last rites," the man said.

The last rites! Berry was horrified. That meant he was about to die! The man's pale eyes stared right through him, and suddenly Berry realized he was not looking at a living human being. Robert Berry ran as fast as he had ever run in his life. By the time he reached his car, his chest was pounding. Without catching his breath, he jumped in his car and raced away to a sleepless night.

The next day, he confided his experience to one of the museum workers at the historic site.

"I would guess that you met Father Whelan," a staffer said, confirming what Berry already suspected. "Whelan stayed here until the very last, exposing himself to a terrible risk of infection. The prisoners here never forgot him. Though Whelan was from the South, he used his own money to buy the prisoners food. He even borrowed four hundred dollars for wheat flour to make bread for men in the hospital. He was a true saint—the only Christian minister to stay at the prison. One prisoner later wrote that because of Whelan's meekness and kindness, he knew that all compassion had not left mankind."

"Yes. I'm familiar with what Whelan did here," Berry said. "In fact, I was thinking about him right before I saw the strange man . . . the ghost. But why was he holding the umbrella?"

"The summer sun beat down with such intensity that Father Whelan always held an umbrella over his head," the museum worker replied. He paused for a long time, then continued, "It's strange, but now and then one of the visitors here will say they've seen the same strange man you did, always in the oddest looking clothes and holding a black umbrella over his head. I tell them I don't believe in ghosts, but to tell you the truth, I know it's Father Whelan."

Berry stood silently, trying to remember exactly what it was that had caused him to spend so much time thinking about Whelan late yesterday afternoon. Though he had read much about Whelan's life, he had never seen a picture of the man and couldn't remember having read anything about his odd appearance. He was sure nothing about the man in black's appearance could have triggered his memory. The more he thought about it, the more he knew there could be no explanation for what had happened to him on the road—the same road so many men had traveled to their death.

"Well, I was just leaving, sir," the museum worker said. He was jangling his keys. "If you're here tomorrow, don't mention my saying anything about Father Whelan, if you don't mind."

ANDERSONVILLE NATIONAL HISTORIC SITE AND THE ANDERSONVILLE CIVIL WAR VILLAGE ARE LOCATED ON GA 49, TEN MILES NORTHEAST OF AMERICUS AND FIFTY MILES SOUTH OF MACON. FOR INFORMATION, CALL 912-924-0343.

THE GEORGIA WEREWOLF

Talbot County (between Macon and Columbus)

Even today, Talbot County, located between Macon and Columbus, is a lonely, heavily wooded part of the state. In the nineteenth century, the county was even more remote and undeveloped, yet it served as a home to some of the state's elite society. One of the most elite of Talbot County's families was the Burt family.

In the 1840s, the Burt family was a highly respected part of the community and sufficiently well off to enjoy European travel and other luxuries reserved for the wealthy. Mildred Owen Burt was widowed at thirty-seven. Her inheritance included sixteen slaves, sheep, hogs, cattle, two horses, a large assortment of books, a barouche carriage, and a brace of fine pistols (she was an excellent markswoman).

Mrs. Burt loved to read, but of her four children—Joel, Sarah, Emily Isabella, and Mildred—only Isabella was as fond of reading as her mother. Isabella particularly enjoyed the books on the supernatural which her mother brought back from Europe.

Isabella's unusual appearance may have driven her toward the quiet solitude of the world of books. Sarah and Mildred were passably pretty and resembled their mother, but Isabella had inherited some of her father's characteristics. He had been a handsome man, though somehow his thick, dark hair, heavy brows, large brown eyes, and tall frame gave him a sinister appearance. However, whenever the curve of his lips parted to reveal a generous smile enhanced by white teeth, any trace of the sinister disappeared. Isabella's hair was thick and dark, like her father's, but shaggier. Her dense brows covered eyes that were smaller than her father's, while her teeth, revealed during rare smiles, were pointed, as if they had been shaped with a file.

On one trip to the dentist, Isabella's mother asked the man if something could be done to improve the appearance of the Isabella's teeth, perhaps by blunting them. The dentist, not a particularly sensitive man, disregarded this suggestion. "Her teeth are perfectly healthy," he said. "After all, aren't we humans basically carnivores?" Mrs. Burt was too irritated to reply.

It was not long after that trip to the dentist that Isabella fell ill. The only substance that seemed to ease her restless nocturnal tossing was a syrup containing opium. Isabella quickly grew dependent on the syrup, often rising from her bed at night in search of the drug. Many a night the family heard her moaning in pain and addiction. Some nights, even the syrup would not ease her insomnia, and she took to roaming the surrounding countryside.

During the long afternoons of December and January, Isabella spent much of her time reading in the family library. In a sense, the girl's invalidism and solitude eased her mother's mind, for at least Mrs. Burt did not have to worry that she would elope or become involved with a young man of the wrong class. The same could not be said for her other two daughters. In fact, Sarah had become involved with a young man named William Gorman. Though Gorman was heir to his father's farm, Mrs. Burt was concerned that the young man seemed more interested in mining for gold than becoming a gentleman farmer. Mildred was away at school for the winter, as was Joel, so Mrs. Burt did not have the opportunity to worry about Mildred and Joel quite as often.

One February morning, Gorman stopped by the Burt house with a strange piece of news. During the night, some of the Gorman family sheep had been attacked. Their shepherd denied having been asleep.

The news greatly distressed Sarah and Mrs. Burt, for they realized their own sheep might also be in danger. However, Isabella simply looked up from her book and asked if the shepherd had seen anything among the herd.

"He says he saw no panther or bear among them," Gorman replied.

"Nor anything else?" persisted Isabella.

"Not that I know of. What do you mean?" asked Gorman.

"Perhaps a wolf?"

"We have very few wolves around here. And a wolf could not attack the sheep without our dogs catching the animal's odor and barking," said Gorman. "That would alert the shepherd immediately."

"What would the shepherd do then?" asked Isabella.

"Frighten it away, or kill it," said Gorman.

Isabella seemed to pause for a moment and consider Gorman's response. Finally she commented, "Well, every animal feeds upon another."

Gorman was now irritated with the young girl, though determined not to show it. "This attack was not for food," he said sharply. Then, changing the subject, he inquired, "Mrs. Burt, I am on my way to the store. Do you need anything?"

"I don't think so, but it is very kind of you to inquire, William."

"Mother, it would be nice to bake some lemon tarts," said Sarah. "If you would like for me to make them, then we need some lemons." She looked at her mother. "And some fine ground white flour for the crust," she continued.

"Of course, I would," said Mrs. Burt. "Ask the store to put it on my bill, William. Four lemons and five pounds of flour."

Later that night, Sarah heard William return from the store and rushed out to the porch to meet him. Mrs. Burt noticed that the two talked on the porch for at least a quarter of an hour before Sarah entered the front door, groceries in hand. That was entirely too long for those two to be alone together, Mrs. Burt thought. Mrs. Burt then heard Sarah speaking with

Isabella. Though Mrs. Burt could not hear Isabella's question, she did hear Sarah's reply.

"Yes. They have found out more, Isabella," Sarah said. "But I don't want to talk about it. It's horrible!"

Mrs. Burt then retired to her room. She walked over to the window and stared out thoughtfully. By now, the men must be making plans to lie in wait for the marauder, she thought, whatever or whoever it was. She knew they would form a posse and shoot it.

On Friday afternoon, two days later, Gorman came by the Burt house again. Sarah had made the lemon tarts that afternoon, and he stayed long enough to join them in a tart and a cup of tea. Isabella persisted in asking him for more news about the animal that had attacked the sheep. He replied that there had been no more attacks on the sheep, but that "something happened at a nearby cattle farm." The news elicited a torrent of questions from the excited young girl.

"Why do you want to talk so much about anything so unpleasant, Isabella?" asked Sarah.

Isabella turned on her sister with fury in her eyes. "You know nothing about it!" she shouted. Then, to everyone's surprise, she grabbed Sarah's plump arm and jerked her violently.

"Isabella, release your sister at once!" Mrs. Burt screamed. Isabella dropped Sarah's arm, but her face was dark with anger.

Gorman made no comment. He thanked Mrs. Burt for her hospitality, said something to Sarah in a low tone, and left. As soon as he was gone, Mrs. Burt said, "Sarah, get the account books. I want to go over our inventory of sheep, hogs, and cattle. We must check each week and make certain all are accounted for. We will start tomorrow matching the figures to your father's will."

A moment later there was a knock at the front door.

"I'll answer it," cried Sarah, jumping up and rushing to the door. Mrs. Burt briefly heard Gorman's voice, then Sarah quickly stepped out on the porch and closed the front door behind her. Why had William come back so quickly? thought Mrs. Burt.

Out on the porch, Gorman spoke to Sarah in grave tones. "We are going to try to solve this problem tonight, Sarah, even if we must use silver bullets to shoot this creature," he stated. "I wanted to leave this little pistol with you for an emergency. Please do not go outdoors during the night."

"Oh, I'm sure I'm in no danger, William. I don't want *you* to get hurt!"

"We shall kill the creature, Sarah, if we can get close enough. I will drop by the house tomorrow to tell you what happened." Gorman then gave Sarah a brief hug and hurried off.

When Sarah returned to the kitchen, she found her mother and Isabella preparing supper. Sarah felt a strange tension in the air. Not long after their meal, Isabella excused herself. Mrs. Burt went up to her bedroom next, and Sarah, also, retired earlier than usual. We all must be more upset by this than we will admit, thought Sarah, trying to explain the tension she felt earlier.

Just after midnight, Sarah was awakened by a strange sound. She hurriedly put on her robe and shoes and eased open the door. No one was in the hall, but two figures were on the stairs. She could see her mother standing perfectly still, concealing herself by the curve of the rail just above the first-floor landing. As Sarah looked past her mother, she saw Isabella slipping out the front door. Her mother soon followed.

Sarah assumed Isabella was simply wandering outside, as she often did when she couldn't sleep. But why had her mother followed? Surely, they both were aware of the danger posed by the mysterious animal roaming the countryside. Determined to find out what was going on, Sarah grabbed the pistol Gorman had left her and followed the pair from a safe distance.

Once outside, Sarah could see that the two—her mother

following Isabella at a discrete distance—were headed toward the winter sheep pasture. Sarah could see Mrs. Burt close in upon her daughter, just as it seemed Isabella was preparing to spring upon one of the sheep. Then she heard the animal's terrified cry. Mrs. Burt shouted at Isabella. The girl spun around and rushed toward her mother with a howl of rage. As Isabella turned, Sarah could see there was a knife in her hand. Sarah was close enough to shoot but could not point the gun at her own sister. Isabella was almost upon her mother when a shot rang out across the pasture. At that moment, Sarah fainted.

The next morning, she awoke to find herself in her own bed. The doctor was bending over her. "I thought I had better check on you again, young lady, just to be sure you were all right," he said.

"What happened?" Sarah mumbled.

"Young Gorman came for me in the middle of the night. It seems he was heading a posse of men hunting a werewolf, and your sister, Isabella, somehow got herself into the middle of it. She's in bed, too. When she wakes up from the dose of morphine I gave her, she's going to be in real pain. One of the men shot off her left hand. She's just lucky the bullet didn't hit her in the heart."

At that moment, a sense of awareness dawned on Sarah, though she couldn't quite verbalize what she knew in her heart. Then she remembered her mother. "Mother. How is she?" she asked.

"Mrs. Burt. Why she's doing fine," the doctor replied. "Has a powder burn on her right hand, that's all. She said she heard a noise outside, got her pistol, and was on her way to investigate when she stumbled. The pistol she was carrying must have gone off accidentally. Women don't know how to handle guns."

This last statement struck Sarah, for her mother was known

as an excellent markswoman. She did not contradict the doctor, though she knew there was no way that gun could have gone off accidentally.

As soon as Isabella's wound had healed, Mrs. Burt sent her youngest daughter to "visit a relative in Paris." Only Mrs. Burt knew the girl was really being sent to Paris to be treated by a famous specialist. The doctor's field was lycanthropy—a psychological disease in which an emotionally disturbed person manages to convince themselves they have become a werewolf.

Some months later, Isabella came home. While she was away, there were no more problems with the local livestock. Some say a minor incident or two did happen after she returned, but these rumors were never proven. "Miss Isabella," as she came to be known, never married. Despite the persistent rumors she was a werewolf, she lived in the county her whole life and managed to avoid serious persecution due to the prominence of her family.

Mrs. Mildred Owen Burt was seventy-eight when she died in 1890. Some years later, Isabella died. Her body is said to be buried on sacred ground in a Talbot County cemetery. Those who live near the cemetery believe her diseased, disordered spirit still roams the land, moaning and howling in the night. All we really know is that somewhere in the vast, undeveloped land of Talbot County, there is grave containing the body of the only woman in Georgia reputed to be a werewolf.

RETURN OF THE GHOST LOVER

Bellevue, 204 Ben Hill Street, and Smith Hall,
LaGrange College, LaGrange

The end of the Civil War found the Union Army slashing
its way through Georgia, with the meager Confederate forces
in the area desperate to stop them. The Confederate com-
mander, "Fighting Joe" Wheeler, believed that Union General
Alexander McCook would head south from Atlanta toward
LaGrange. Without enough men to defend a large area, it was
crucial for the Confederates to guess correctly where to inter-
cept McCook. Wheeler calculated that McCook would swing
his troops wide to avoid Newnan, then cut back and take the
road from Newnan to LaGrange. When McCook's troops re-
took the road, the Confederates must be ready to stop them—
but where?

If any officer could guess correctly, it was Colonel Henry M.
Ashby. His miraculous intuition had been right numerous times
in the past.

Wheeler could spare only two hundred men to send with
Ashby against McCook's army. When Lieutenant John Griffin heard the command, he immediately recognized the danger of accompanying such a small force. However, he idolized
Ashby and was elated to follow his hero.

Colonel Ashby and his men rode through the center of
Newnan on the main road toward LaGrange. After a quick
survey of the surrounding countryside, Ashby positioned his
troops at a point along the road. Once again, Ashby's intuition was remarkable; when the Federal troops stepped onto
the LaGrange Road, Ashby and his small force were awaiting
them.

General Wheeler was bringing up his men in dense woods
some distance away when a scout arrived with a message: "Sir,

I have made contact with the head of the Federal column and General McCook is preparing for battle. Respectfully, Colonel Henry M. Ashby."

Wheeler sent the scout back with his order: "Attack, Colonel Ashby!" When Ashby received the order, he immediately ordered the assault. The well-positioned Confederates' fire was so heavy that, believing they faced a far greater force, the Federal soldiers panicked. But they soon regrouped, and the two sides quickly found themselves in a bloody conflict. All afternoon, Federal and Confederate troops fought bitterly, with the advantage passing from side to side. Later, the engagement would be called the Battle of Brown's Mill.

Lieutenant Griffin found himself in the middle of the battle. As the fighting continued, he saw many of his friends and comrades fall. Josh Smith fell from his horse; Murdoch MacRae lay on the ground nearby, probably dead; and Andrew Farley sat slumped forward on his horse, blood spurting from a great gash on his forehead. Both sides sustained heavy losses. Some men had their horses shot from under them. Others, badly wounded, screamed for help as they lay writhing on the ground. Cries of the wounded mingled with the terrified whinnies of the horses.

Griffin became determined to do something about the wounded. "Get the injured to Newnan!" he commanded a platoon of medics. His order was drowned out by the roar of artillery, and as he started to make the command again, he felt a searing pain in his right shoulder. He collapsed to the ground but was able to collect himself in a few moments. Though he knew the wound would need treatment, he could tell no vital organs had been damaged. In any case, he thought, there were men all around him in worse shape. Once again, he started shouting orders to his men. "Don't leave the men who have fallen in the woods," he commanded. "Get them out of here, boys. Take them to Newnan . . . and hurry!" Finally, after he was satisfied everything possible was being done for the wounded, he placed his second lieutenant in command of his men and went to seek treatment for his injury.

He knew he was losing blood but still did not think he had been seriously wounded. LaGrange was further away than Newnan, but he wanted to try for it. There was a good hospital in LaGrange, and his sister, Indiana Griffin, was in college there as well.

The ride was almost thirty-six miles. Blood from the wound spread out in an ever-larger stain on his jacket. He could tell he was not always aware of his surroundings. But his steed was on the right road, and the loyal animal carried him steadily. Finally, he saw other wounded men riding in front of him. He followed them a few miles to some waiting ambulance wagons, where his mount was gently taken and he was eased onto a waiting stretcher. He heard a girl's voice say, "That's Indiana's brother! Take him to Smith Hall." Just before he slipped into unconsciousness, he looked up at the girl and saw that she was beautiful.

He awoke to find a terrible pain searing through his shoulder and a strange man looking closely into his face. At first, he thought the enemy was upon him and raised his arms feebly to ward off the man. Then the pain became unbearable. He opened his mouth to scream, but at that instant, a bottle was forced between his lips and a clear fiery liquid was forced down his throat. Strong hands held his arms to a table. The corn whiskey—one of the few anesthetics available to the Confederates at the time—seemed to spread quickly through every vein in his body, making the shoulder hurt just a little less. He realized a surgeon was swabbing his wound. "Sorry, young man. I'm going to have to hunt for this one," the doctor said. As the man began to probe the inside of his shoulder for the bullet, Griffin lost consciousness once more.

After the surgery, Griffin was placed in Smith Hall, the

Smith Hall

building which had been converted into a hospital. For a week, he hovered between life and death. Sometimes he regained consciousness long enough to see a lovely face above him. At first, he thought it was his sister, Indiana, but later he recognized the girl from the ambulance wagon. He gradually improved enough to say a few words to the girl and learned her name was Lorena. Griffin began to look forward to her daily visits. She would sit with him and cool his raging fever with a damp cloth. Griffin was certain she stayed with him just a little longer than she did with the other soldiers. Despite his condition, he knew he was falling in love with her.

After a few days, more serious casualties were brought into Smith Hall. Griffin was told he would be taken to a house called Bellevue, where recovering men were being treated. This distressed him greatly for it meant separation from Lorena,

Bellevue Plantation

but she assured him she would visit daily. At Bellevue, Griffin was placed in the ballroom, which had been converted into a large ward for the soldiers whose wounds had improved. Here he did not have to listen to the cries of the newly wounded, nor did he have to suffer the anguish of watching some of his own men die.

Lorena came to visit him often. He wanted desperately to express his love for her, though he was beginning to worry about his shoulder. He was making no more improvement, and the flesh around his wound had turned an angry red.

Soon, his high fever returned. Sometimes, he forgot that Lorena had visited him during the day. At night he would cry out, "Lorena is over at Smith Hall, and I must go see her. I know the room she is in." He began to rise out of his bed each night and roam the halls. During his nightly wanderings, he startled young nurses by grabbing their arms and saying in the most pitiful tone, "Lorena! Why didn't you come today." Of course, Lorena had already been there.

It was barely a week before he died.

In the years since, there have been countless incidents involving a mysterious presence at Smith Hall. Some have said they heard a man's voice calling "Lorena, Lorena," softly and insistently outside the building. Girls have reported someone gently touching their arm as they walk back to Smith Hall alone at night. Some have even seen the ghostly figure of a Confederate cavalry officer in a room on the building's second floor.

At Bellevue, the ghost of a Confederate officer has been seen in the ballroom. Though it may be a romantic embellishment, there are reports that the officer is arm-in-arm with a beautiful young girl. Perhaps Lieutenant Griffin has finally found his Lorena!

BELLEVUE, THE MAGNIFICENT ANTEBELLUM HOME OF BENJAMIN HARVEY HILL, IS A NATIONAL HISTORIC LANDMARK AND ONE OF THE FINEST EXAMPLES OF GREEK REVIVAL ARCHITECTURE IN GEORGIA. THE HOME IS OPEN TO THE PUBLIC; FOR INFORMATION, CALL 706-884-1832. SMITH HALL NOW SERVES AS AN ADMINISTRATIVE BUILDING FOR LAGRANGE COLLEGE.

THE HAUNTED SPRINGER OPERA HOUSE

The Springer Opera House, 103 Tenth Street, Columbus

The Springer Opera House is one of Columbus's most famous buildings, renowned both for its historic past and as the current-day home of the State Theatre of Georgia. Among the many outstanding performers who appeared at the Springer were Agnes de Mille, Lillie Langtry, the legendary Shakespearean actor Edwin Booth, John Philip Sousa, and Ethel Barrymore. With such an impressive history, perhaps it's no surprise that some of theatre's current performers are ghosts.

The theatre opened in 1871. Its lavish interior featured red plush seats, gilded fixtures, darkly polished wood, and ornate chandeliers. Top performers were lured by its beauty, and soon it had a reputation as the finest theatre between Washington and New Orleans. Before performances, patrons arrived in a glittering parade of carriages with liveried drivers. Men with silver-headed canes and collapsible opera hats escorted women in elaborate velvet-and-satin gowns from the gaslit streets of Columbus into the capacious Victorian lobby. Then it was on to the orchestra seats, or to a seat in the curving double balconies, where patrons viewed performances by the greatest actors of the day.

The Springer was not only home to top-notch theatrical performances. Many great American orators—men such as William Jennings Bryan, Will Rogers, and Franklin D. Roosevelt—also enthralled audiences at the theatre, adding to its prestige. However, the theatre's glory was not to last. During the Great Depression, the costly touring circuits that were the lifeblood of the stage became economically impossible. The once-glamorous Springer Opera House fell on hard times, eventually becoming a lowly movie house.

In the early '60s, there was talk of demolishing the old theatre, but the community rallied around the building. A massive restoration effort was soon underway. In 1965, the Springer, now designated the State Theatre of Georgia, reopened and once more became a year-round working theatre featuring top quality performing arts. Today, the theatre's many offerings include the Springer School of Theatre Arts, the Library of Theatre Arts, and a theatre museum.

The first of many strange events occurred after the restoration. A traveling company was having a closed rehearsal, and the company's director was distracted by the sound of a door repeatedly opening then banging shut. The irate director rose from his seat and shouted at the actors to stop the performance.

Just then, the stage manager stepped out from behind the curtain to the footlights and shouted, "Look up there!" The entire company could see a man standing in a box on the third level angrily banging the door. The director and the stage manager ran to the third level from different directions, reaching the door at the same moment. No one was there, and since the two men had approached the door from each of the two possible stairways, it would have been impossible for the man to escape past them.

People familiar with the theatre suspect the frustrated ghost was that of Edwin Booth. Edwin was the brother of John Wilkes Booth, and his career suffered inestimable damage after his brother's assassination of President Lincoln. Each time Booth performed in a different city, he was nervous about the reception he would receive as the brother of an assassin. Not long after the assassination, Booth arrived in Columbus to play Hamlet, the role for which he was most famous. Though he rehearsed for hours, he appeared extremely nervous before the performance. However, he performed the role to perfection, and when he took his curtain call at the end of the play, the audience stood and gave him a thunderous ovation. This enthusiastic reception seemed to be a turning point in his career, restoring the actor's confidence and erasing the stigma of his brother's deed.

If Edwin Booth is, in fact, the cause of some of the supernatural occurrences that have happened at the theatre, many of the theatre's workers are convinced it is because he is indignant over the omission of Shakespearean drama from the Springer's current repertoire.

Even if Edwin Booth is responsible for some of the strange incidents at the theater, it is unlikely he is the cause of all of them. Ralph Wimberly, a young genius who is in charge of the impeccably neat and well-organized prop room, has seen the ghost, and he is convinced it is a "her."

"I have learned that if I just ask 'her' for what I can't find, it suddenly will appear right in front of me!" said Wimberly. "For instance, I knew there was a black web belt up here. I had looked at all the belts, and it was nowhere to be seen. I finally gave up my search and called out 'I must have the black belt!' Then I turned, and there it was, lying right on top of the pile of belts." Wimberly insists "the 'presence' is very real."

The list of strange events goes on and on. On a few occasions, the stage lights have blinked, though they are not wired to behave that way—the theatre's lights can be dimmed or brightened but there is no way to make them blink.

And then there was the morning workers arrived to find that each pair of shoes from the costume room was placed as if it was walking up the hall stairs with feet inside them. At the end of the trail, a pair of cowboy boots were positioned as if they were walking directly into a wall. On another occasion, the cast of a play was preparing to go on stage. Just before the show, they discovered that each and every pair of gloves used in the play had disappeared!

One day, a theatre worker named Amy Bishop brought each member of the cast a box lunch, placing them in the actors' dressing rooms. By lunchtime, three of the boxes were missing. The boxes were later found hidden in the prop room untouched.

During rehearsals for one play, a young actor was changing in the men's dressing room when he looked up to see a man hovering over his head. During other rehearsals, strange

Springer Opera House
PHOTO BY GEROGIA SCENIC SOUTH CO.

figures have been seen walking behind the theatre's last row of seats, and music has been heard coming from the empty theatre at night.

Though much rarer, audience members also experience run-ins with the theatre's ghosts. During an evening performance of the 1996 season, Robert Carrollton was sitting in one of the theatre's boxes and heard a mysterious noise coming from the box's door. He looked over and was surprised to see a gentleman standing in the doorway watching the play. Carrollton was about to rise and speak to the man when the fellow turned his face toward Carrollton as if to introduce himself. As Carrollton looked at the face, he felt a cold chill travel down his spine. The man's expression was an angry one, Carrollton noticed, but his features could have been carved from marble—they were as immobile as those of a corpse in a casket. The man's attire was old-fashioned. In fact, the man's black-velvet cape and elaborate, lacy shirt had a theatrical appearance; Carrollton suspected the man was part of the play, even though it had a contemporary setting.

The man's odd appearance made Carrollton uncomfortable. He rose to get the manager, but as he did so, the man vanished, leaving behind only a faint musty odor. Later, Carrollton realized the scent reminded him of being in a room full of antiquities.

Events like this involving the theatre's audiences are rare. However, there's a ghost of a chance that, along with some of the best fine arts performances in the South, visitors to the Springer Opera House will get a supernatural experience thrown in with the cost of admission.

THE SPRINGER OPERA HOUSE IS LOCATED IN DOWNTOWN COLUMBUS. FOR INFORMATION ON TOURS OF THE THEATRE, CALL 706-324-1100; FOR PERFORMANCE AND TICKET INFORMATION, CALL 706-327-3688.

HISTORIC
HEARTLAND

Hay House (see story on page 203)

PHOTO BY WOODY MARSHALL

THE ROOM AT HERITAGE HALL

Heritage Hall, 277 South Main Street, Madison

Tour guide Hattie Mina Hicky often tells of the strange things visitors experience when they tour Heritage Hall. But according to Mrs. Hicky, to understand how such strange things could happen at the house, one must first hear the story of Dr. Elijah Jones and his ill-fated family.

The story begins on the night Virginia Jones woke her three sisters to show them her new engagement ring.

"It's beautiful, Virginia!" exclaimed Georgia, who was recently married herself.

"Oh, let me see it," begged Florine, the youngest of the girls. "Oh, it is beautiful."

Mary Jane, the oldest girl, gasped at the size of the diamond. "It's so big! Is it real?"

Virginia took the ring off her finger, and they all hurried through the hall to the bedroom window.

"Let me be the one to try it," begged Florine, giving Virginia a hug. She was an animated, affectionate girl, and she and Virginia were very close. "Please. Please let me do it." Her yellow curls bobbed with excitement as she leaned toward the window and moved the diamond against it. "It's real," Florine cried. "Look how well it writes!"

Elizabeth Jones had heard the excitement of her daughters and stood watching Virginia from the doorway. Mother and daughter had the same lovely dark hair, shy charm, and radiant smile. However, on this occasion a look of worry was on the mother's face. Virginia had only known her suitor for a few months, and Elizabeth wondered if things were moving too fast. Charles Nesbit was a thin young man with dark hair, and there was a burning intensity in his eyes when he gazed upon Virginia that many people commented on. He had shocked Dr. and Mrs. Jones by announcing his intentions to marry Virginia on his third visit to the Joneses' home. Nesbit was from out of town, and the Jones knew nothing of his family. He talked about them as if they were quite wealthy, and he appeared to work hard at his job in town. The parents had some suspicions, but they were willing to give the young man the benefit of the doubt.

"I wish my husband James could take a lesson from the way your fiancé handles his money," Georgia said to Virginia. Georgia had been married in June, just two months before, but already there was a hint of sadness in her voice.

"If James needs anything it's poker lessons," Florine blurted out. "Everybody in town knows he loses all his money gambling."

"Hush Florine! I am surprised at you," reprimanded her mother, giving away her previously unnoticed position.

"But it's true, momma," Florine protested. Unfortunately, as time would tell, Florine was right. In a poker bet, James Mann would go on to lose the house given to the couple by Georgia's father.

"That's enough! Get back in bed, Florine," Elizabeth com-

Heritage Hall

manded. Then with a nod toward the other sisters, Mrs. Jones said, "You girls go up with Florine and be sure she goes straight to her room." She then heard her husband stirring in their bedroom. She was not surprised he was awake.

As the girls' footsteps faded on the stairs, Elizabeth returned to the bedroom. "Virginia's young man has given her a ring, my dear," she said to her husband.

The doctor frowned. "I have nothing against Charles Nesbit, except that I wish I knew more about his family than what he tells us. Virginia has always been a merry, happy girl, and he seems so austere."

"He doesn't smile often, does he," said Elizabeth. "Does anything else bother you about him?"

"He was interested in marriage so quickly that I didn't

think he gave himself time to know Virginia. It was as if she simply fit into his plans for the future . . ."

"And he was too aware of her financial assets?" Elizabeth said, completing her husband's thought. "Well, we should consider his assets, too. We have three unmarried daughters. I am sure you agree they will need security."

"And for a woman, I suppose that means a husband," muttered Dr. Jones, obviously unhappy with the popular sentiment of the day. "I understand why my girls are so anxious to marry, but what they don't understand is that they will be far worse off with a rascal. Take Georgia's husband for example. I'm already hearing stories about his gambling." He paused. "I'd like to be sure Virginia marries a sound fellow. Will she not wait for awhile?"

"Charles is pushing her to set the wedding date for September," said Elizabeth, repeating something she had overheard the girls discussing by the window, "unless you have serious objections."

"That soon!" exclaimed Dr. Jones. He sighed. "If Virginia loves him . . . but somehow I can't see her happy with this long-faced young man."

"I'm not sure you like Mr. Nesbit, my dear," Elizabeth said, and secretly she felt the same way. Still, the parents decided not to stand in the young couple's way, and plans for the marriage were soon underway.

The wedding took place on September 20, 1849, and Virginia's first baby was born a year later. Sadly, the baby lived only one month. In 1851 her second baby was born at the home of her parents. A few weeks later, before the family had retired, they heard the crack of a pistol from upstairs. It seemed to come from Virginia's room. Everyone rushed to the second floor, and Dr. Jones jerked open the door. Charles stood in the center of the room holding the smoking pistol, his faced flushed with anger. "An accident, sir. It is a good thing I checked this pistol or it might have hurt someone." Virginia was pale with terror.

The parents' mistrust of Charles continued to grow, though Virginia refused to accuse him of any mistreatment. Not long after this incident, Virginia became ill. One afternoon Dr. Jones found himself pacing back and forth outside the door of her room. He knew his daughter was growing weaker, and none of his usual remedies seemed to have any effect. On this day, as his daughter lay in bed with a high fever, icy fingers of fear closed around the doctor's heart.

His wife mounted the stairs with a tray. "Is she worse, my dear?" she asked, seeing the frown on her husband's face. At that moment a scream came from the room. Dr. Jones threw open the door, and found Virginia crumpled on the floor, the baby in her arms. She had been walking the baby and her weakness caused her to collapse.

Elizabeth lifted the baby from her daughter's arms, and Dr. Jones carried Virginia back to bed. "Elizabeth, we must take the baby out of the room," he said. "Virginia is in no condition to care for it." He lifted the kerosene lamp and examined Virginia. Thankfully, the fall had not damaged his daughter. However, his examination of the infant was not as positive. The young child appeared to have been shaken badly by the fall.

Later that day Elizabeth brought some chicken broth to Virginia's room and attempted to feed her. In a few minutes, though, she exited the room shaking her head sadly. Florine and Georgia followed their mother into the room, and Florine managed to get her sister to eat a little of the broth before Virginia pushed it away. That night Charles entered the room. Dr. Jones, keeping watch by the bed, left the husband and wife alone, closed the door behind him, and found his wife waiting for him in the hall.

"He never even sits on the side of the bed," Elizabeth said

to her husband. "He just stares down at her from the foot of the bed, always wearing that horrible black suit of his."

"What horrible suit do you mean?" Dr. Jones asked.

"The one he bought for the baby's funeral last year. It's not very cheerful," said Mrs. Jones.

"I understand how you feel, my dear," Dr. Jones said angrily. "He is not very kind to Virginia, and it pains me to see it."

At that moment the door to Virginia's room opened and Charles called out, "Doctor, I think you should go in. Virginia is very weak." The doctor hurried past him. Some minutes later his portly figure emerged with shoulders bowed in grief. Elizabeth rose quickly and went to him.

"She is gone, Elizabeth," he said, putting his arms around his wife and pressing his face to her hair. She began to cry quietly. Charles, who was also waiting in the hall, showed no emotion at all.

Charles and Virginia's second infant died two months later, leaving Charles as sole heir to the property Virginia received from her father upon her marriage. Though the Joneses had no proof, they suspected Charles's harsh treatment of Virginia contributed to her death. They opposed his possession of the property, but legally there was nothing they could do.

Virginia's death was the first in a long line of tragedies for the Jones family. All of the daughters, so attractive and full of life, seemed ill-fated. All four died at a young age. Dr. Jones's health, however, was remarkable. After Elizabeth Jones died, he married a second time, fathered two more children, and lived on until he was eighty-one. In all those years, he never forgave Charles Nesbit, and he grieved for his beautiful Virginia until the day he died.

When she directs tours at Heritage Hall, Hattie Mina Hicky relates all the details of the Joneses' family history. Most visitors are interested in the house's tragic history, so they are enthralled by Mrs. Hicky's supernatural stories. The stories center around the upstairs bedroom located directly over the music room. According to Mrs. Hicky, this is the room which is believed to be the one where Virginia died.

On one occasion an Atlanta Alliance actor stayed in the room after other members of the group went on for the rest of the tour. Mrs. Hicky found him standing in a trance in a part of the room she calls the "special spot" because so many have felt the presence of a young woman there. Finally she said to the actor, "Do you feel her touch?"

He replied, "Yes. I felt the touch of a woman."

On another occasion two women came to tour the house. They went in the room with the rest of the tour group but did not exit when it was time to move on. When Mrs. Hicky went in to get them, one of the women was standing in the special spot. "May I tell you what I'm feeling right now?" she asked Mrs. Hicky. Mrs. Hicky agreed, and the woman said, "A girl who was very sick died in this room, and someone is standing at the foot of her bed crying at this moment."

Still another time, Mrs. Hicky noticed a woman who was chaperoning a group of scouts standing in the special spot. The woman interrupted Mrs. Hicky's presentation and said, "I see a young girl with very dark hair lying in bed. She is burning up with fever. A thin man, dressed all in black, is standing at the foot of her bed." Mrs. Hicky tried to soothe the woman by saying others had felt the same thing, but the woman left the room trembling.

Once Mrs. Hicky had a luncheon at the house, and afterwards, while she was trying to get everyone on the tour bus, someone called out, "Wait! Someone is still upstairs."

Mrs. Hicky went up to get the woman, who immediately apologized. "I didn't realize I was holding up the tour," she said. "I'm a diviner. I have a pendant that swings to one side or the other when I ask it questions. When I asked it whether the presence in the room was the girl named Virginia you told us about, the pendant said it was."

Mrs. Hicky recalled the day a man saw a strange stain on the hearth in Virginia's bedroom. The docents had noticed the stain before and tried to clean it, but it kept reappearing. The gentleman bent down to look at the stain and claimed he saw the shape of a woman holding a baby in her arms—a shape Mrs. Hicky also believes she can see in the stain. "I think the young lady fell and hit her head against the mantle," the man said to Mrs. Hicky. "That could have caused the high fever, and ultimately her death."

Mrs. Hicky also remembered the time a mirror flew off the dresser in the room, sailed over the bureau top, and fell onto the floor. Then there was the time a carpenter, working alone in the house, reported hearing a piano being played and seeing a doorknob turning.

Mrs. Hicky can't help wondering about the cause of all these strange incidents. Is the figure in the stain one of the Jones girls? Does the distraught spirit of Virginia still reside in the bedroom? And does the black-clad Charles Nesbit continue to watch over her?

Despite the many strange incidents in the house, Mrs. Hicky remained a skeptic of the supernatural until one day when she was leaving the house.

"I bent down to lock the tall front door," Mrs. Hicky said, "and suddenly I was aware of a second shadow right beside mine. It was the outline of a woman—very sharp, very dark—against the white of the paint. I looked behind me, but no one was there! Now that did give me a start."

FOR INFORMATION REGARDING TOURS OF HERITAGE HALL, CALL REGAL TOURS AT 706-342-1612.

WHAT THE BUTLER SAW

The Hay House, 934 Georgia Avenue, Macon

Perhaps there is no one more privy to a family's secrets—intimate moments, quarrels, and skeletons in the closet— than its butler. That must have been the case with Chester Davis, a devoted servant to the P. L. Hay family. During the twenty-nine years he worked at the house, he never broke the family's confidences. He maintained that silence until 1984, when he revealed to the *Macon Telegraph* that the house was haunted.

Davis's story caused a commotion in Macon since the Hay House has been a centerpiece of the city for over a hundred years. Called the "Palace of the South," the Hay House is renowned for its Italian Renaissance Revival architecture, a style uncommon among the South's antebellum homes. Built in 1855, the house had a number of cutting-edge amenities. Its "modern" features included three bathrooms with hot-and-cold running water, central heat, a fifteen-room speaker-tube system, a large in-house kitchen, walk-in closets in the bedrooms, and an elaborate ventilation system. The majority of these features did not become commonplace in American homes until well into the twentieth century. The house is enormous, covering eighteen thousand square feet over four levels. An eighty-foot cupola serves as a final reminder of the home's grandiose proportions.

The home was designed by a New York architect for Colonel William B. Johnston, whose fortune was earned through investments in banking and railroads. It later became the home of the Felton family before it was bought by the Hay family—the family Chester Davis served loyally for so many years.

According to the story Chester Davis told Terri K. Smith,

the author of the story in the *Macon Telegraph*, his first ghost sighting occurred early one spring morning. Davis began the day with the knowledge that there was to be a party at the mansion that night. One of his duties was to ensure the home's silver was gleaming and bright. He noticed that the silver door-knob on the door of the dining room was tarnished and set about to polish it. He was standing beside the tall doors of the dining room, his cloth deftly swirling around the knob, when he glanced up and noticed a gentleman in his early fifties standing nearby.

"He had on blue pants, a white shirt, and looked like he was about fifty-five years old," Davis recalled. "He had an open collar like mine, and his hair was pepper gray." Davis noted that it was a very good haircut, parted in the center and "no hippy haircut." The gentleman stared at him "as if he wanted to ask what I was doing." Davis remembered that he looked away with an involuntary startled movement, and when he looked back the man had vanished.

"I don't believe in ghosts," Davis told the reporter. "I didn't say anything (about the incident) because people would have believed I was crazy."

Davis went on to describe another occasion when he happened to look out the front window and see an elderly lady walking toward the front door. "She looked to be in her sixties and was wearing a long blue-and-white checked dress," he said. The woman's clothing made Davis believe she was gardening. "She had on a straw hat with a wide brim, kind of a yellow gold color, like a field hat," Davis remembered. Davis watched the woman approach the front door and reach for the doorbell. When she did, Davis rose from a chair in the hall to see what he could do for her. At that point, the lady disappeared.

The next day, Chester Davis had an equally unsettling experience. He was polishing the large brass hinges on the front door when he looked up and noticed a slim, graceful woman standing at the edge of the lawn near the front driveway. Davis recalled she was "in her late thirties or early forties" and was wearing "what looked like a net dress." Davis saw the woman long enough to tell her dress "had a thin, gauzy appearance and was a light purple," while her hat was perched on one side of her head and "matched the dress." This was all he could notice about the woman before she vanished.

Many people have speculated on the identities of the mysterious figures seen by Davis. Some believe the man in the dining room may have been Judge William H. Felton, the mansion's second owner. The judge was a tall, distinguished man who loved to entertain, which may explain his appearance on the morning of the party. The description of the woman on the lawn seems similar to that of the lovely and elegant Luisa McGill Gibson of Baltimore, who married William Felton, Jr., in 1915. William and Luisa lived in the house with William's parents for several years.

Chester Davis did not mention what he had seen to anyone. He kept his secret until Mrs. Fran LaFarge, the former director of the Hay House, mentioned that she and several other personnel at the Hay House had seen apparitions in various part of the house and experienced cold chills at one place on the stairs. Only then did Chester Davis disclose his encounters to the public. Other employees then came forward with their own stories. One maid reported seeing someone in the basement she thought was another servant, only to have the figure vanish when she approached it. A worker said he once met a man in a black overcoat coming down the stairs from the fourth floor. He stepped aside to let the man pass, then remembered it was the middle of summer! He turned quickly and looked back, but to his astonishment, the man in the overcoat had disappeared.

Chester Davis is dead now, and if any of the ghosts he,

or the others, saw are still there, no one will talk about them. Since 1978, the home has been run under the auspices of the Georgia Trust for Historic Preservation, and those now in charge unequivocally deny ever having seen a ghost on the premises, despite the stories of the former employees. However, the Hay House is open to the public, so you can look for ghosts there yourself. It's possible that while you're touring this magnificent home, you, too, will spot some of the same ghosts that the butler saw.

THE HAY HOUSE IS ON THE NATIONAL REGISTER OF HISTORIC PLACES AND HAS BEEN CALLED "ONE OF THE MORE OUTSTANDING HOMES IN THE UNITED STATES." THE HOME IS OPEN FOR TOURS DAILY; FOR INFORMATION, CALL 912-742-8155.

SYLVIA, SWEETHEART, YOU'RE BACK!

Panola Hall, North Madison Avenue, Eatonton

Georgia is full of magnificent antebellum houses, some of which are also haunted. This description certainly fits Panola Hall in Eatonton. What sets Panola Hall apart, aside from its unique architectural features, is that it is the home of the snootiest ghost in Georgia.

The Greek Revival–style house was built in 1854. Its three floors, with four rooms on each level, encompass over seven thousand feet. The house's impressive foyer is noted for its handsome wainscoting, the inlaid Greek key pattern decorating the edge of the floor, and the nine-foot-high windows with original glass panes. Each of the house's large rooms contains a huge fireplace and beautiful pine floors. One of the home's most interesting features is the dovetailed, hand-chiseled beams in the attic that are secured with wooden pegs. Another fascinating feature is the tunnel leading from inside to an underground room and a well on the grounds. During the Civil War, Confederate soldiers hiding from Union forces used the passageway to travel from the underground room to the house, where they would hide in another secret room located in the attic.

Though the house was built in 1854, it did not receive the name Panola Hall until Dr. and Mrs. Benjamin W. Hunt moved there in 1876. Dr. Hunt was a wealthy New York scientist and horticulturist who met Louise Reid Pruden, a beautiful young woman from Eatonton, when they were both staying at the same New York City hotel. He visited her several times in Georgia. The two soon fell in love, married, and settled in Eatonton.

Mrs. Hunt was an accomplished musician and a published poet. She also had a taste for elegant clothes and wore the first Parisian dress ever seen in Eatonton—a handsome Worth gown. On the couple's honeymoon in Philadelphia, they had gone to an exposition where the designer's dresses were being shown. Afterward, Dr. Hunt bought his wife every dress in the collection!

Dr. Hunt was a distinguished scientist with many interests. He was fascinated by dairying and once imported cows from the Isle of Jersey. He also studied botany and received an honorary degree in horticulture from the University of Georgia. Even today, there are still traces of Dr. Hunt's horticultural projects on the grounds of Panola Hall.

Dr. and Mrs. Hunt settled into an enjoyable life at Panola Hall, but it wasn't long until they discovered their house was haunted. On one occasion, Mrs. Hunt was reading in the library when she looked up to see a lovely young woman at the foot of the hall stairway. The woman wore a white, hoop-skirted dress and a red damask rose in her dark hair. The woman seemed to be laughing as she stood beside the bannister watching Louise Hunt.

Mrs. Hunt rose and shouted indignantly, "Why are you laughing at me in my own house." But the strange girl disappeared the instant Mrs. Hunt spoke to her.

Over the years, the strange girl became familiar to the Hunts and some of their guests, though it was said she only revealed herself to those she considered her social equal. For this reason, the ghost developed a reputation as a snob.

Mrs. Hunt named the ghost Sylvia, and a poem she wrote about the woman ensured the name would live on through the years.

> Sylvia's coming down the stair—
> Pretty Sylvia, young and fair.
> Oft and oft I meet her there,
> Smile on lips and rose in hair.

The first person outside the Hunt family to actually see Sylvia was a young man named Nelson, who came from Ohio to discuss a creamery project with Dr. Hunt. Mr. Nelson had started up the stairs when he met a young lady on her way down. She was dressed in a white hoop skirt and wore a red damask rose in her dark hair. As she approached him, he stood aside and bowed courteously to her. With the merest trace of a delightful smile, she inclined her head to acknowledge him and went on down the stairs. Mr. Nelson recalled being very much aware of the intense fragrance of the rose in her hair. Nelson assumed that she was another guest and that he would meet her at dinner that night. When he entered the dining room, he saw only Dr. and Mrs. Hunt and noticed only three places were set. When he questioned the Hunts about the girl

Panola Hall

whom he had met on the stairs, they explained to him that the young lady was an apparition.

This explanation did not seem satisfy Nelson. After he left the Hunts, they received several letters from the infatuated young man addressed to "Sylvia, Dr. and Mrs. Benjamin W. Hunt, Eatonton, Georgia."

In the years that followed, others saw Sylvia. One was Alice Wardwell, a librarian in Eatonton. Alice was a down-to-earth lady, known both for her integrity and skepticism. The library where she worked was located next to Panola Hall. One evening, Alice happened to glance through a window and see into the house. "I could see into their living room quite clearly," said Alice. "Mrs. Hunt sat sewing and Dr. Hunt sat nearby reading. Behind his chair stood a lovely young girl in a white dress. She was bending over as if to see the pages of his book. The strange thing to me was that neither of the Hunts, who were extremely courteous people, were paying the slightest attention to their visitor. They seemed completely unaware of her presence.

"As I stood watching this scene, a group of children came into the library. I asked them to come over to the window and tell me what they saw. The first child saw exactly the same thing I had. Then I made sure each child saw her, just for my own satisfaction. In all this time, the girl never moved, nor did the Hunts acknowledge her presence in any way!

"The next evening, Dr. Hunt came into the library. I mentioned to him quite casually that I had noticed he had company last night. He gave me a long look and then said, 'No. We were alone all evening, Alice. That must have been Sylvia whom you saw.' I was so shocked, I didn't know how to reply. Then Dr. Hunt said, 'All I can say is that you have been highly complimented. Sylvia, as we have come to call her, reveals herself only to the finest people.'

"The Hunts had learned to accept her presence themselves," Alice continued, "but they didn't talk about her to strangers who might think they were queer. If you knew Dr. and Mrs. Hunt, you would know that wasn't true at all, for they were highly intelligent, cultured people."

Over the years, there has been much conjecture about the identity of the woman. One of the most plausible explanations is that she was a guest of the Trippe family, who lived in the home during the Civil War. Apparently, the young woman was at the house when she learned her fiancé, a Confederate officer, had been killed in battle. Overcome with grief, she threw herself off the balcony, landing on the brick steps below.

Miss Bessie Butler was a friend of the Hunt family who inherited Panola Hall after Dr. Hunt died in 1934, since the Hunts had no children. Miss Butler first ran into Sylvia one afternoon in 1929.

"I had heard about Sylvia for many years," said Miss Butler, "but never expected to see her. It was the afternoon of

Mrs. Hunt's last illness. I went across from my room into a guest room to see if it was in readiness for relatives expected on the next train. The only people in the house at the time were Dr. Hunt and the nurse at Mrs. Hunt's bedside downstairs, and the cook in the kitchen. I was the only person upstairs.

"I had walked into the center of the guest room and was taking a swift glance about when, from the corner of the room behind me, came the sound of someone tiptoeing. Then a sweet, musical voice called, 'Miss Bessie. Oh, Miss Bessie.' Just that and no more, but it was enough. . . . I ran past the white blur in the corner that I knew had to be Sylvia. I didn't want to see her."

Sylvia's words seem to have been an omen of Mrs. Hunt's death, for she died that same afternoon.

Arlene Griffith is yet another person who saw Sylvia. Ms. Griffith lived in a small Victorian cottage on the grounds of Panola House. One day, Ms. Griffith briefly saw Sylvia in the cottage's dining room. The apparition stood staring into a corner cupboard, looking at a display of china teapots. Griffith remembered sensing that Sylvia was curious at the changes occurring to the house and grounds at the time.

Panola Hall is currently owned by Rick Owens, who has worked hard to restore the home to its original beauty. Due to all the work going on inside, Owens does not yet live in the home, though he looks forward to the day with anticipation. He first heard about the home's ghost from the previous owner. Owens regarded the ghost story with amusement, never dreaming anything unusual would happen to *him*. However, he has changed his mind.

"Some unusual things have happened that I would rather not share at this time. After I am actually living in the house, I may see her, but I really don't know whether I shall talk about it, even if I do see her," he says with a twinkle in his eyes. "After all, people who claim to see her are sometimes accused of snobbery, since Sylvia is said to associate only with aristocrats."

Though Owens is tight-lipped about his house's famous resident, he does mention one memorable incident. "On a morning in December of 1996, I entered the house when none of the workmen were there. Suddenly, I was enveloped by an odor as overwhelming as if the door of a florist's refrigerator had opened beside me. The air was redolent with the fragrance of fresh roses."

Owens's story is similar to that of the young Mr. Nelson, who was overcome with the intense scent of roses as he passed the mysterious girl on the staircase so many years ago.

PANOLA HALL IS A PRIVATE HOME AND NOT OPEN TO THE PUBLIC.

THE HAUNTED COLLEGE TOWN

Athens

Everyone who visits Athens, home of the University of Georgia, notices the city's beautiful homes and campus buildings. What most don't notice are the ghosts said to inhabit many of these structures. For instance, the Lustrat House, now an administrative building on the north campus, is said to be haunted by an old Confederate major. A young man who died an accidental death at the Sigma Nu house supposedly still roams the fraternity house's halls. Just about anywhere you scratch the surface of this tranquil college town, you are liable to turn up a ghost story. Below are a few compelling stories from this haunted college town.

The Barrow-Tate House
436 Deering Street

"I've heard the rattle of wheels on boards and the clatter of horse's hooves when they ran over the cemetery bridge at night," recalled Mrs. Susan Barrow Tate, "yet no carriage or horses were visible." As she speaks, the conviction in her voice is enough to make the hairs rise on your arms and a cold chill shiver down your spine.

The diminutive, white-haired Mrs. Tate is a graduate of the Lucy Cobb Girl's School and the University of Georgia. After graduating from the university, she continued to serve the school, spending her career working as a librarian in the Georgia Special Collections portion of the school's library. Now and then, the library still calls her with a question they believe only she can answer.

Mrs. Tate has lived in the Barrow-Tate House her entire life and has had several strange experiences there. One afternoon, she was lying on the bed in her room with her eyes closed, trying to resolve a difficult problem. She heard an odd sound, and as she started to rise, she looked toward the doorway. "I was astonished to see York, a black gentleman who had worked as a yard man for us," she said. "As children, we would walk along with York and ask him questions while he worked. He was always patient with us. York had been dead for many years, yet there he stood, holding his hat in his hands while he looked over at me. He said quite clearly in the kind way he always spoke, 'It's going to be all right, little Missy,' and then he disappeared. And you know, it *was* all right. I think he came back to keep me from worrying so.

"On another occasion, our dog was lying by the front door. The dog suddenly got up and ran back to the rear of the hall near a door. She paused there, then began walking slowly along, looking up all the time. When she reached the entrance to the parlor, she stared up expectantly. My aunt and her husband were there watching this, and she said, 'Whom do you think she sees?' I replied that I didn't know. The dog was now sitting by the fireplace, still looking up expectantly as if into someone's face. My aunt said, 'I know who it is. That must be, Papa.'

"At that moment, the dog got up, walked over to my father's empty chair, and stood beside it for a moment as if puzzled. Then she shook herself and went back to the patch of warm sunlight by the front door where she had been lying before.

"Not long after this incident, a student asked me, 'Mrs. Tate, who is the elderly gentleman who sits on your front porch?' I told her that we didn't have any elderly gentleman living in the house. 'No one with a beard?' she asked. I replied no again, though I knew she was describing my father who had been dead for years."

THE BARROW-TATE HOUSE IS NOT OPEN TO THE PUBLIC; PLEASE RESPECT THE PRIVACY OF THE OWNER.

The Alpha Gamma Delta House
530 South Milledge Avenue

The women at the Alpha Gamma Delta sorority house not only have a ghost who is very protective of them, she's also a real matchmaker.

"I think the only reason my friend is engaged is because she lived in that room," said one of the sorority members, referring to the room the ghost seems to prefer. "She hardly dated before she moved into the room, and then she had this big romance!"

The ghost is said to be Susie Carithers, whose father donated the Alpha Gamma Delta house to the sorority as a wedding gift to his daughter. The beautiful house on South Milledge Avenue even resembles a three-tiered wedding cake. On the afternoon of the ceremony, Susie was a vision of loveliness in her white satin gown. The wedding was to take place in the sorority house at four o'clock. By 4:10 the groom had not appeared—the young bride was very nervous, and the guests grew restless. At 4:30, he still had not appeared, and by five, the guests were saying their good-byes in hushed tones more appropriate for a funeral than a wedding.

While her parents stood in the decorated entrance hall trying to conceal their humiliation, they did not notice Susie slip up the stairs. The young girl ran directly to the attic of the house and hanged herself.

There are several versions of what happened to the groom. According to one, he suffered a carriage accident and arrived a short time after the guests had left. Apparently, the young man arrived just as the girl's shocked parents discovered her body in the attic.

Residents of the room on the top right side of the house, located just under the place in the attic where Susie hanged herself, have been the beneficiaries of Susie's matchmaking skills. A current sorority member said, "The girls all want that room; it's awesome the way the ones who get it become pinned or engaged during the time they're living there." The sorority members now call it "the engagement room." It seems the ghost of Susie Carithers is trying to play Cupid to make up for her tragic end.

The Phi Mu House
250 South Milledge Avenue

The Phi Mu House, also on South Milledge Avenue, is home to the ghost of Anna Powell. According to a sorority member, Anna sometimes gives three knocks to indicate she is present in a room. "The knocks really startled me the first time I heard them," the sorority member said, "but luckily someone else was with me. If it happened when I was alone, I think I would leave in a hurry!"

"The story I've always been told," said another Phi Mu member, "is that the woman (Anna Powell) died after her husband accidentally shot himself here in the house. It supposedly happened at the bottom of the stairs. When the sunlight comes into the front hall at just the right angle, a cross appears very clearly on the floor. According to our sorority legend, that cross marks the spot where her husband died."

This member went on to recall a time she heard the ghost. "One time, I heard someone sobbing their heart out. It sounded so close when I stood near the stairs, and I looked everywhere thinking it was a sorority member I might be able to comfort. But there was absolutely no one there—no one on the whole floor."

CLASSIC SOUTH

Callaway Plantation (see story on page 223)

STRANGER ON CAMPUS

Augusta College, Augusta

THIS STORY IS BASED ON THE STRANGE EXPERIENCE OF DR. KEITH COWLING, A PROFESSOR RECENTLY RETIRED FROM AUGUSTA COLLEGE. DR. COWLING, A DELIGHTFULLY COURTEOUS, WHITE-HAIRED, SCHOLARLY MAN, IS A NATIVE OF ENGLAND.

Most students and professors walk the campus of Augusta College unaware of its colorful history, although classes take place in buildings that were once a federal arsenal.

The arsenal buildings, seized by Confederates at the start of the Civil War, were the hub of Augusta's wartime activities. Confederate General "Fighting" Joe Wheeler galloped over this ground as his cavalry made a desperate attempt to screen Augusta from Sherman's superior forces.

Near the campus is the Walker home. Two men of this family became Confederate officers, and both would die from wounds received in battle. Their remains rest in the small cemetery in back of the Walker house.

When the federal government closed the arsenal in 1955, the quaint old buildings became part of Augusta College.

Not long afterwards, Keith Cowling arrived from England and joined the faculty of Augusta College as a professor of

English. He had decided to try a "taste of American academic life," and he found he liked it. When it came time to retire, Professor Cowling no longer had any desire to return to England. Augusta had become home.

Although Americans think the British see ghosts in every castle, Dr. Cowling never saw anything supernatural during the years he lived and taught in England. "The only thing that has happened to me was right here in Georgia," he says with a wry smile.

"I had long been skeptical about ghosts and the supernatural," says Cowling, "particularly after an experience I had in the Civil Defense in England during World War II. I was the duty officer and received messages about injuries in order to dispatch ambulances to the scene. There was a girl there who also worked for the Civil Defense, and when there were no raids on, we would chat through the serving hatch between the dining room and the kitchen.

"She would often talk to me during the night about going to séances. I felt very sorry for her because she was greatly upset by messages from her husband sent to her through a medium. Messages that he was dead. When I last saw her, she had not heard from him for months and was convinced the medium was right.

"After the war I met her on the street, and we talked for awhile. That night I said to my father, 'I saw Ann this afternoon. Did her husband ever come back from the war?'

"He replied, 'Of course. He may have been wounded, but he's fit as a fiddle.'

"That confirmed my skepticism about the supernatural. It was not until years later, when I was a professor of English at Augusta College, that an event happened to change my mind.

"I was on campus one spring night in the Fine Arts Department building, still hard at work. It was about 8:15, a time when there wouldn't have been any students around, when

I left the building and went to the parking lot. As I turned the ignition in my car, I noticed at a distance a man on foot. Recently there had been a series of minor thefts on campus. Because of this I watched the man closely and with some suspicion. He was wearing what appeared to be a gray, English-style overcoat, and a yellow scarf was tied around his waist. His hat had its brim turned up on one side in that carefree, dashing manner that immediately made me think of the way Australians wore their hats. Since he was dressed in such an unusual fashion, I thought he might be on his way to return props to the drama department.

"As I watched, the fellow walked diagonally across the road near the Fine Arts Building, but he did not enter the building. He strolled on, heading in the direction of one of the gateways to the Walker cemetery. I drove very slowly some distance behind him, and he did not look back or seem at all aware of me. As he continued beyond the trees, his yellow sash was a bright spot of color which I could easily follow. I watched from the road as he headed in the direction of the small cemetery. When he reached it, he seemed to vanish. I could only guess that he must have walked behind a tree and passed from my range of vision. But I was left with the feeling that the whole thing was very odd.

"The more I thought about it on my way home, the more strange the incident seemed. It was on my mind to such a degree that I rang up a friend of mine and said, 'I have just seen a ghost.'

"'You must be drinking,' he replied with an embarrassed laugh, refusing to take me seriously.

"But the first thing I thought about the next morning was the dashing, gray-clad figure with the flowing yellow sash. I left my classes early that day and soon reached the area where I had seen him the previous evening. I had no plan as to what to do other than walk over the ground, retracing the path he had taken.

"When I was on the little side road that we call Arsenal Avenue, it occurred to me that from the start the figure was headed in the direction of the small graveyard. It belonged to the old Walker house, which had fallen into disuse as a home and later became part of the arsenal. An arsenal I knew little about at that time except that it had closed in 1955 and the college had become the beneficiary of its buildings.

"As I walked along the campus road toward the gate on Arsenal Avenue, I noticed some grass seed had just been sewn. To keep anyone from walking on the new stand of grass, a heavy strand of wire was stapled between the trees. This wire was about waist high. There was no way to continue to the cemetery without pausing and stepping over it, or stooping and crawling under it. I am somewhat taller than average, so I halted and stepped over it rather than ducking my head and going under. This made me realize that I either should have seen the fellow's hat go down out of sight and then appear in view again or his body turn sideways to throw a leg over the wire. But I saw neither. Without a break in his stride, the figure had passed right through the wire!

"At the same time, I noted that there were no trees on either side of the wire. He could not have disappeared behind a tree. Walking on a few feet, I reached the cemetery. It was here I saw him vanish. I tried the gate only to find it securely locked. The cemetery was enclosed by a ten-foot-high fence that was impossible to scale without a ladder.

"Later I began to think more about what the fellow was wearing, and I realized that although I first thought it was similar to the garb I had seen Aussies wearing in England, this of course was not England. Judging from my reading and the movies I've seen, the man's outfit resembled a Civil War officer's uniform. It was then I thought of the activity that must have surrounded the arsenal during the Civil War, with Confederate officers constantly coming and going.

"My excitement mounting, I recalled another point. In *Gone With the Wind*, Scarlett makes a yellow scarf to give to Ashley for his Christmas present—just the sort of scarf the young man had tied around his waist! What a figure he cut in his gray uniform, with his jaunty hat and the ends of the yellow scarf fluttering in the evening breeze. I was convinced then that I had seen the ghost of a Confederate officer."

Other stories of ghosts on the Augusta College campus have been reported, perhaps because of the two cemeteries on campus. One is the Augusta Arsenal cemetery, where Union and Confederate soldiers killed in the skirmishes between Wheeler and Sherman lie side-by-side in death. The other is the private burial ground of the Walker family.

And if the gray-clad figure Dr. Cowling saw was the apparition of one of the two Walkers who served as a Confederate officer, what place more natural for either man to return to than the family graveyard?

CONFEDERATE SOLDIERS IN THE MIST

Callaway Plantation, Washington

Callaway Plantation has fascinated Michael Horgan from the time he started driving past the estate on the way to law school at the University of Georgia. Initially, he admired the appearance of the plantation house, with its majestic red brick and tall, white columns, but as time went on, he became fascinated by its history. Michael learned the house had been built in 1869 and was one of the few plantation homes that had remained in the same family, passed down from generation to generation for more than a century. Its restoration had become a project for the city of Washington, Georgia, and Michael would note the progress each time he passed the house on his way to Athens.

In 1985, after he finished law school, Michael started to practice law in Washington. His search for a place to live ended abruptly when he was asked if he would live at the Callaway Plantation as a caretaker; of course, he accepted with delight. He is still there today.

Horgan likes to tell visitors about people who have lived in the house over the years. One of his favorite stories is of Aristide Callaway, the wealthy planter and trader who built Callaway Plantation. When Aristide was thirty-four-years old, he took a fifteen-year-old bride. Michael often wonders whether the girl really wanted to marry a man who must have seemed ancient to someone her age. She was to bear her husband nine children before she died at age forty-five.

Aristide Callaway began building his plantation home in his early thirties. Interestingly, the home was built in the years after the Civil War, during a time when the fortunes of many planters were devastated. According to some accounts, Callaway was able to preserve his fortune, in part, through a favorable coincidence and good planning. The story goes that Aristide had a large shipload of cotton in the harbor at Savannah when the Civil War broke out. Aristide quickly set sail for England, where he sold the cotton at a good price and banked the money.

Michael also likes to tell people about the Gilmer House. The house, located on the land adjacent to the Callaway Plantation, was the boyhood home of Georgia governor George Gilmer. It was during Gilmer's first administration that the Cherokee Indians were removed to Oklahoma.

But Michael's favorite story about the region is of the buried Confederate treasure said to be hidden in the Washington area. At the end of the Civil War, the remaining Confederate gold was hidden from the Union troops. Union forces tracked down the gold and found $100,000 of the original amount stored in a bank in Washington, but the rest of it disappeared. Legend has it that the remainder of the gold was buried along the old stagecoach road near Washington. After the war, fortune hunters scoured the area looking for the gold. Even today, people still look for the hidden bounty, though according to Michael, these fortune hunters aren't always from our time.

One night Michael and Jack, an out-of-town friend, double-dated. After the date, Michael invited Jack to stay overnight at his trailer so he wouldn't have to make the long drive home. As the two friends settled down for the night, the conversation soon turned towards one of Michael's favorite topics—the lost Confederate gold.

"Legend has it that the balance of the Confederate gold is buried somewhere in Wilkes County. I think fortune hunters still look for it on the old stagecoach road, but the chances are that someone knew quite well where it was hidden and reclaimed it," Michael said.

"Michael, I'm dead!" Jack replied. "Let's wait to talk more history in the morning. Maybe you'll let me see the inside of that fine house before I have to leave."

They fell asleep quickly, but sometime before daybreak, Michael awoke to the sound of his dogs barking loudly. He jumped up and looked out the window to see the dogs, running back and forth, barking at something behind the house.

"Jack!" Michael said, shaking his friend who was already partially awake. "Let's go out there and see what's happening."

"Sure thing," Jack replied, and they both put on jackets. Michael dropped his gun into his pocket and opened the trailer door. They walked quietly toward the back of the house.

"I don't think I've ever heard them barking like this before," said Michael. "Wait a minute, Jack. Let's not step out before we—" He meant to peek around the corner, but Jack was ahead of him and it was too late now. As they stepped out into the moonlight behind the house, they were face to face with four mounted riders. Through the mist swirling around the horses legs, Michael could see the riders wore black, brimmed hats and the well-worn uniforms of Confederate soldiers.

"The riders stared at us and we stared back," Michael remembered later, "but not a word was spoken. Then they reined in their horses, turned away from us, and rode off in the direction of Washington. The dogs went crazy barking but they made no move to follow."

Michael and Jack stood in shock. Finally, Michael said to Jack, "They looked like soldiers in Confederate uniforms."

"Yeah," Jack replied. "But they didn't make a sound. Did you notice that?"

"I sure did," said Michael. "Not a creak from their saddles or the noise of metal from their spurs, not a whinny or a snort from any of the horses."

"Quiet as the dead," said Jack, his face filled with awe.

"What a sight that was," said Michael. "You know, I'll bet they were here to guard the Confederate gold that was brought to Washington."

"Or dig some up for themselves!" said Jack.

To this day, Michael Horgan will tell you, "I don't believe in ghosts." But then he says, "When I hear the dogs bark at night, I always think about those four horsemen."

CALLAWAY PLANTATION BRINGS HISTORY TO LIFE WITH ITS THREE RESTORED HOMES AND ADJOINING FARM. THE PLANTATION IS LOCATED FIVE MILES WEST OF WASHINGTON ON U.S. 78, ACROSS FROM THE WASHINGTON-WILKES AIRPORT. FOR INFORMATION ABOUT TOURS, CALL 706-678-7060.

NORTHEAST
MOUNTAINS

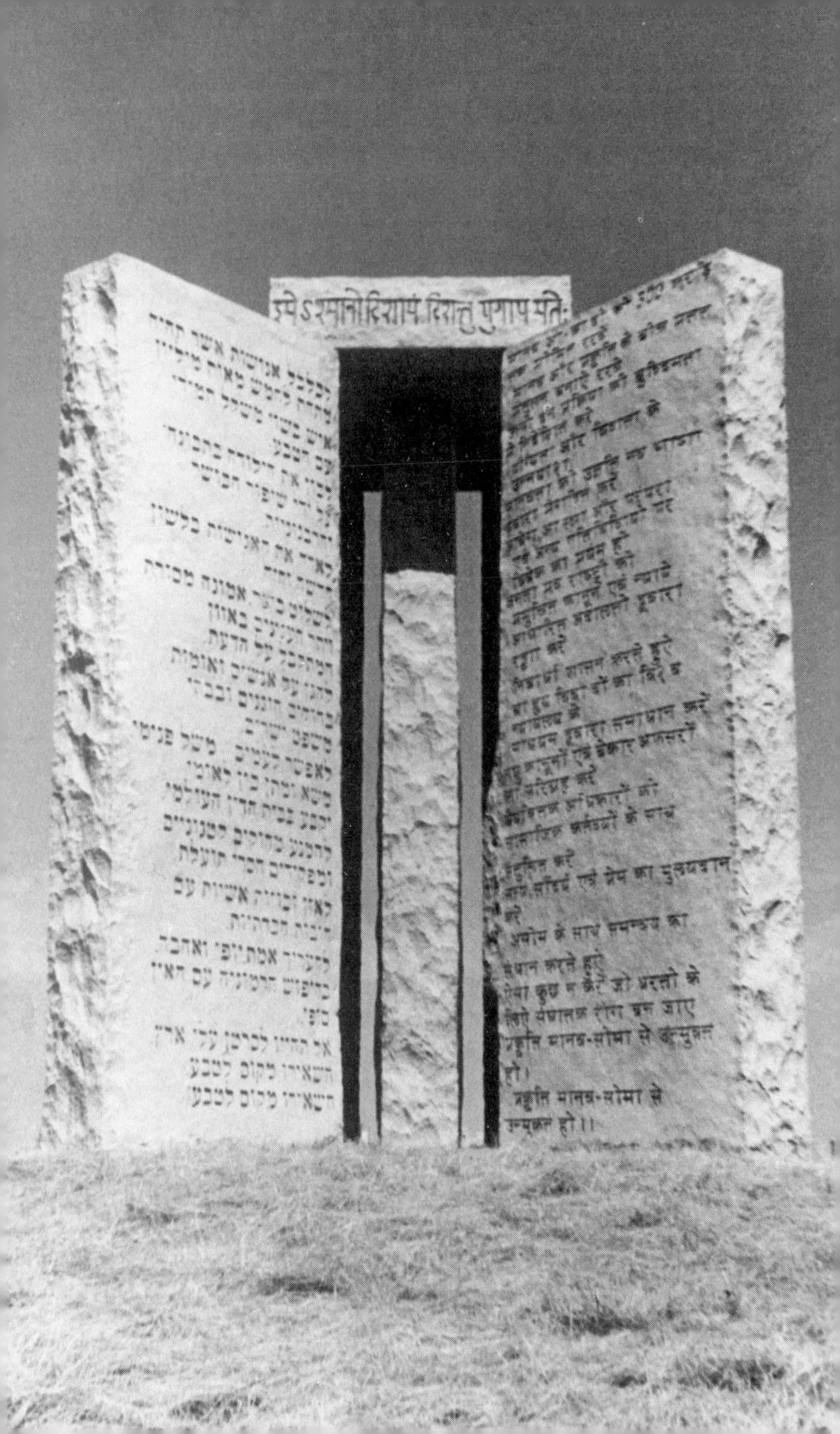

WHERE GHOSTS STILL LINGER

Dahlonega Gold Museum, 1 Public Square, Dahlonega

As the church women finished two hard workdays of cleaning up the Mount Hope Cemetery, Madeline Anthony stood back and felt a deep satisfaction. It was amazing how much better the cemetery looked with the grass mowed, the weeds pulled, and the dead underbrush removed. She went back to the car and got out her camera. Mrs. Anthony liked to record things. She had taken some pictures before the work started, and now she wanted to shoot one showing what had been accomplished.

Mrs. Anthony could take extra satisfaction in knowing she was helping to preserve a historic part of Dahlonega's past. Many of the area's early settlers were buried there—men, women, and children who had come to Dahlonega to make their fortune in the Georgia gold rush that started back in 1829.

She shot several pictures of the cemetery that day. After finishing the roll, she wrote the day's date, April 15, 1953,

e Georgia Stonehenge
e story on page 246)

on the film and took it to Gainsville to be developed. As an avid photographer, she was familiar with the developer and confidant of his judgement. "Just enlarge the best one and make several prints," she told him, anxious to pass the enlarged pictures around to her friends.

When she picked up her pictures, she initially was very pleased with the quality. But as she looked at it longer, she couldn't believe her eyes. The longer she looked, the clearer the mysterious images became. In the distance, she could see a girl in a long, old-fashioned dress silhouetted beside a tree. But that wasn't all. She also saw the faces of bearded young men, grizzled older men, and even a baby wearing a ruffled cap—face after face out of the past!

She took the picture back to the studio in Gainesville and accused the developer of tampering with it.

"Ma'am, I couldn't do this if I tried a million years," said the man who had processed and printed her film. "I would have to find pictures of all these people somewhere, cut them out, and reduce or enlarge them to scale so they would be in the right proportion to each other. Then I would have to arrange and paste them on something, blur the edges of each picture, photograph it, and print your negative and that one on the same sheet, being sure the tones of each one matched. I would have to be crazy to try something like that for any amount of money."

Convinced that the man was telling the truth, Mrs. Anthony asked him if there was any way he could explain how the faces got on her picture. "In my opinion," the man answered, "where these faces and figures came from is an absolute mystery—unless it was from right out of the grave!"

Mrs. Anthony gave the picture to the Dahlonega Gold Museum, where it was framed and hung in the office. The original negative of the print has been lost, making the photo impossible to reproduce clearly for this book, but a picture made from the original negative is still on display in the gold museum.

Many pictures are purported to be of ghosts, but there are some compelling reasons why this one may be legitimate. For one, Mrs. Madeline Anthony was an amateur, who truly did take the picture only to document her church committee's cemetery clean-up day. It was not made with infrared film, which is too often used to create "fake" ghost photographs, and no prints of this picture were ever sold by Mrs. Anthony, who simply regarded it as a curiosity. Since the outlines of the people in the photograph are so amazing, perhaps this time the camera really did capture the images of ghosts!

FOR INFORMATION ON THE DAHLONEGA GOLD MUSEUM, CALL 706-864-2257.

OLE SNAKE
233 East Broad Street, Winder

The old cream-colored-brick building at 233 East Broad Street in Winder is now the home of several county offices, but as one can probably guess from the wide windows and large porch across the front of the building, it was once a hospital. As a reminder of the building's historic past, it still houses a morgue on the ground floor, and a local resident claims that the morgue, and the rest of the building, is now haunted.

When questioned about the ghost, the man begins, "I can remember a friend of mine lying in bed sound asleep on the second floor one night, when all of a sudden he woke with a start. He heard the sound of a man's feet racing down the hall past the door of his room. It was about two or three o'clock in the morning, so he jumped up, threw open the door, and stuck his head out to see who it was. But there wasn't a soul in sight down the length of the hall.

"Well, he told some people the next day and they didn't hardly look up from their work. 'It was just Ole Snake,' one of the fellows who worked in the building back when it was a hospital told him. 'You'll learn not to pay him any mind.'

"My friend then asked, 'Who is Ole Snake?'

"The man replied, 'Not is, *was.*' The man then said Snake was an orderly who used to work in the building when this place was a hospital. His whole life revolved around that job. Apparently, he was proud of it, and he was a good orderly.

"After Snake died they tried to throw his favorite chair out on the trash heap, but that chair would just keep reappearing. They would find it back in the basement where it always sat when he was alive. Like many people who work at the building, I've seen my share of strange things there, and everyone seems to think they're caused by Snake.

"One night I heard noises coming from the ground floor and hurried down to check on what it was. As I reached the ground floor where the morgue is, I saw a pair of feet sticking out from under a sheet rolling toward me out of the darkness. It was frightening, but it turned out it was just one of the bodies from the morgue.

"People talk about doors opening and closing of their own accord, or shadows passing across a threshold when no one is out in the hall. But everyone will tell you there's nothing to be afraid of. Why as far as I know, Snake has never committed a malicious act. He's a goodhearted fellow who just keeps on doing his work as a hospital orderly and relaxing in his favorite chair when his rounds are over. He might like to play a trick every now and then, but you can't fault him for that."

THE GHOST OF BRENAU COLLEGE

Brenau College, 1 Centennial Circle, Gainesville

"I always thought of Agnes as looking like one of the girls in my grandmother's college annual," said Brittany Bell, a junior at Brenau College. "She was a real person, you know. She went to school here at the same time my grandmother did. That was during the 1920s, when everyone was dancing the Charleston, watching Chaplin's first movies, and reading F. Scott Fitzgerald's new novel, *The Great Gatsby.* What a cool time!

"I guess I'm one of the best people to talk with about Agnes," Brittany said as I interviewed her over spaghetti and a glass of wine at Pasquale's. "There's some crazy new story about her every year, but my grandmother actually knew her. At least as well as anyone did. They were both freshmen, but it wasn't until the second year that they became friends.

"Right before my freshman year, Gran tried to tell me a little about Agnes. Gran said you could see right away that Agnes was not really like the other girls, with their short skirts and cloche hats. There was something innocent and old-fashioned looking about her. Everyone else was wondering how short they could get away with wearing their skirts while Agnes wore long, full-skirted, muslin dresses. Gran said she didn't even bob her hair.

"I was packing my suitcases and only half listening while my grandmother talked. She said I would probably hear more about Agnes after I got to Brenau.

"When I arrived I was assigned a roommate and a room that happened to be in Pearce Hall. I liked being over Pearce Auditorium. You could hear the music and all.

"It wasn't until my return after Christmas that I moved into another room on the same hall. A girl in a single had left school, and the dorm mother was able to move me into her

Pearce Hall, Brenau College

room. It's easier to study and go to sleep at night when room-mates and their friends aren't coming and going. Not that I'm antisocial—I'm just very serious about my studies in business. But if someone yells at me as I pass their door, I may go in for awhile and hang out.

"That's what happened the night when the story of Agnes came up. According to what one of the girls in the dorm said, Agnes fell for a music instructor, but no one seemed to know any more details about what happened except me. I told them my grandmother and Agnes had lived on the same hall and were friends. They were really impressed.

"I didn't learn anything else about Agnes until my grandmother visited me at school later that semester. When we reached my floor and room in the dorm, Gran looked around and said, 'Don't tell me this last room on the hall is yours?'

"I said, 'Of course.' And then she told me the room had belonged to Agnes.

"Gran said Agnes's parents had all her bedroom furniture trucked from home and moved into the room. According to Gran, her brass bed was between the windows. Her chest of drawers was against the opposite wall, and near the closet stood her dressing table with its gathered pink skirt. There was an upholstered bedroom chair that had pink roses on it, a student's lamp, and a straight chair.

"Grandmother said the ceilings were a lot higher then, and the light fixtures in the rooms were different. The fixture in Agnes's room was a Victorian-type metal rod with a horizontal bar at the bottom and glass lampshades on each end.

"I asked if she knew the music teacher Agnes fell for, and she said she did. According to Gran he looked like a poet. She said that back then the more strange or unstable a boy seemed, the more romantic the girls thought he was. One day Agnes told Gran something that happened while the music teacher was giving her a harp lesson. Apparently, he suddenly clasped his hand over Agnes's fingers. She thought she had done something wrong, but when she looked up at him, he pulled her to him and kissed her. 'Fiercely' was the way Agnes described the kiss to my grandmother. A short time later she told Gran that his intentions were serious.

"Agnes said that he talked about destiny, and that meant he was going to propose. But she got angry when Gran told her not to be too sure of that.

"It was two weeks later that everything happened. The music teacher announced his engagement to a real flapper who didn't know one note from another. Agnes's door was locked that evening when Gran went by her room, and she didn't get to talk to her.

"The next day the administration called an assembly of all the students and announced that Agnes had suffered a tragic accident. They used the word 'accident' because they didn't want the students to know the truth, at least not right away. Of course the students learned later that she was dead, and everyone was terribly shocked.

"After Gran told me about Agnes's death, I wasn't too happy about living in the poor girl's room. But then I thought, Well, that was a long, long time ago.

"But something strange happened about a month before school was out for the year. One night I woke up thinking I heard someone sobbing. I called out, but no one answered. The crying grew softer, then finally stopped. This happened again on several nights. I asked people about it in the rooms near mine, but no one ever heard the sobbing sound.

"Then one night there were several terrifying claps of thunder. The noise caused me to wake suddenly and sit up in bed. Flashes of lightning made the room almost as bright as day. Gradually I became aware of a shadowy form in the center of the room. It was the figure of a girl in a long, white dress. A rope was about her neck, and her head was lolling over to one side. The other end of the rope was attached to the light fixture, and she was swaying very slowly back and forth, back and forth.

"I watched, unable to take my eyes from her, and then I began screaming. I must have awakened the entire hall because all the girls came streaming into my room. Someone turned on the light, but I still screamed at the top of my lungs. I didn't even recognize anyone at first.

"Lisa, who lives next door to me, said she thought I was being murdered, and some people asked whether I was having a nightmare. Then everyone was talking at once and trying to reassure me. I just let them think that it was a bad dream. It was daylight outside before I got back to sleep, and I slept with a bright light on every night afterward. When I went home at the end of the school year, I told Gran what had happened.

"She said that everyone heard Agnes had committed suicide, but she didn't tell me how or where because I seemed so happily settled in there. At first I was furious with Gran for not telling me when she came to visit, but the second term was over, and I was moving to a new dorm. I decided Gran had done the best thing. I probably would have failed my exams if I knew I was sharing my room with the ghost of a girl who had hanged herself.

THE LADY OF THE LIBRARY

Chestatee Regional Library, 127 Main Street, N.W., Gainesville

Is it possible that Chestatee Regional Library is haunted? The ultra-modernistic style of this formidable red-brick building makes it such an unlikely looking home for a specter that five years ago people would have laughed at such a suggestion. But that was before the sightings.

The first suspicion that a ghost was roaming the halls occurred one night about four years ago.

"After closing the library upstairs," said a staff member, "my coworker was to go down the front elevator, and I was to go down the one in back. When I reached the bottom and stepped into the hall, a strange young lady stood near the elevator. All the lights were off, with the exception of the security lights.

"You can imagine how startled I was—and frightened. She was only a few feet from me! Her brown hair, which was soft around her face, fell to her shoulders. She was about medium height and wore a long, dark dress, either navy or black. For an instant I considered stepping into the elevator behind me, but when I turned back toward her, she had disappeared! I'm not going down that elevator after closing time again."

Could the woman be a patron rather than a ghost?

Library employee Ella Jean Smith replied, "I don't think it's possible for strangers to wander about after hours. We are very careful when we close the library each night and before holidays. The procedure we go through is a detailed one."

Ms. Smith, who had worked at the library for seventeen years, then described the routine staffers follow for closing.

"We alert people that the library will be closing in ten minutes, and then we check for any open windows. During this time people are taking their books up to the desk to check them out before leaving. When the last patron has gone, we turn off the computers. We look at all the emergency exits to make sure they are secured and walk through the stacks to see that no one has inadvertently lingered there. Then we check the rest rooms. One of the last things we do is turn on the telephone answering machine, making sure the message indicates the library is closed to the public for the night.

"As we leave each level, we turn off all the lights with the exception of the security lights. Then one person goes down the back elevator and one goes down the front. The person in the front elevator sets it on 'hold' in order to have it there to ride up the next morning. Then, just before we go out the front door, we stretch the chain across the foot of the stairs leading to the second floor. And the last thing we do is turn on the motion sensor.

"If someone gets in the library and begins walking around, or if the books are disturbed, a security alarm goes off down at the police station," Ella Jean said.

But another member of the staff said that several peculiar events were mentioned at library meetings. One person said that on a night when she closed the library, she was certain that all the books in the bookcase at the bottom of the stairs were in order. The next morning when she opened the building, she was amazed to see a pile of books on the floor, as if they had tumbled from the shelves and been left there the night before!

Had the motion detector responded to the books tumbling from the shelves by ringing an alarm at the police station? The answer was no.

Recently, the library was empty except for two employees who were closing. One of them, a staff member who had never seen "The Lady of the Library," as the apparition was called by some of the staff, turned off all the lights upstairs except for the security lights.

"It was then I saw the girl with her long brown hair and long dress standing at the end of the aisle," she said. "Suddenly the lights blinked, and I glanced up. I'll admit to being frightened. When I looked back, she had disappeared."

The library has even had trouble with the telephone. A patron called the library on Martin Luther King's birthday asking, "Are you open."

"Yes. We will be open until nine o'clock tonight," a pleasant, feminine voice answered. Accordingly, the patron went to the library only to find it locked and a sign saying, "Closed for the Holiday."

If it is true that buildings can be influenced by the site upon which they stand, this may be what is happening at Chestatee Regional Library. There are several possible origins for the mysterious young lady who haunts the library halls: the Minor Brown family home, a cemetery, and a hotel all once occupied the library site.

As the commercial growth of Gainesville began to encroach on the residential area, Minor Brown, a respected Gainesville settler from the gold rush days, sold his property. After the sale, the home was razed. Then the Wheeler Hotel was built on the site. The hotel was more utilitarian than elegant, but many guests stayed there because it was the only hotel in the town from the 1930s to the 1960s. The Wheeler was patronized by parents and friends of the students and faculty at Brenau College, as well as by visiting businessmen.

But in its last years, the Wheeler's reputation was clouded by talk of a murder that may have occurred there. A former hotel employee says that a pretty girl was found dead in her room. Even today he is reluctant to talk of it.

"Hotel management didn't want us to say nothin' to nobody!" he said, "or we'd lose our job. But the maid who unlocked the door and found her was my wife!"

According to this employee, now in his sixties, by the time the girl's death was reported to the police, it was almost ten in the morning.

"The bell boy said he saw that girl in the hall the night before. It looked like her boyfriend was telling her off, but he said it wasn't none of his business. I asked the boy were they going to charge anyone, and he said by the time the police got there, wan't nobody to charge.

"Word got around fast, and those guests had checked out. My wife, Fronie, was shaking and crying when she ran out of that room. She said the girl had big ugly bruises 'round her throat and was dressed and lying across the bed. Funny thing, she only had on one shoe."

Did the young woman die in this room or in one of the dimly lit halls of the old Wheeler? Does she return to the site now because of a crime that went unpunished?

THE HAUNTED FIRE STATION

Corner of Short and Price Roads, Gainesville

THE FOLLOWING STORY CAME FROM TODD ORR, ONE OF THE TWO FIRE-
MAN WHO HAD THIS EXPERIENCE. MR. ORR IS STILL A FIREMAN, BUT HAS
BEEN AT ANOTHER STATION FOR SEVERAL YEARS. HE WILL NEVER FORGET
A CERTAIN SPRING NIGHT WHEN HE WAS ON DUTY AT SARDIS COMMU-
NITY STATION. AS HE RELATES THE FOLLOWING STORY, IT IS OBVIOUS HE IS
STILL PERPLEXED BY THE EVENTS OF THAT NIGHT.

Our fire station was located where city and country meet.
There were some houses right next to us, but when you looked
out the front window, you saw a well-kept farm with cows
grazing in a meadow. It's a nice little station, blue with white
trim and two roll-up doors on the side for the bays. That's
where we parked the ambulance and a bright red Gruman fire
truck. Steve Wilbanks and I spent our time between calls in
the living quarters at the front. Most calls were pretty routine, but I remember one that wasn't.

The series of crazy events that night began when Steve
and I were watching an Atlanta Braves game. Otto, the
firehouse dog, lay at my feet. Purebred he was not. A huge
white animal with a face like a bulldog and the red spots of a
bird dog, he would bark every time we got excited over a play
in the game.

Suddenly, above the sound from the television, we heard
noises coming from the bay—terrible crashing and shattering
sounds. Otto rushed toward the bay barking furiously. Jumping up to see what had happened, Steve looked in and gave an
awestruck whistle. "I never saw anything like this," he said.
Nor had I. Broken soft drink bottles were strewn from one
end of the bay to the other, and there was glass everywhere.
We still got our bottles in wooden crates then, and there were

a few crates that had all their bottles. The next thing I noticed, one of the crates flipped over on its edge and all of the bottles spilled out of it!

How it happened I'll never know. There was no way for anyone to get in. The dayroom where we were sitting was the only entrance to that part of the station. Steve and I were pretty spooked, but we decided we'd better clean up. It took awhile to sweep up all the fine splinters of glass. Otto was whining the whole time wanting to get in there with us. "If there was a stranger around here that dog would go for him," I told Steve, and he nodded. By the time we were finished cleaning, the game was over so we hit the sack. I hadn't been asleep long when a shout from Steve woke me.

"Get up, Todd! Fire call," he exclaimed.

"No," I said. I prided myself on never sleeping through an alarm. "You're imagining things. The pager didn't go off."

"I'm sure it went off. The dispatcher said there's a fire on Yellow Creek Road."

"Steve, our pager did *not* go off. Now go back to sleep."

A few minutes later he shouted at me again. "Todd, Todd! Look at that!"

"At what?" I said, raising my head. Steve was sitting bolt upright.

"I just saw a man standing at the foot of your bed staring at you."

I was angry until I realized Steve was scared to death. "If the man's still there I don't want to look at him," I said.

"He's not," said Steve. "He's gone."

"Good. Well maybe we can get some sleep now. If we do get a call we'll be too beat to go to the fire." I made him lie down, and despite the fact that all of this was bothering me more than I wanted to let on, I closed my eyes. About two minutes later the pager really did go off.

Then the dispatcher's voice came over the loudspeaker saying, "There's a fire on Yellow Creek Road." Steve went white as a sheet. I swung my legs over the side of the bed and began pulling on my clothes.

"Call him back on the phone and tell him we're on the way," I said.

Within a few minutes we were driving down Yellow Creek Road with our siren on wail, but I'll be doggoned if we saw any flames or smoke. It's a bad feeling to be dispatched on a call and unable to find the fire. Finally we saw a car with a blue light on it, and an officer waving us to follow him. We pulled in behind him.

In a few miles we saw the fire. It was in a van parked a short distance from the road. Flames poured from its windows, motor, and roof. As we climbed out of the fire truck, people gathered around and asked us why we took so long to get there.

"Came soon as we got the call," I told them, "but we didn't see the fire at first. It's good you sent that patrol car up the road to lead us."

"What patrol car?" asked one of the people. "We didn't send any patrol car, and none's been out this way."

"Yeah," someone else cracked, "like fire trucks, never around when you need one."

That was a surprise, but we didn't stop to think about it then. The first thing we needed to determine was whether anyone was still inside the burning van. We grabbed the hose line and began to knock down the fire with water from our tank.

"Anybody in the van?" I asked some bystanders. Voices answered "No," but you could never be sure, and there was no way to see inside it because of the flames. Someone might be lying on the floor unconscious. It took about thirty minutes to knock down the flames and dig out all the hot spots. Fortunately, nobody was inside.

Driving back to the fire station, Steve and I kept going over what had happened: His waking up the first time thinking that the dispatcher had sent us on a call to Yellow Creek Road when the pager hadn't even been activated. His seeing somebody standing at the foot of my bed. Then the activator *really* going off and the dispatcher sending us out on a call to the same road. What kind of crazy coincidence was that? And what about a patrol car that nobody sent and nobody saw leading us to the fire?

I wish I could say we were able to figure out an explanation for everything that happened that night, but we never did. I've always heard fire stations have a reputation for being haunted, and Sardis Sation sure lives up to it.

SARDIS COMMUNITY FIRE STATION IS AT THE CORNER OF SHORT AND PRICE ROADS ON THE EDGE OF GAINESVILLE.

THE LITTLE GIRL'S SONG

Gainesville

In the hill country west of Gainesville is a beautiful, wooded place called "War Woman Dell." The Indians named it after a mother who dressed as a man so she could join her patriot sons in battle. And deep at the end of the dell is a section called "Apple Orchard." It was here that a couple lived with their adored only child.

The little girl loved to play, but there were no families nearby. And although it was not her desire, she became a solitary child. Her father selected an ancient oak on a rise overlooking the road and built a tree house for her. He hoped that from the tree house she might see the approach of possible playmates. But playmates seldom came, and so she was thrown upon her own resources for entertainment.

On a platform among the branches, she would play with her corncob dolls and sing happily to herself. She always sang the old songs, the hymns and Scottish airs, in a sweet voice that passersby loved to hear. The first year after her father built the tree house, she played there the year around, but the next year she was there only now and then. She had contracted consumption.

Within a short time she was dead. Her grieving family chose the foot of the ancient oak, right below the tree house, as her final resting place.

In the months and years that followed, many who walked the road where the tree stands claimed the girl's plaintive melodies were still carried on the wind.

Apple Orchard is deep in War Woman Dell, on the other side of the stream. The early settlers in this area were pure Anglo Saxon, and up until recently, the isolation and reliance on oral tradition enabled much of their legends and folklore to be preserved. One of the last of the old mountain women to live in War Woman Dell was named Aunt Sudie.

Folklorist Bimbo Brewer would sometimes talk with Aunt Sudie about the little girl. According to Brewer, Sudie would look off toward the big oak tree and, lifting a work-calloused hand to quiet everyone, would say, "On a real quiet day you can hear her sing. Can't you hear her strike up that pretty air? Listen now!"

At this point, everyone gathered around would strain to hear. "She's out there," Aunt Sudie would say, her faded blue eyes kindling with light. "What a sweet voice the child has."

Many have listened and some have heard.

THE GEORGIA STONEHENGE

Elberton

Approaching Elberton is like driving through a moonscape, or perhaps the playground of some ancient race of giants. Enormous boulders lie on either side of the road. These outcroppings of granite are the chief resource of the area, and they continue to lure skilled stone craftsmen from places as far away as Italy and Spain. The stone also attracted a man that Joe Fendley and the town of Elberton will never forget.

It was Friday in early June of 1979, and it was already hot. The floor fan hummed, its breeze stirring the papers slightly on the large, old-fashioned desk. Joe Fendley had just leaned back in his oak captain's chair to study a sales report for his granite finishing company when he heard a light knock at his office door. Looking up, he saw a well-dressed stranger in his forties.

"I would like to buy a monument," said the man.

Fendley got up out of his chair. "Sorry. We don't sell directly to the public, Mr. . . ."

"Christian. Robert C. Christian," the man said with a curious smile. "Are you the owner, sir?"

"Yes. Joe Fendley's the name."

"Perhaps monument wasn't quite the right word. I meant something similar to Stonehenge in England, sir. You've heard of it, I'm sure."

Joe Fendley suddenly sat down. Surely he was alone with a crackpot, but hopefully not a dangerous one.

Christian continued, "I would like to know if you could build something that I want to dedicate to the preservation of mankind." He took out his pen and started to outline his project. As he discussed specifications, Fendley was even more dumbfounded. Each stone was to weigh approximately twenty-eight tons. Most of the monoliths at Stonehenge are more than thirteen feet high, but these were to have a height of nineteen feet.

"Now how much will this cost?" Christian asked as he finished describing his design.

"No monument that size has ever been quarried in Elberton, so it's difficult to estimate," said Fendley. By now he had recovered enough to make notes, and he was beginning to have some respect for the stranger's intelligence and sincerity. "I can only give you a rough estimate, and I'm afraid a very high one at that."

This did not seem to discourage Mr. Christian, who listened to the estimate with no show of emotion. "That sounds fine," Christian replied, "but I would like to see your bank references before you are hired."

Fendley understood that Christian wanted to make sure his company had the resources to mine the amount of granite needed for a project this ambitious and pay the skilled labor to cut and carve such huge stones. "Gladly," Fendley replied. "My banker is Wyatt C. Martin."

Thirty minutes later Christian was introducing himself to Mr. Martin at the bank.

"Is this project your idea?" asked Martin.

"No, not entirely. You see, I represent a small group of loyal Americans who believe in God and simply wish to leave a message for future generations."

"And what is the name of this group, and where are they from?" asked the banker.

But Christian would not say. "I am sorry, but we feel that our identity would detract from the monument and its meaning. We wish it to remain forever a secret," said Christian. "The message to be inscribed on the stones is to all mankind and is neither sectarian, nationalistic, nor in any sense political. The stones should appeal to believer and nonbeliever."

Christian then asked the banker to be a financial intermediary for the project.

"But why has Elberton, Georgia, been chosen for this?" asked Wyatt Martin.

"For several reasons," Christian replied. "The Indians believed this to be a place possessing extraordinary energy. We think it's a site that would be highly visible from the air because of the elevation, and because it's devoid of trees. The mild climate here will not be as damaging to exposed stone, and we also believe this area would survive any nuclear conflagration due to its distance from Atlanta."

Christian went on to reveal, "Of course, Robert C. Christian is not my real name." Martin was taken aback at this disclosure, and he refused to act as an intermediary unless the stranger provided his real name, along with information that would enable Martin to investigate Christian both personally and financially. Christian agreed, but only after swearing the banker to the strictest secrecy.

Then the man who called himself "Christian" left Elberton, promising to return. Some time passed and nothing was heard from him. Fendley and Martin began to believe it had all been a huge practical joke.

But Christian finally reappeared, and this time he brought a wooden model of the monument. Both model and specifications bore an amazing resemblance to the inner portion of England's famous Stonehenge. Martin notified Fendley that the funds for the project were in an account and work could proceed. The cutting of the stones began. Key craftsmen and special crews were employed for the project.

Stonehenge carries no written message, but these mammoth stones do. Expert sandblaster Charlie Clamp was chosen to etch the more than four thousand characters into the blue-gray stone. The stones bear the message in eight different tongues: English, Russian, Mandarin Chinese, Arabic, Classi-

cal Hebrew, Swahili, Hindi, and Spanish; as well as four ar-
chaic languages: Sanskrit, Babylonian Cuneiform, Classical
Greek, and Egyptian hieroglyphic. These languages were selected because they are spoken by the greatest number of
people in the world, and translations were done by authorities
from several countries and universities. Clamp said that as he
carved the letters into the blue-granite slabs, he sometimes
heard "strange music and disjointed voices."

The purpose of the monument, says their inscription, is
"to convey our ideas across time to other human beings . . .
which will silently display our ideas when we have gone. We
hope . . . they will hasten in a small degree, the coming Age
of Reason."

There are ten commandments, or "guiding thoughts," on
the stones. The English translation of the guiding thoughts is
as follows:

1. Maintain humanity under 500 million in perpetual balance with
   nature.
2. Guide reproduction wisely, improving fitness and diversity.
3. Unite humanity with a living new language.
4. Rule passion, faith, tradition, and all things with tempered reason.
5. Protect people and nations with fair laws and just courts.
6. Let all nations rule internally, resolving external disputes in a world
   court.
7. Avoid petty laws and useless officials.
8. Balance personal rights with social duties.
9. Prize truth, beauty, love . . . seeking harmony with the infinite.
10. Be not a cancer on earth—leave room for nature.

A detailed explanation follows each of these guiding
thoughts. Among these explanations are calls for an effective
world government that is willing to accept a system of world
law. According to the inscriptions, this law will stress the

responsibility of individual nations in regulating internal affairs and in the peaceful management of international frictions. "With such a system we could eliminate war," the stones read. "We could provide every person an opportunity to seek a life of purpose and fulfillment. There are alternatives to Armageddon. They are attainable. But they will not happen without coordinated efforts by millions of dedicated people in all nations of the earth."

And who is the small group who paid for this monument out in the far reaches of the Georgia countryside? No one knows. Years have passed, and the individuals remain unknown. For some, it is a temptation to attribute these principles either to superior beings or to beings who have mistakenly trod the same road nations are traveling today.

The mysterious stones were unveiled in March of 1980. Is it coincidence that on September 12th of the same year, a round, brightly illuminated object was reported hovering in the air near the monument? The object was described as being about twenty feet wide and having green lights around it. There were widespread sightings of this object over an area of several counties.

Both Fendley and Martin describe R.C. Christian as appearing to be well traveled and intelligent. He claimed to have served in World War II and described himself as "a patriotic American in every sense of the word." Nothing else is known of him save his own words: "My name is not Christian. I only use that name because I am a follower of Jesus Christ."

Confidentiality has been so carefully preserved that it is doubtful the identity of Robert C. Christian will ever be known. Martin personally censored all communications from Christian to Fendley, even concealing the stranger's true identity from his own secretary. On completion of the monument, he shredded all records and letters, eliminating any trace of the sponsors.

Martin's only statement on the identity of Christian has been, "I never expect to see or hear from Mr. Christian again."

TO REACH THE GEORGIA STONEHENGE FROM ELBERTON, DRIVE SEVEN MILES NORTH ON GA 77. FOR MORE INFORMATION, CALL THE ELBERTON GRANITE ASSOCIATION AT 404-283-2551.

SPIRIT OF AMICALOLA FALLS LODGE

Amicalola Falls State Park, Dawsonville

Amicalola Falls Lodge is on the peak of the mountain at Amicalola Falls State Park, and one of the highlights of this park is the 729-foot-tall waterfall. The road leading to the falls and lodge is steep and winding. During my visit to the lodge, I was not surprised to learn that long ago Indian braves sought visions on the crest of Amicalola Mountain, praying to the great spirit that lived here. As I traveled the invisible, fog-shrouded road ascending to the lodge, I had my own vision—that we would drive right off the side of the mountain. However, my husband and I arrived at the impressive stone lodge safe, but shaken.

While we were in the dining room, our server pleasantly inquired how we happened to be visiting the lodge. My husband explained that I was looking for ghost stories for a book. Apprehensive about the weather, we had decided to stay overnight at the lodge rather than drive on.

"A young woman here named Diana Reagan is part Cherokee Indian. You might be interested in hearing her story," our waiter said. "She's busy in the kitchen now, but I'll ask her to come out and talk with you when she can."

Diana finally appeared as the dining room emptied, and she agreed to describe her experiences to us.

"I felt something strange the first time I came up here, five years ago," she said. "My blood surged with a sense of excitement and uneasiness as I reached the top of the mountain that afternoon. The lodge was enveloped by a cloud resting on Amicalola's peak, much as it is tonight," she recalled, "and it was impossible for me to tell whether the figures moving about in the mist were men, women, or spirits!"

She stood beside our table in the lodge dining room as she spoke, twisting her hands nervously in front of her sturdy figure. Her face, with its shining brown eyes and broad, high Cherokee cheekbones, was a pleasant one, but for the moment she appeared troubled.

Before speaking again, she looked out the immense picture window beside our table. The world outside was one of shifting white clouds. Our only assurance that there was ground below the lodge was the dark, ghostly shapes of fir trees briefly coming into view through the window, then disappearing behind the mist.

"Like tonight, it was a dream world the day I arrived. In the eye of my mind, I could see Amicalola's massive head jutting into the sky and water from the gash in his side, tumbling down hundreds of feet. I imagined Cherokee braves climbing the trail up the flank of this sacred mountain and stopping to drink from the small springs that feed the falls. The braves would climb to this peak to fast and wait for their vision, each solitary figure wrapped in the white breath exhaled by Amicalola."

She had painted a picture of the distant, mystical Cherokee past, and she looked at us hoping for understanding.

Finally she continued. "I wondered if the mist that covered everything that day was the reason why I had such strange feelings," she said.

"And was it?" I asked.

She shook her head. "No. I think I was instantly aware of the spirits up here, although I never would have admitted such a thing at the time. I tried not to think about anything but my duties. My job was in the kitchen, so I made myself as busy as possible."

"And did that work?"

"Yes, for awhile. If there were things I didn't want to notice, I tried to tell myself it was just due to being in a strange place with new tasks—learning unfamiliar recipes, helping with food preparation, being sure that trays of freshly baked desserts were ready for the servers. But I eventually experienced things I could not ignore.

"Because of the cooking, the air in the kitchen was often warm, particularly in the area where I sometimes loaded the dishes. And it was near the dishwasher that I had my first extraordinary experience. As I stood there one night, enveloped in the dishwasher's steamy warmth, I suddenly felt an icy column of air beside me. The contrast was even greater because of the heat from the machine.

"I was so startled that I cried out and moved away from the cold air. My coworkers turned and stared with curiosity, but they said nothing. Later I found that other people in the kitchen had experienced the same thing. It's usually when tempers are stretched to the breaking point that things begin to happen. We get along well together most of the time, but occasionally someone is in a bad mood, and they take it out on others.

"One night, I don't even remember what the argument was about, but at its peak a large frying pan went flying through the air toward the arguing pair. It almost hit them, too. We all turned to see who had done such a thing. It came from a hook on the other side of the room, but no one was near it. Everyone was shaken; as a newcomer, I was the most startled of all. After closing time that night, I questioned a friend who worked with me.

"She said the icy air and the flying pans had happened before. When I asked her why she thought it happened, she said, 'It's as if someone we can't even see finally becomes totally disgusted. Pots and pans begin to fly! It's upsetting at the time, although people are usually much quieter afterward.'

"The next week I was off, and I spent a night at my mother's. My Cherokee grandmother was there at the house on a visit. When I asked her about the strange goings-on in the kitchen, Grandmother said, 'You're part Indian. You ought to know why things happen up there, Diana.'

"'I know the spirits of the ancient ones are up there,' I answered.

"My grandmother replied, 'They are there because the lodge was built on one of our sacred mountains. The spirits are trying to say that they were a contented people until the white men came searching for gold, making us leave our home for the long, painful walk west.'"

This seemed to be the end of Diana's story, so my husband asked, "And why do you think the spirits are up here?"

Diana paused. "I think my grandmother's right. Sometimes I can feel the presence of spirits as close to me as you are."

"Is there any way to make them happier?" I asked.

"I'm not sure. There's really no way to change the past, but I hope we can show a greater respect for all people," Diana Reagan replied with quiet dignity. "One thing that makes me happy inside is the beauty up here on the mountain. The park people are trying to keep the woods and streams a place everyone can enjoy. I know the spirits must like that."

AMICALOLA FALLS STATE PARK IS LOCATED ON GA 52, FIFTEEN MILES NORTH-WEST OF DAWSONVILLE. IN ADDITION TO THE LODGE, THERE ARE COTTAGES AND CAMPSITES. FOR RESERVATIONS, CALL 800-864-PARK.

NORTHWEST MOUNTAINS

Godfrey and Julia Barnsley

END OF THE BARNSLEY CURSE

Barnsley Gardens, 597 Barnsley Gardens Road,
Adairsville

How does one know whether he or she has been cursed? Most people don't take the matter too seriously, but the story of the Barnsley family may cause some to revise their opinion.

Julia Henrietta Scarborough, the beautiful daughter of a prosperous Savannah shipping magnate, and Godfrey Barnsley, a dashing Englishman, were married in what was regarded as the most romantic match of Savannah's 1828 social season. The marriage was a happy one except for Henrietta's domineering mother, who had opposed her daughter's marriage to the handsome young cotton broker from the start. Godfrey's mother-in-law became such a nuisance he took his wife to England to avoid the woman's meddling.

The couple lived in Liverpool for two years, though Godfrey constantly traveled between Liverpool, New York, and Savannah on business. England's constant demand for cotton made Godfrey's cotton-brokering business a prosperous endeavor. In 1830, the Barnsleys returned to Savannah with Anna, the first of their seven children. In Savannah, Barnsley's business thrived and soon his fortune was substantial. Still drawn to his English heritage, Godfrey decided to return England once more and build a suitable home for his growing family.

Just as the Barnsleys were set to return to England, a severe recession dashed their plans. Cotton prices plunged, and banks in both the United States and England failed. Godfrey's fortune was shattered. Fortunately, though, the recession was short lived, and with his wife's encouragement, young Godfrey Barnsley started over.

He built up a second fortune, and once more he and Julia pored over designs for a home. Their dream was to build an Italian villa surrounded by elaborate gardens. Meanwhile, Julia gave birth to two more children, Reginald and Harold. By this time, weakened from frequent childbearing, Julia's health was beginning to suffer. In 1838, she became ill with consumption.

Rather than expose his beloved wife to the damp climate of England, Godfrey decided to build a home in northwestern Georgia. He purchased almost four thousand acres that, until recently, had belonged to the Cherokee Nation. In a letter, Godfrey described his first visit to the land he had purchased. The letter describes how, to his surprise, he found an old Cherokee man living on the land and briefly hired the man to work for him. "I assured him kindly that he need not move but could stay. However when I explained to the old Cherokee brave that I was going to shear off the bluff above the spring and build a mansion there, the Indian said, 'This land is sacred to the Cherokees. You must not destroy it. I fear it would not please the forefathers.'

"'I will not change my plans,' I replied, and when I said that the Indian cursed me," Godfrey wrote. A short time later, the Indian disappeared and was never heard from again.

Barnsley brought his wife and their six children to the beautiful, rolling land of northwest Georgia, quartering the family in a large log house while the villa was being built. When Julia saw this part of Georgia for the first time, she was awestruck by its wild, romantic beauty. She would soon discover how truly wild this part of Georgia's frontier remained.

Godfrey named their new estate "Woodlands Manor," preferring the English term "manor" to plantation. Work on the villa began at once. The couple shared a mutual interest in plants, and they never tired of discussing their plans for the grandiose and elaborate gardens which would surround the house. Godfrey imagined Woodlands Manor as an estate that would rival any gentleman's country seat in England. His taste in landscaping was to avoid straight lines and symmetry. Instead, he designed serpentine paths and an acorn-shaped boxwood garden that reflected his international influences.

During this period, another child, Godfrey, Jr., was born to the Barnsleys. As their home began to take shape, the Barnsleys experienced a period of happiness. However, Godfrey's business concerns soon drew him away from the home for long periods of time. During his absences, construction on Woodlands Manor lagged. Life in the wilderness was hard on Julia, particularly when Godfrey was away. Julia's poignant letters to her husband reveal that she and the children missed him greatly during his prolonged absences. To make matters worse, she missed the pleasant, civilized social life with her friends in Savannah. Julia enjoyed the summers at Woodlands Manor, but the cold, damp winters were hard on her spirits and her health.

In October of 1844, Julia wrote her family in Savannah that she was too sick to answer their letters. A few months later, she was carried back to Savannah and placed under the care of her family's physician. Unfortunately, it was too late;

she died soon after her return in the city.

Overcome with grief that was compounded by guilt over his frequent absences from the side of his beloved wife, Godfrey lost all heart in the completion of Woodlands. Without Julia nothing mattered. To assuage his grief, he threw himself into his shipping business, traveling constantly between his seaport offices in New Orleans, Mobile, Savannah, and Liverpool.

On one trip to Mobile, an event happened that changed his life—he went to his first séance. The spiritualist conducting the séance convinced him it was possible to communicate with his dead wife.

At once, he renewed his work on the villa and went forward with his designs for the gardens of Woodlands. Now he was convinced that Julia was again part of his life—that she not only appeared to him during his dreams, but that she was constantly by his side, talking with him and giving him suggestions about the house and gardens. Sometimes he even would pass along "her" instructions to his carpenter, Robert Freeman. "Robert, Miss Julia would like for you to do it this way," he would say to Freeman on certain mornings, referring to something Julia had told him in his communication with her the night before. According to Freeman, Godfrey spared no expense in constructing the fourteen-room Italian villa according to his dead wife's slightest desire. Godfrey's diaries indicate that she "talked" with him most often when the two of them sat beside the fountain in the boxwood garden.

In May of 1864, Federal troops under the command of General James B. McPherson arrived at Woodlands. The general was so impressed by the gardens that he gave orders for the soldiers not to damage the boxwoods, but instead to march *around* them. The fact that Barnsley raised the British flag and claimed neutrality regarding the war probably helped save the mansion from being set on fire. Later, when it was discovered that his safe was full of Confederate bonds and that he had two sons fighting for the Confederacy, his storage buildings were ransacked by the Union troops.

Neither manor nor gardens escaped the hard times suffered by the South after the Civil War. Godfrey and his family lived on in genteel poverty. He returned to New Orleans in 1871 in a fourth, and this time futile, attempt to revive his cotton business and recoup his fortune. He died there in poverty in 1873. In letters written to his daughter Julia, Godfrey said that he looked forward to joining his wife in the spirit world.

Julia returned his body to Woodlands for burial. Some New Orleans acquaintances must have followed the body home, for vandals dug up his grave and severed his right hand. Many believed the hand was then used in voodoo rituals.

As always, Woodlands needed money to maintain its beauty after Godfrey's death. Godfrey's granddaughter, Addie, had a son named Preston who had been a successful prizefighter under the assumed name of K.O. Dugan. Preston loved Woodlands and used much of his earnings to help maintain the estate. Due to his violent temper, and probably because of head injuries suffered during his career as a pugilist, Preston was committed to the state asylum at Milledgeville. Security at the asylum was lax, and one evening Preston simply walked back to Woodlands. Preston had become convinced during his confinement that his brother Harry was trying to steal his share of the Woodlands estate. When he reached the estate, Preston entered the house, a gun in hand, and fired at Harry several times. Harry tried to escape, but one of Preston's bullets found its mark. Harry died in his mother Addie's arms.

To the end of her days, Addie believed Harry's spirit, along with that of Godfrey Barnsley, inhabited Woodlands Manor. According to Addie, Harry's ghost warned her of the Japanese attack on Pearl Harbor a week in advance. She passed the warning along to Colonel Thomas Spencer, a syndicated columnist from Atlanta. Spencer included Addie's warning in his column, but every newspaper except one that published his column deleted it, thinking the prediction too bizarre. On December 7, 1941, exactly one week after Harry's warning, the Japanese attacked the Hawaii base.

Addie reported many other ghost sightings at Woodlands Manor. She claimed to have seen her grandmother Julia in the boxwood garden and to have heard Godfrey push his chair back from his desk when he was through with his work, then walk across the floor, just as he had so many times in life.

As the years went by, the family could not afford to keep up the house, nor could other families who took their place. A legend began that the tragedies experienced by the Barnsley family in the century following Julia's death were the result of the Indian's curse. The house fell into ruins, while the grounds, covered with underbrush and vines, became a depressing sight. The once beautiful villa and the gardens slumbered. But a prince was on the way to awaken Barnsley.

Prince Hubertus Fugger Babenhausen of Augsberg, Germany, had already invested in Georgia timberland and was interested in further investment in the northwestern part of the state. A friend described Woodlands Manor, and although Fugger had several castles on his hands in Germany, he purchased the property sight unseen.

The prince's first trip to inspect his new property was a shock, but he immediately saw the property's beauty and potential. He put into motion a plan not only to restore Barnsley Gardens to its original splendor, but to carry out Godfrey Barnsley's own plans for its future, as revealed in Barnsley's meticulous letters and records. Miraculously, a number of old photographs and plans have been donated to assist the project.

The Barnsley family motto was, "Life is Like the Rose." During the estate's prime, Godfrey planted hundreds of roses around the house, which were choked out over the years. Wishing to remain true to Barnsley's wishes, Prince Fugger planted more than 180 varieties of the same heirloom roses that would have graced England's finest gardens of the 1800s. An 1820 log cabin has been moved to the grounds to serve as a plant shop. The greenhouse and nursery on the estate specialize in various heirloom plants.

The original right wing of the mansion has been turned into a museum, where clothing and furniture of the period, some belonging to the Barnsleys, are exhibited. Stains of Harry's blood remain on the floor in the front room, as do bullet marks from Preston's gun in the woodwork. The overgrown family graveyard has been cleaned and landscaped, with a stone in the style of the period placed at the previously unmarked grave of Godfrey Barnsley.

However, before all this restoration began, there was a problem. Whether the Cherokee Indian's curse was the reason for the downfall of Woodlands and the Barnsley family was impossible to determine, but the people in charge of restoring the estate were willing to do anything necessary to protect their sizable investment. Before they, too, suffered the same fate as the Barnsleys, they set out to exorcise the curse.

Since the rumors about a curse would not go away, a decision was made to have two Cherokee chiefs come to Woodlands to remove the curse. One was from North Carolina and the other from Oklahoma, representing each branch of the Cherokee Nation. According to the chiefs, Cherokees are not in the habit of putting curses on people, but to give peace and serenity to Woodlands and bring the estate into harmony with the Great Spirit, the two men performed the solemn and impressive Eagle Dance. Now, there is every reason to believe the sad years for Woodlands are over.

Though the Eagle Dance apparently brought peace and harmony to the estate itself, its magic did not do away with

Woodlands many ghosts. Julia can still be seen and felt near the fountain in the boxwood garden, the same place where she "discussed" her plans for the estate with her beloved Godfrey. Godfrey himself has been spotted walking about the house's ruins, while poor murdered Harry can be seen roaming the grounds. There have even been sightings of the Confederate colonel who was shot dead by a Yankee while he tried to warn the family of the approaching Union army. Perhaps these members of the Barnsley family, and their friend, can not bear to leave the estate they loved so much.

ADAIRSVILLE IS LOCATED NORTHWEST OF ATLANTA. FOR INFORMATION ON BARNSLEY GARDENS, CALL 706-773-7480.

A LIVELY DEAD INDIAN

Big Canoe Resort (near Jasper)

Billy Howard has been working at the Big Canoe resort in the Georgia mountains for fourteen years. Affable and friendly, he runs the Sconti Clubhouse and knows most of the golfers. All day long he listens to them exchange jokes, talk about the stock market, and analyze their golf game, all comfortably unaware that anything unusual occurs here.

Big Canoe is a family-type community, and people of all ages live in this resort area. Most of them commute to nearby towns from homes nestled by the lake in a forest of pines, oaks, and maples.

Billy had been working at the Sconti Clubhouse only a few weeks when he was in the men's locker room late one afternoon. He looked up to see a tall, slim figure standing near the door. He stared at it trying to figure out what it was, only to see it vanish. This happened on several occasions before he finally was convinced it was a man. Then the apparition, which appeared to be shy at first, gradually became bolder.

As time went on following the first sightings, the specter's appearance became much better defined. Howard was able to see that he had long gray hair, and that the brown garment he wore seemed to be animal skins. His visitor, Howard decided, was an Indian.

"He is most likely to appear when this place is quiet and nobody else is around," says Howard. "On Wednesday mornings, when I go in to work about three or four o'clock in the morning, he is at the clubhouse. He's always curious about what I'm doing and wants to watch everything."

Billy says, "I saw him only two days ago. He is not nearly as shy about my presence as he once was. He moves around quietly in the pro shop, the kitchen, and the downstairs banquet room. I'm always aware of when he is around, but recently I heard him make a noise for the first time. I was straightening up the banquet room after a meal when I heard a clinking sound. There he was, sitting over at a table, holding a porcelain sugar holder in each hand and buffing them together.

Billy and the Indian became so comfortable with each other, that the Indian even moved in with Billy for awhile. "In the fall of 1995 they remodeled the clubhouse, and during all the nailing, sawing, and confusion, the Indian went home with me," says Billy Howard. "My three-year-old grandson, Christopher Clayton, kept saying, 'Granddady, who is that man with the long gray hair? Is he going to live with us?'

"The Indian stayed at my place until the remodeling was completed and the clubhouse was back to normal," says Howard. "Then he returned. One day when I was driving a golf cart toward the clubhouse to put it up, I saw the Indian standing in the double doorway. I was going toward the entrance faster than usual to park the cart, and he ran. I had no idea that a ghost could be afraid of anything, so I talked to a friend who is something of an expert on the supernatural.

"'Why did he take off running?' I asked. 'Nothing can hurt him now.'

"My friend answered, 'Well, when you drove straight toward him, I think he had exactly the same reaction a live person would have had. Your Indian may not even know he's dead'."

Howard believes the spirit belongs to a Cherokee whose grave may be under the clubhouse, or one who once lived in the area. He does not regard it as strange that he is one of the few who have seen the Indian. Billy Howard is the seventh son of a seventh son, and according to some folklore tradition, these sons have a special insight into the supernatural. Billy Howard believes he has been endowed with a spiritual gift— a special awareness of what others do not always see.

Lending credence to Howard's sightings are the experiences of fifty-year-old Gail Jones, a red-haired, hazel-eyed woman who lives in Dawson, three miles away from Big Canoe. Gail has been clubhouse housekeeper for the past five years. She has not seen the figure quite as clearly as Howard, but she says that at first she saw something with a "shadowy or misty appearance, which appeared and then disappeared as fast as it came." To be on the safe side, she utters a courteous greeting when she enters the Sconti Clubhouse to clean at night, "just so it knows I am there," Jones claims. She says there is a relationship of mutual respect between her and the spirit.

Recently, Gail experienced an incident in the men's locker room. "There are swinging doors in there," she explains. "One night I was on one side of a door, and it was on the other. We were nose-to-nose, so to speak. I went one way and the ghost went the other!"

But the incident that seems to have terrified her the most

happened one night. "I went out to my car and saw an upright shape standing in front of it," says Gail. "It just stayed there for about five minutes and gradually took a form that showed me it was a person. I was so scared I thought I would die!

"Once I thought the vacuum cord had brushed me," Jones continues. "Then I realized the cord was not even close to me. It was the ghost that brushed me."

Would Gail prefer to work somewhere else? she is asked. "Oh, no. I like Big Canoe. The apparition has never harmed me," admits Gail. "It's just startling at times."

IF YOU WANT MORE INFORMATION ABOUT FACILITIES AT BIG CANOE, YOU CAN CALL 1-800-652-6091, 770-268-3333, OR SEND A FAX TO 706-268-3459.